Broken Road

Shannon Lane

This book is dedicated to my family and friends who have stood by my side as I brought this story to life. Your overwhelming support means the world to me and I couldn't have gotten this far without you all. Thank you!

Chapter One: The Job

We sit at a counter along the window in our favorite, hole-in-the wall sandwich shop across the square from PPG Place, as we do most of days for lunch, and enjoy the bustle of people in the streets. Men and women in corporate attire, medical staff in scrubs, students, and joggers a pass by and skaters glide around the ice rink as I gaze around at them like they are a movie on a screen.

People watching is one of my favorite pastimes and my best friend Dakota, is the perfect company for it. There's just something interesting about being surrounded by strangers and not knowing their story. To watch someone and not know what's been going on in their life; it's a complete mystery, and the city is the perfect setting for that, especially with the holidays having just passed.

Pittsburgh isn't anything compared to other major cities, like New York, but I know it well and for me, it is the perfect place to call home. I had grown up on the outskirts of the city, and my sister and I used to come out on the weekends all the time with our friends. I instantly fell in love with it, and that's why it had been the best place to start over fresh after everything happened a few months ago. Life was starting to feel normal again.

After the incident, Dakota and I found an apartment together so she could be my support system. She was also tired of the commute from our hometown in Bethel Park, and our apartment on Liberty Ave is just around the corner from her job here in the square. It has been one of the best decisions we've made because she got me through some of the toughest months after my divorce and I don't know how I would have done it without her.

I look out the window to the right and catch sight of my mother and Clarissa coming from Market Square, already bickering about something. My little sister is getting married in the fall and begged me to meet up with them for lunch to help with some of the plans. I know how

crazy Mom can get with things like that, so I reluctantly agreed as long as they didn't mind Dakota joining.

None of us wanted anything fancy for our lunch date, so Dave's Deli was a perfect spot to get together. It's one of mine and Dakota's favorite lunch spots. They've got a unique selection of sandwich combos, and their avocado toast is to die for. I set our food out on the counter and then watch as Mom and Clarissa silently make their way in the door and toward our counter.

Looking at Mom, you'd never think she was 55. Instead, one would guess she was our older sister. She is a tiny woman, five feet tall and very fit, who always dresses to impress, no matter the occasion. She could be camping in the middle of nowhere, and you can bet she'd still look like a model for Vogue. There's never a blonde hair out of place or wrinkle on her perfect face.

Clarissa is practically Mom's mini me, with the exception of her wardrobe which is much more casual. She has the same sunflower blonde hair and bright, baby-blue eyes, whereas I look more like our father with honey-brown hair and light-brown eyes. At least, that's what the pictures tell me.

Our biological father passed away when I was two years old, while Mom was pregnant with my sister. He was a firefighter and gave his life getting two children to safety one night on the job. Shortly after, Mom and I moved back in with my grandparents until she was able to care for us on her own again. I had just turned eight when Mom met our stepfather, Eamon, who had just moved to the US from Ireland. And, well, the rest is history.

Mom likes to say that Eamon was immediately smitten with Clarissa and me, and she's pretty sure that's half of the reason he fell in love with her. Since they got together, he has been nothing short of the perfect father, and I have the greatest relationship with him. He took on a huge role that he didn't have to and I'll always respect him for that. He's the dad I almost didn't have growing up.

"Hello, girls." Mom hugs Dakota and me and takes a seat at the end of the counter, hanging her purse on the back of the chair.

"Hey, Nelly!" Clarissa wraps her slender arms around my neck for a hug and then greets Dakota before taking the seat in between Mom and me. "How have you been?"

Clarissa and Dakota are the only two people I let call me Nelly, which is a nickname for Ellen. I'm not crazy about the name, but it was my late great-grandmother's name, so Mom insisted on using it for her first-born daughter. Most people just call me Ellie, which I prefer much more than Ellen or Nelly, but I wouldn't tell my best friend and sister that.

"Eh, same old, same old." I shrug with a smile.

As I look at my sister, I can see the relief on her face, and I know she is glad I agreed to meet them for lunch. I hate to admit that I've been avoiding them lately because I know how Mom gets when she's in planning mode: Overbearing and demanding. However, there is another reason, and it's just that I haven't been in the spirit for wedding stuff.

It's not that I'm not happy for Clarissa, because I truly am. She's my baby sister and her happiness means the world to me. But, ever since my own marriage fell through, the whole concept is a vacant idea in my mind.

"So, how's Dad?" I ask my mom after taking a bite of my toast.

"Oh, he's well." She smiles. "You know him, just taking it one day at a time."

"Of course." I shake my head in amusement. Dad has always been the kind of man to just take everything as it comes to him. He's got a lively spirit, and that's one of the things that made Mom fall in love with him. He's a very adventurous and spontaneous man, and Clarissa and I have a lot of great memories because of it.

We fall silent for a few seconds as we each take a bite of our food.

"And, Clary, how has Gareth been?" I ask my sister, referring to my soon to be brother-in-law, who is probably the sweetest guy I've ever met.

I haven't been able to spend a lot of time with Gareth, but I know he's perfect for Clarissa. I was a bit nervous at first because he's from a wealthy family, but it doesn't seem to affect their relationship at all. He is very down-to-earth and humble and, most importantly, he makes my sister happy, which is all I could ask for.

"He's great!" Clarissa says with a huge grin. "He's actually been very helpful with the wedding plans, and it's all just getting so exciting for both of us."

She bounces around in her seat as she talks, and I can't help but smile. Seeing her this giddy makes me so thankful that she found someone great to spend the rest of her life with. When I first learned about their engagement, I was shocked because they hadn't been together very long and I didn't want her to make the same mistake I did by rushing things. That's what I did with Jake, but Gareth is nothing like him, and there isn't a doubt in my mind that he and Clarissa will be happy together.

I rest my hand on hers and smile. "That's wonderful, Clary. I'm so, so happy for you."

"Thanks, Nelly. I hope you can find someone else who makes you just as happy." Clarissa gazes at me with caring eyes and I smile at her again. Her concern always makes me feel a thousand times better.

Dakota leans in and rubs my arm quickly. "She will."

"Eventually." I sigh. "But for now, I'm just worrying about me." I glance over at the fountain in the square across the street, hoping for a change of subject so I don't have to think about my past.

Mom finally looks up from her cellphone to cut in. "Speaking of, how is the job hunt going, Ellen?"

Cue internal eye roll.

"Not much different than when you asked two days ago, Mom." My eyes meet hers, and I smirk. "I'm still getting some hours at the café, but it's not where I want to be right now."

I'm currently working part-time at a local coffee shop down the road from my apartment, but I've been trying to find a job in child care. I'm not trying to be too picky or ungrateful, but I want to enjoy what I do. After all, that's the whole reason I got a degree in child development.

I love working with children and am set on getting a job in that field. I had a great job at a daycare in Philly, but after everything happened with the divorce, I decided I couldn't stay there anymore. I needed to come home. Since then, I've had a few babysitting gigs on the side but nothing permanent just yet.

"Oh my gosh, Nelly!" Dakota blurts out before my mother can do her usual interrogation. "I can't believe I forgot to tell you!"

"Tell me what?" I ask, intrigued by her excitement and the timing of her statement.

"My boss is looking for a nanny." She says with exhilaration. "I don't know the exact details, but I heard him talking with one of his associates a few days ago, and I instantly thought of you. I told him I knew someone who may be good for the job and he said we could try setting something up!"

My jaw drops and I stare in disbelief as I take in what Dakota just said. "Your boss?" I ask. "As in, Brennan Grant?"

Dakota leans over and closes my mouth. "That's the one." She laughs. "Brennan Grant is looking for a nanny. Are you interested?

"Of course, I'm interested!" I say as if it's the most obvious thing in the world. "I can't believe you forgot to mention it to me. We live together!"

"I know, I know!" She keeps laughing. "We just got caught up in other things it just slipped my mind. Here, I'll call him right now and see what he wants to do!"

She grabs her phone and hits a number on speed dial. Mom, Clarissa, and I watch her step out to the sidewalk to make the call, and then we exchange glances.

"Brennan Grant. Why does that sound familiar?" Clarissa looks at both of us for an answer.

"He's one of the biggest transactional lawyers in the city," I reply. "Extended his dad's firm from the Poconos and opened up his own office here."

"Oh yeah!" Clarissa snaps her fingers as the lightbulb clicks on above her head. "Dakota works for him?"

"She's the receptionist at the firm." I nod, pointing down the street to the left. "Right next door, actually."

Dakota had gotten lucky with her job. She was attending college at the University of Pittsburgh and just happened to be looking for a job at the right time. Brennan had just opened up his firm and was hiring all new staff when Dakota was sending applications around. It's been about six years now, and she still loves every minute of it.

I watch as Dakota hangs up and waltzes back toward us with a swing in her step. She gives me a thumbs up as she reaches us. "He's interested! Wants you to come in for an interview."

Clarissa claps her hands excitedly, and the smile grows on my face.

"Great! When?" I ask.

"Today at two o'clock," Dakota says, peeking back down at her phone. I do the same and see that it is already 12:30.

"Wow, okay," I say. "I can do that. I'll just have to run home quick to change and grab my resume."

"Sounds great!" Dakota beams and takes a sip of her drink.

We finish eating while we discuss various wedding arrangements like venues, photographers, and color schemes. By the time we are finished, it's almost 1:30 and we all part ways. I tell my mother and sister I'll see them soon and they walk off in the direction from which they came.

"Well, I'll be seeing you in a little bit." Dakota winks at me and heads back to work.

From the sidewalk, I glance at the building next door and see the figure of a man standing in the large window on the second floor. I'm not positive who it is, but my stomach fills with butterflies as my nerves arise again. I could become a nanny for one of the biggest names in the city, and I'm not entirely sure what to think of that. I take a deep breath and turn to head home.

As I walk to my apartment, I think about how fast this is happening and try not to let the nerves get to me too much. I've done so many interviews before, and this one would be no different. At least, that's what I hope.

Chapter Two: The Interview

I check my phone when I get home to see the time is 1:40 and I barely have time to get myself ready. I'm not dressed for an interview, so I throw on a nice blouse with some black slacks and pull my long curls into a low bun. I touch up my makeup and, after a quick examination in the mirror, head out.

Even though my best friend works there, and the fact that it is right around the corner from where I live, I've never been to Brennan Grant's office. It will only take a few minutes to get there, so I don't walk too fast. Although it's the middle of winter, the cold doesn't bother me and I enjoy my stroll through the people out and about.

I approach PPG Place and slow my pace as I near the end of the square to the tan building which has "Grant & Associates: Law Firm" written in big letters. From the outside, it doesn't look like much, so I am surprised when I step into the immense two-story lobby. The entire office has a modern style and is gorgeous from the tan, tiled floors to the brown, marble wall behind the L-shaped reception desk.

There's a waiting room to the left of reception which has a round, glass table with magazines organized neatly on top and two huge, white couches around it. For decoration, there are potted plants and a beautiful landscape photo of Pittsburgh, which hangs on the wall behind one of the couches.

Behind reception, a wide hallway, with an array of locked doors along it, leads straight back to what appears to be a kitchen or lunchroom. Just to the right of the hallway entrance, through glass windows, I see three massive conference rooms, lined with bookshelves and furnished with long, elegant tables in the center of each room.

On the far right of the lobby, across from the waiting room, is a grand staircase that leads up to a balcony where there is a hallway which leads to what I assume are the offices of all the associates. Along the wall going up the stairs are some scenic paintings of seasonal landscape.

I'm so caught up in the beauty of the office that I almost forget why I am here until Dakota stands up and greets me.

"Nelly!" She smiles, and I'm awestruck. She fits in perfectly with this type of scene and looks very professional. Her rich brown hair with creamy blonde highlights is styled in an asymmetrical bob, and her makeup is subtle to enhance her bright, hazel eyes. She has such a pleasant face to be greeted by.

"My goodness, Kody, this place is gorgeous," I say as I approach her desk, slipping my jacket off as I walk. "No wonder you love it here so much."

Her smile grows even wider. "It's great, right?" She glances at the clock on the wall next to us. "You're actually a few minutes early, and Brennan is in a meeting with some clients that ran a bit late."

"No problem at all. I don't mind waiting." I smile and walk over to the waiting room, taking a seat on the white couch by the window. I'm actually very thankful for the extra time to calm my nerves. I must have been walking quicker than I thought, because I hadn't expected to arrive early.

"I'll let you know when he's ready," Dakota says as she sits back down to continue working on her computer.

I sit in silence, fumbling with the manila folder on my lap and looking around the room. I feel completely out of my element here, like I don't belong in such a nice, polished setting. People like Brennan Grant don't usually associate with people like me. Dakota is an exception because she has always been confident and headstrong. But me? I've always been more reserved and self-conscious. Why would a big shot lawyer want someone like me caring for his kids?

My thoughts are interrupted by my phone buzzing, and I look down to see a text from Clarissa.

Hey, sis! Let me know how it goes! I know you're going to rock it!
Love you xoxo

I smile to myself and peek out the window, but before I can take in any of the sights, I hear a door open, followed by the sound of men talking. I glance up at the balcony and see a few people coming out of the first office at the top of the stairs.

I can't make out what they're discussing, but the two older gentlemen are laughing about something with the younger, who I instantly recognize from the TV ads and billboards as Brennan Grant. Trying not to pry, I look back down and open my folder to sort through my papers again.

When I glance back up at the men again, they're still at the top of the stairs, shaking hands and saying goodbye. As the older gentlemen walk down the steps, Brennan catches sight of me and just stares for a second, making me feel frozen in my spot. Even from a distance, his gaze is intimidating, and I have to remind myself to breathe. How does Dakota work with that?

After breaking eye contact, Brennan waves goodbye to his clients one last time and strides back into his office, shutting the door behind him. The clients look my way and nod with a smile on their way out the door, and I smile in return.

I patiently wait for a few minutes until the phone at Dakota's desk finally rings. She answers and watches me as she listens. As she hangs up the phone, she stands up and looks my way.

"Alright, girl. You're up." She gestures toward the stairs. "Just up the stairs and he's the first office on the right."

I don't bother telling her that I already know which office is his, and quietly make my way across the lobby.

"Thanks again," I whisper to Dakota as I pass her desk. "This means a lot to me, whether or not it works out."

The walk up the stairs seems to take forever but finally, I'm standing in front of a door with Brennan's name written on the frosted glass. I knock and wait for his reply while my heart beats out of control.

"Come in," Brennan calls from inside.

I slowly open the door and step inside to see him sitting at his own L-shaped desk, organizing paperwork and sliding folders into different drawers in the filing cabinet next to him.

He stops everything and walks around his desk to greet me, fixing the buttons on his jacket as he moves. He's definitely taller than I thought he'd be and, next to me, standing at 5'3", he has to be at least six feet tall.

"Ms. Mannis, it's nice to meet you." He extends his hand to shake. "I'm Brennan Grant."

I take his hand in mine and smile. "The pleasure is mine, Mr. Grant. Thank you for seeing me."

He holds onto my hand for a second and nods when he finally lets go, not saying anything. He doesn't smile and keeps a professional appeal that is just as intimidating as the gaze he had given me a few minutes earlier. He seems very resolute, and I can't tell if that will make this meeting easy or extremely awkward.

"Well, then." Brennan gestures to the chairs in front of his desk. "Shall we?"

I take a seat in one of the chairs and look out the window beside the desk while he settles into his chair. The window takes up most of the wall and overlooks the street below, with a great view of the square and sidewalk below. Clearly, Brennan was the man I saw earlier.

He relaxes in his chair, slowly running a hand through his dark hair. He is much more attractive in person than cameras capture, and I'm trying my best not to stare. I don't want to come across as a strange girl who is infatuated with him like every other woman in the city probably is.

It's hard to ignore the perfect features he possesses, though, and I find myself continually glancing at him to take them all in. He's got a strong build and windswept, dark-brown hair which swoops perfectly above the chiseled face where his crystal-blue eyes glow.

"I appreciate you coming in on such short notice and apologize for the delay." Brennan finally speaks again, snapping me out of my little daze. "Today has been very busy for me."

"I understand." I nod, feeling a little guilty for taking up his time. "I could have come at another time if it were easier for you."

He puts up a hand to dismiss my statement and shakes his head.

"No, it's fine. I need these interviews done because I've been working a lot lately and need to find the kids another nanny." He reaches out for the folder I'm still holding. "May I?"

I hand him the folder and watch him intently as he opens it and skims through my papers, completely silent. I find myself unable to focus because my mind is still wrapped around the fact that he said 'another nanny'. How many has he gone through already? And why?

Eventually, he begins reading some information aloud.

"Alright. Ms. Ellen Mannis. Childhood and Early Adolescent Education degree. Graduated from Penn State in 2011." He peeks up at me. "Great school. I got my Bachelors in Economics there. Graduated 2006." He gives the slightest smile for the first time since I entered his office and it eases the tension a tiny bit.

Looking back down, he continues reading. "And after that, it looks like you worked in Philly for a few years before you moved here to Pittsburgh."

He silently skims through the rest of the papers while I wait patiently, yet anxiously.

"Looks great to me. You're CPR, and first aid, certified and have some years of experience which is what I'm really looking for." He sits back in his chair and studies me for a second, making me feel like a bug under a microscope. I feel my cheeks beginning to turn red as he finally speaks again.

"And your friend speaks very highly of you. If you don't mind my asking, why the sudden move?"

I had anticipated the question and already have my answer planned out in my head.

"It wasn't the job at all, I can assure you. That was probably the only good thing going for me in Philadelphia. Everything else just didn't work out, and I had some personal family matters to attend to, so I moved back home."

Brennan just looks at me and nods, and I can tell he's working things out in his head. He is a very serious man, and I assume it's because of his line of work. I just hope he doesn't think I'm avoiding the question. There are some details he, as my potential boss, doesn't need to know.

"Thank you for explaining. Now, let me give you a quick rundown of what I need right now." He stands up and walks over to the window as he begins.

He saunters along with a purpose and I intently listen to him as he speaks. He just has that alluring quality to him.

"I have three children. One daughter and two sons. Sophia is almost eleven, Asher will be eight in a few months, and Noah just turned four. Unfortunately, their mother passed away two years ago, and I've been through two nannies already who just didn't work out. I'm looking for someone who can help with the kids at home, but also assist here a few days a week to give me an extra hand." He finally turns back to look at me. "Is this something you think you'd be interested in?"

I nod. "I can certainly help with the kids, but I'm not sure how much help I would be here. I don't know the first thing about criminal justice."

"No need for that, I promise." He remains standing with his hands behind his back. "It would be more for organizational purposes. A personal assistant type of position to help me keep everything in check."

I nod as I receive his response, though I still find it interesting that he wants a nanny who can work as an assistant as well. It seems a bit unorthodox, but I won't complain.

"Okay, then that is no problem. I can handle everything."

Brennan saunters back to his chair and sits down. "I'm glad to hear that. You're the first person I've interviewed because I just posted the position a few days ago and any applicants I spoke with fell through. I guess they weren't serious about the job."

"I can assure you I'm very serious," I say, trying to sound reassuring but not too desperate. "And I'm very sorry for your loss."

He leans forward on his elbows, hands interlocked and an even more serious expression than usual if that's even possible. I almost can't believe how intense he is. And yet, I don't feel completely uncomfortable in his company. It's the strangest thing, but there's something about him that makes me feel relaxed in a way.

"Thank you." He croaks a bit and then moves off topic immediately as if the topic of his wife is something he wants to avoid at all costs. I can respect that. "About your salary." He continues with such ease like this is a normal business arrangement.

"On average, a live-in nanny makes about $6-700 weekly, but with the size of my house, three kids, and the additional duties here at the office, I figured $1,500 weekly would suffice. That's $78,000 annually and includes other expenses such as food, transportation, etc." He explains, and all I can do is stare at him, dumbfounded. The salary is amazing, but that isn't what caught my attention.

"I'm sorry, Mr. Grant." I'm not quite sure I heard him correctly. "Did you say live-in nanny?"

Brennan looks confused by my question, seemingly wondering why I would ask. "Yes, you would be moving into the guest room and working as a full-time, live-in nanny. You do that kind of work, right?"

Heat rushes to my face as embarrassment washes over me. I know for a fact Dakota didn't mention anything about a living situation, but I don't want to throw her under the bus.

"Actually, I've never done a live-in situation before. There must have been a misunderstanding. I'm so sorry." I shift uneasily in my seat, angry at myself for not considering the fact that someone like Brennan Grant would be looking for a more established contender.

Brennan begins rubbing his face vexatiously, and I just sit in silence, unsure of what he will say next. I've come to realize that he's a very unpredictable man.

"No apology necessary." He finally says. "I may have forgotten to mention that detail of the position to Dakota."

He refuses to make eye contact with me, and I can sense his frustration. I would say this was the most awkward interview I have ever done, but that would be a lie. It definitely falls within the top five, though. I can't believe I made an idiot of myself in front of this professional, and incredibly handsome, man.

"I'm terribly sorry." Brennan finally meets my eyes again as he runs a hand through his hair like he did earlier. I am surprised by his apology, and don't know what to say, but he stares at me pensively before speaking again. "I take it that's a deal breaker?"

His voice is hushed, and I think I see a hint of disappointment in his face. He's obviously in desperate need of a nanny, and if I say no, he'll be back to square one. Plus, I can't imagine the pain he must be feeling after losing his wife.

I open my mouth, but nothing comes out. I have no clue what to say. It really isn't a deal breaker because what else have I got to lose?

I can see how much we both need this, but a live-in nanny? Could I really do this kind of job? He seems like a nice enough man but I've known him for no more than fifteen minutes, and I haven't even met the kids yet. So, how can I just jump on the opportunity and move in with them?

Almost $80,000 a year, though. I could get a good savings account going and live comfortably until I find more work. This situation almost seems too good to be true, despite the living with strangers aspect.

A million more thoughts are running through my mind, but I sit up straight, meet Brennan's eyes again, and take a deep breath. The answer is obvious.

"I can do it." I put on my best poker face to show him I am serious, even though my thoughts are racing out of control.

Brennan's eyes sink into mine, and I see the relief flood through him.

"Really?" He asks hopefully.

I glance down at my lap for a second, trying to decide if this is truly what I want. When I finally look back up, I give him a genuine smile. "You need a nanny, and I need this job. I don't see any reason we can't make this work."

"Are you sure?" He sits forward, leaning on his desk. "I mean, you'll have personal time for yourself, but I really need this to be a live-in situation."

His eyes quickly look to my left hand as though searching for something. "No husband or other family members to worry about?"

I instantly shake my head at the word husband.

"Nope. Nothing." I say quickly, considering my decision again. "I'm all yours."

Brennan smiles genuinely for the first time, and I notice his entire body relax like a weight has been lifted off his shoulders. He seems much more at peace and his bright, blue eyes have a gleam in them that makes me smile in return.

"You have no idea how much this means to me." He sighs and shakes his head.

"I'm happy to help." I nod and smile once more.

"Well." Brennan starts, checking his watch quickly and pulling out a packet from one of his desk drawers. "As long as you're sure, we have a little bit of paperwork to review, and then we can decide when you'll start."

"I'm positive," I reassure him. "No problem at all."

He continues to grin, and I feel a lot better about my decision. "Great." He says, placing the packet on the desk in front of me. "I have another meeting soon, but we can get this done quickly."

"Sounds good," I answer, and within twenty minutes everything is settled.

As I walk back downstairs, Dakota stands up and examines my face. "Well?" She asks eagerly. "You were in there forever! What happened?

I shrug and smile. "Well, I have a job."

Dakota runs around her desk and pulls me into a hug. "Yay! That's so great, Nelly!" She exclaims.

Her voice echoes in the lobby, and she instantly covers her mouth and giggles. She hasn't even heard the most interesting news yet and she's already squealing. I'm in for it now.

"I'm just curious." I look her in the eyes. "You didn't know it was a live-in position?

"Wait, you're moving in with him?" She gushes, bringing her voice down to a whisper. "Like, you'll be living at his house?"

I nod and study her face for a crazy reaction, but she just seems surprised.

"I had no idea." She shakes her head. "I would have told you if I had, honestly! Either way, you'll do great!" She smiles again and gives me another quick hug before returning to her place behind her desk.

"You'll also be seeing me around here because he wants me to be his personal assistant on top of the nanny duties."

Dakota's eyebrows shoot up, and her smile grows. "No kidding? That's so incredible!"

She looks genuinely happy for me, but then her expression shifts a bit. She almost looks like she has bad news to tell me.

"Um, so what do you think your parents are gonna say?"

My smile vanishes as the realization hits me. "Ah, crap," I mutter and blow her a small kiss. "I'll see you later. Thanks again!"

I rush out the door and stop in front of the building, taking another second to think about everything that just happened. I glance up at Brennan's office window and see him standing there, gazing out at the people on the streets. His eyes find me, and we stare at each other for a second before I nod and start walking back toward Market Square.

I take another deep breath and reassure myself as I pull my cell phone out of my purse. I dial Clarissa's number and wait for an answer.

"Hey, are you at Mom and Dad's?" I ask when she finally picks up. "Good, I'm coming over right now."

Chapter Three: The Move

"What!?" My mother, father, and sister all shout in unison.

"What d'ya mean you're movin' in with Brennan Grant this weekend?" Dad asks, doing the overprotective father ordeal. He may not be our biological father, but he definitely cares about my sister and I as if he were. His eyes are burning into mine, and I can feel his irritation overwhelm me as he stands against the fireplace with his arms crossed.

Dad is like Mom and keeps himself fit, so he can be intimidating. Throw in his thick Irish accent, and it just makes it a thousand times worse. He was born and raised in Dublin but decided to make a big change and move to the United States when he came of age. When Mom met him, she fell hard and fast, just like I had done with my ex-husband. It's different with them, though. They're perfect for each other and I'll always be thankful Mom found him.

Dad is only three years older than Mom, but his grey-brown hair makes him look more his age, and he has prominent facial features that enhance his bright, green eyes.

"Dad, it's not like that at all. It's a job. I'm not dating the man; he's just my boss." I explain, knowing perfectly well that it's going to take a lot more than that to convince him. Things did not go well with my ex-husband, and I know my parents are skeptical when it comes to the decisions I make with men.

Mom sighs and looks at Dad. "Oh, Eamon. Calm down." She shifts her gaze back to me, speaking with a calm timbre. "You know, Ellen, this isn't exactly what I had in mind when you said you were looking for a job in child care."

"Of course, it wasn't, Linda," Dad exclaims. He is definitely not calmed down. "I don't want her livin' with a complete stranger, either."

"Guys, it's not like this was my plan. But, it's a job and a good paying one at that." I take a seat in the lounge chair across from the sofa as I explain.

"Look, we were just going about the interview, and things were great until he mentioned the live-in part. At first, I was going to say no, but I could see how desperate he was for a nanny and hell, it's not like I'm really leaving anything behind. I'm almost thirty years old, I'm divorced, and I'm living in a one-bedroom apartment with my best friend. Not exactly a thrilling lifestyle. And I'll still have some time to myself to see you all."

Mom and Dad exchange a look, and I can tell where this is going.

"Ellen." Dad sighs, rubbing the bridge of his nose in defeat. "You're a grown woman and we can't tell ya what to do. We just hope ya know what ya doin'."

"It is nothing like that!" I defend myself immediately, unable to fathom the idea that they would relate any of this situation to my failed marriage. If I were dating Brennan, I would understand their concern, but this is just a job. Why don't they believe that?

"That's not what I meant," Dad states in his stern voice.

"It's exactly what you meant." I stare daggers at my dad as my mother chimes in.

"We just want you to be careful." Mom's expression remains calm and serene, and it calms me. I know they care about my well-being, but they have this all wrong. I am not repeating my previous mistakes.

"I am being careful. I promise." I lower my voice to just above a whisper. "This is just a job. Nothing more. I can handle it."

"I know you can, honey. We just care, that's all." Mom nods. "If this is what you want, we will support you. Won't we, Eamon?"

She looks to Dad with an expression that pleads for his agreement. One great thing about my mom is that she always lets me make my own decisions, regardless of whether she agrees with them. She would never interfere with my life, unless she thought it would have catastrophic results.

Dad eventually sighs and nods. "Of course, we will."

He doesn't sound completely positive, but the fact that he's trying makes all the difference to me. Clarissa, who has been sitting next to Mom on the couch silently listening to our exchange, leans forward to speak.

"Can I say something now?

"Do I wanna hear it?" I sneer at my little sister. I'm not sure I'm ready for any more criticism right now.

Her face breaks into a smile. "I'm really excited for you! This sounds like an awesome job, and it's a new adventure!"

"Thanks, Clary." I can't help but smile.

My sister always sees the good in everything. She has always been the one person who would support me in any decision I made, no questions asked, and I love her for that. Despite the two-and-a-half-year age gap between us, we've always been close, and she looks up to me as a role model. I want to make a good impression for her when it comes to my career since I didn't do so well in the relationship department.

Mom stands up and fixes her shirt. "Ellen, will you stay for dinner? I can throw something together quick."

She plays it off with a gentle smile, but I know what's really on her mind. Although I'll have some time for myself, this job is taking me away from them again, and she wants to make up for it now.

"That sounds great, Mom." I smile and stand up. "Do you need any help?"

"Oh, no, no. I'm fine. You just hang out with your sister, and I'll let you know when the food's ready!"

She practically hops to the kitchen and Dad sits down in front of the TV to watch a movie on HBO, like usual. In the meantime, Clarissa and I decide to go sit out back on the screened porch and talk while we wait for dinner.

"So, are you nervous?" She asks, sitting on the canopy swing just outside the door.

The evening is chilly and I immediately question our decision to go outside when there is still snow on the ground. I shiver and rub the goosebumps on my arms. I sit down beside her, and we start to slowly rock back and forth.

"I'm not gonna lie, I really am." I look down at my hands and twiddle my thumbs. "This is a really big change. I just met Brennan and now I'm going to be living with him. And, what if his kids don't like me?"

Clarissa immediately grabs my hand to stop me. "Hey, don't think like that. First of all, I know for a fact that the kids will love you! You're incredibly sweet and funny, and I've never seen a child who hasn't fallen under your spell."

I faintly smile and listen as she continues. "Secondly, I can't imagine living with someone as gorgeous as Brennan Grant is that big of a problem!"

"Clarissa!" I gasp, slapping her shoulder, and we burst out laughing.

"Seriously, though, you're gonna be so great!"

She flashes her megawatt smile, and I think about how much I miss our little talks. She has this way of making everything seem better, and times like this are far and few between these days. It's just going to change even more once I start this job and she's finally married.

"Thank you, that means a lot."

She lays her head on my shoulder with her hand still locked with mine. "I love you, Nelly."

"I love you, too, Clary."

***

"Well, this has been fun," I say after taking the last bite of my spaghetti. "I should probably get going, though. I have a lot to get done."

Dad stands up to give me a hug. "Let me know if ya need help with anything for the move."

"I will," I grin and lean onto my tiptoes to kiss his cheek. "Thanks."

I say goodbye to my mom and sister and walk out to my black mini-van, which I've had since I got my degree. I never thought I'd be driving a soccer mom car, but it's convenient for the line of work I'm in, and I guess it will pay off now since I'll be taking care of three kids.

I open the door but before getting in, I look up at the house I grew up in. It's a two-story, brick-front home on a big lot with a detached two-car garage and fits in well with all of the other nice houses in Bethel Park. It had been a great place to grow up, and I had always hoped to someday have a similar home for my own family. It's amazing how much can change in just a few years. For now, my focus is Brennan and his family.

The drive back home takes about 30 minutes, and by the time I arrive, I'm so worn out that all I want to do is sleep and it isn't even eight o'clock yet. I walk into the dark apartment, flicking the light on the moment I reach the tiny living room. Light illuminates from under the bedroom door, so I know Dakota is home, but I won't bother her. I glace around at my belongings, thankful that there isn't much.

The living room has essentially been my bedroom since we moved in, because I had hoped to find my own place sooner rather than later. It was almost like Dakota lived here, and I was the roommate who just ate, showered, and slept on the couch while spending the rest of my time at work. Therefore, aside from the big stuff like the couch, recliner and TV stand, which Dakota is keeping, I don't have a lot to bring with me.

It only takes about an hour to pack my belongings, and then I situate myself on my 'bed' to watch a movie before I go to sleep. Dakota eventually comes out of the bedroom and waltzes into the kitchen.

"I thought I heard you come in." She pours herself a cup of juice and leans against the counter. "How'd your folks take the news?"

"About as good as you can imagine." I sigh, skimming through the guide on the TV. "They'll come around, though, so I'm not worried."

Dakota plops down on the couch next to me. "I can't believe you're leaving me." She pouts and lays her head on the back of the couch. "But I know how great this is gonna be for you."

"I have you to thank for this." I look her in the eyes with a smile. "I really appreciate this. You have no idea."

"Anytime, girl." She smiles. "At least I'll see you at work. Heck, I'll probably even see more of you now!" She chuckles.

"You're probably right." I shake my head and laugh along.

Although we've been living together, our schedules have always been so conflicting that we really don't see much of each other. I feel a guilty leaving my best friend, especially since she moved here for me in the first place, but she's right. I will probably see her more now that I will be at work with Brennan, and who are we kidding? She'll probably love having the apartment to herself.

"So, what are we watching?" She stares at the screen while I scroll and then points with excitement. "Yes! Let's get some laughs in before you leave me forever!"

I turn on the TV show we've re-watched countless times, and glare at her as she hops off the couch and skips back into the kitchen.

"I'm going to pretend you didn't say that"

Dakota throws some popcorn in the microwave, and we both get situated under my comforter, enjoying this last bonding moment before I leave. A few episodes later, my eyes feel heavy after such a long day, and I feel myself slowly doze off.

***

After two busy days of getting things organized for my move, I am woken up on Saturday morning by the sound of my phone's alarm blaring from the kitchen. I jump off the couch, dig through my purse, and shut off the ringer, trying not to wake Dakota.

I quietly shower and get dressed in jeans and a nice shirt, combing my hair out to air dry. After applying a little bit of makeup, I do a quick check in the mirror and nod. I want to look nice for my first day meeting the kids, and this is perfect. I manage to get my van packed up before Dakota wakes up and joins me for breakfast.

When it's time for me to leave, I look around at the apartment a final time. It all seems to be happening so fast, and the nostalgia washes over me. This had been my residence for some of the hardest months of my life while I coped after everything and although it is small, it was home to me. A part of me is going to miss living with Dakota

Once everything is taken care of, I climb into my van and plug Brennan's address into the GPS. I check the time on my phone again and see that it is 1:20 pm, which is perfect since I told him I'd be there around two.

Before pulling onto the road, I take a deep breath and look at my reflection in the mirror. A lot of changes are rapidly happening, and I am both excited and nervous to begin this new chapter in my life.

Chapter Four: The Children

I've never been to Sewickley Heights before because, well, it's a bit above my pay range. I have heard great things about it, though, and I know it's a nice place to live. I am starting to see just how nice as I enter the area, passing huge, luxurious homes. It is no surprise that someone like Brennan Grant lives in such an elite location.

I pull onto the road his house is on and slow down as I look for the numbers on the mailboxes. When I finally find it, I turn into the driveway and am greeted by the most gorgeous house I have ever laid eyes on.

The driveway leads two ways. One way goes to a three-car garage with a walkway attached to the main house and the other way wraps in a circle by the front door. I decide to pull up near the door for the time being while I get my stuff unpacked. I step out of my car and appreciate the huge house which has a brown, veneer stone front and dark-tan siding. The entire two-story house looks like something out of a movie and it seems too good to be true.

I approach the entryway and ring the doorbell, still admiring my surroundings. Even the large front door is impressive, made of a sturdy, dark wood with a large elliptical transom window above, and sidelights along each side.

After about a minute of waiting, the door opens and Brennan stands there with a small smile. It's strange seeing him out of business attire and it almost feels out of character for him to be wearing jeans and a plain, grey t-shirt. I mean, he looks great either way, but that is beside the point.

"Ellen, good to see you. Come on in."

He steps aside for me to enter and I stop just inside the door and stare at the soaring two-story foyer and grand, curved staircase that leads up to a balcony. I look around, taking in every inch of my new home, noticing the sitting room to the left and dining room to the right.

"So, I figured you could meet the kids first and then I'd give you the tour." Brennan says, closing the door behind us. "They're just in the living room. Right this way."

He leads me straight past the staircase and steps down into a large room with vaulted ceilings and long, tall windows that overlook the back deck. As we enter the room, a little boy with shaggy brown hair runs over and hugs my legs.

"Hi! I'm Noah!" The boy smiles and looks up at me with big, brown eyes. I kneel down to his eye level and look into his little face with a grin.

"Hi, Noah. I'm Ellen." I say. "It's very nice to meet you." He giggles at my words and runs back to join his siblings on the couch, where they sit watching TV.

"Sophia, Asher, please come here for a second." They hop off the couch as they're asked and slowly walk in our direction. "Kids, this is Ellen. She's going to be our new nanny."

Asher's lip curves into a crooked smile, exposing a missing tooth.

"Hi!" He waves in one quick motion.

He's a bigger version of Noah with shorter, brown hair and light-brown eyes. Sophia, on the other hand, looks completely different from her brothers. Her dirty-blonde hair is tied into a ponytail with bangs falling in her face, almost covering the bright blue eyes that are identical to her father's. She doesn't seem as happy as her brothers to see me, and I get a mumbled hello before she looks at her feet in silence.

"Now, I need you to be on your best behavior whenever I'm not here, okay? Whatever Ellen says, goes" Brennan looks back and forth between his children and they both nod. "Good. Now go on and finish your movie." He says, tousling Asher's hair before they run back to the couch.

"And you've already met Noah." Brennan points toward Noah who is engrossed in the movie.

What a cute kid. Brennan looks at me again.

"They'll warm up to you. But for now, let's get you that tour."

We start upstairs, where Brennan shows me the loft which sits above the sitting room and overlooks both the foyer and living room. It has a lounge area with a large bookshelf full of a mix of adult novels and children's books. There's a hallway that leads in the other direction towards the bedrooms.

Sophia's room is on the same side of the hall as the room the boys share and they are connected by a shared bathroom which is a nice touch for kids so young. Sophia's room looks like a typical girl's room, painted light pink with floral decals and pictures in white frames scattered around the walls. The boys have a basic boy's room, painted blue-green with stars on the ceiling, bunk beds, and toys thrown all over the floor.

The last room upstairs is across the hall from Sophia's room and is where I will be staying. The room itself is almost the size of the living room of my apartment and has its own private bathroom. It has a cozy feel to it with warm, coral-colored walls and chestnut furniture.

The queen-sized bed has a two-toned, brown comforter and decorative pillows with white-colored flowers on them. The room doesn't have a whole lot in it, but I'm not going to complain. It is the nicest thing I've had in a very long time, and it will be enough to make me comfortable for the time I'll be staying here.

"I hope the room is to your liking." Brennan says, snapping me out of my daze.

I look at him with an appreciative smile. "It's really great, thank you."

Actually, it's better than great. It's amazing.

"After I finish showing you the house, we can bring your stuff inside and I'll let you get settled in." He says, leading me out of the room and back downstairs.

We walk back towards the living room and enter the kitchen to the right. The kitchen has to be about four times bigger than the one at my apartment and has a huge island in the center. All of the countertops are black granite and the tall, mahogany cabinets make the room look nice and homey. It's probably one of the nicest kitchens I have ever stepped foot in and it will take me a while to get used to cooking in it.

The kitchen has an archway that leads into a hallway where you can either go straight across to the dining room, or left down a small hall toward the powder room, laundry room and garage. Across from the laundry room is Brennan's room which, of course, is the nicest bedroom in the house. It's a large room painted light-blue with a king-sized bed, master bathroom, and sitting area by a bay window overlooking the backyard.

Lastly, Brennan brings me out onto the deck where there is a screened porch, table set, and lounge area. A few steps lead down to a stone patio where there's an in-ground pool which is currently covered for the winter. Beyond the pool is a vast yard with a jungle gym, trampoline, and lots of room for the kids to run around. A white fence surrounds the yard and has a gate leading out to a pond behind the house.

I walk over to the deck railing and look out at the landscape as I finally begin to speak.

"You have such a beautiful home." I shake my head in disbelief. "I couldn't imagine having a place like this to call home."

I turn to glance at Brennan who is now leaning against the railing beside me.

"It's amazing" I smile, managing to get a small grin in return.

I know it's going to take a while to alleviate the awkwardness, but I just hope it doesn't take too long. He seems like a nice enough guy, and the seem great, too. At least, the boys do anyway.

"It was my wife's dream home." Brennan says, facing forward and looking out at the frozen pond. I keep my eyes on him, trying to decide if I should move onto a new subject or not.

"Can I ask what happened to her?" I finally ask, hoping he won't be mad by the intrusive question.

I know nothing about him or his family, but I think it would benefit us all if I understood them better. Brennan stares down at his hands for a second and then at me. There is complete sorrow and grief in his blue eyes as they sparkle bright in the sunlight.

"She was in a car accident a little over two years ago." He answers, and looks down at his hands again.

I immediately regret my decision to ask. That must have been very hard for him to endure and now he has a complete stranger digging up the past.

"I'm so sorry." My voice is barely a whisper as I apologize. "I didn't mean to –"

"No, don't apologize." Brennan shakes his head and meets my eyes once more. "It's better that you know. She was on her way home from the store one evening when a drunk driver ran a red light and struck her side of the car. She died on impact."

I look down at the ground and listen to Brennan's story. How terrible it must have been for him to get the phone call when it happened. I can't imagine the pain he felt, and how hard it probably still is for him to cope with that loss.

"I'm sorry that happened to her." I turn and look in the windows of the house and see the kids laughing in the living room. It breaks my heart to watch them, in all their innocence, and think about everything they've lost. "And to all of you."

"Things have been a lot different since it happened," Brennan follows my gaze to the house and shakes his head. "Honestly, the boys are so young and I don't think it hit them as much as it did Sophia. She's been more reserved the last two years, but the boys didn't take long to bounce back to their energetic, zany selves."

"They seem like really great kids." I say sincerely. I can't wait to get to know them better and build a good rapport with them.

"They are, I promise." Brennan nods and smiles briefly. "They're a lot of fun."

I look at Brennan as he watches his children with admiration and can't help but smile to myself. It's great to see him talk about his kids with so much love. I can tell he has a great relationship with them and that is going to make my job a lot easier. We stand in silence for a minute before he lightens the mood with some small talk.

"So, how long have you known Dakota?" He asks.

"Way too long." I chuckle to myself, receiving another grin from Brennan. "We met in the second grade and she's been my best friend ever since."

"That's nice." Brennan nods. "She's a great woman and I've enjoyed having her at the firm."

"She's fantastic. And very driven." I agree. "She won't let you down."

"She hasn't yet." He nods and glances at me. "And I'm very thankful she found me a nanny."

"Me too. I've been looking for this type of job for a while."

I look down at my hands, where I have unconsciously been digging at my nail beds while we talk. It's such a bad habit when I'm nervous but I can't help it.

"Speaking of, I should probably bring my stuff in now."

"Do you need help?" Brennan asks as he leads me back over to the door and opens it for me.

"No, thanks." I step back into the living room and walk toward the front door. "I don't have that much stuff with me."

"Okay, well let me know if you need anything. I'm just going to order a pizza tonight so take your time getting settled." He tells me as we enter the foyer.

"Thank you." I'm about to open the door when I remember something. "Oh, quick question. Where should I park my van while I'm here?"

Brennan opens a drawer on the small entryway table. "I have a spot open for you in the garage." He hands me a garage remote. "It's the spot on the far right."

I take the remote and nod with a smile. "Thanks."

I slip out the door and open the back of my van to grab out a box, but before I do, I glance up at the house again. A smile creeps to my face as I think about how lucky I am. This is such a beautiful place and I can hardly believe it's my temporary home.

It doesn't take me long to bring my stuff inside, considering there are only two boxes. I organize the room the way I want and once I'm done, I walk over to the window and sit down. The sun is starting to go down and I watch the rays reflect on the ice that shields the pond. It's a beautiful view and reminds me of the times Clarissa and I used to go ice skating on the Monongahela River.

After a few minutes of relaxation, I decide to go back downstairs and get myself more acquainted with the family I'll be taking care of.

I walk into the living room and find the kids playing a dancing game on the Xbox and Brennan is nowhere in sight. I take a seat beside Noah on the couch and watch Asher and Sophia dance. The little guy next to me is giggling up a storm and dancing in his seat to the music.

I lean down for him to hear me. "Where's Daddy?"

He looks up at me, never losing his adorable smile, and points toward a closed door on the opposite side of the room from the kitchen. That is Brennan's office and the only room he told me not to worry about during my time here. He said the place is a mess but he knows where everything is and it's best to just leave the clutter.

The song ends and Asher gives his sister a high five, laughing, while they wait for the results to tally up. I must have surprised them because Asher's smile grows even bigger when he spots me next to Noah.

"Hey, Ellen!" He says in a loud voice. "Wanna dance with us?"

His smile falters a little bit when Sophia discreetly elbows him in the shoulder and I instantly pick up on the hint. One thing at a time.

"Maybe another time. I'm enjoying watching you guys." I smile and Asher turns back to help his sister select another song to dance to. I hear the office door open and turn to see Brennan on his cell.

"…that's fine. Great, thank you." He hangs up and tucks his phone into his pocket as he waltzes over to the couch. "Pizza's on its way."

He takes a seat on the other side of Noah and watches Asher and Sophia with a smile. Once again, I find myself filled with admiration for his relationship with his kids.

Brennan, Noah, and I watch two more songs before the pizza arrives and we gather at the island to eat. There isn't much conversation as the kids all devour their slices and then run upstairs to take their baths before bed. I help Brennan clean up the dishes and that's when the talking begins.

We discuss the routines he has for the kids and what his schedule is usually like so I can get an idea of what to expect. I'll bring the kids to school and then head to the office for a few hours a few days a week, and then pick them up after school. On top of that, I'll take care of meals, cleaning, and other household chores. So far, just some basic nanny duties.

Brennan tucks the kids into bed, and I finish cleaning up the kitchen before sitting back down at the island to wait for him. When he returns, he leans against the opposite side of the island facing me.

"So, what about you?" I ask, throwing him off guard.

"What about me?" He analyzes my face, confused by my question.

"Well, you gave me a rundown of the routine with work and the kids, and that's great, but what about you? Don't you ever get some personal alone time to do whatever?"

His expression softens and he sighs "Honestly, I don't even know what alone time is anymore. I've been so busy with work and the kids that I've accepted the fact that I don't get a lot of time to myself."

"I see." I respond, feeling guilty for some reason. It makes me sad that he has to work so hard every second of every day just so his kids can be happy. His happiness is important too, and it doesn't seem like he cares about that now that his wife is gone.

"Well, you have me here now. So, if you ever just need a night to yourself, I've got everything covered."

Brennan stares at me and a small smile forms on his face. "I really appreciate that. Thank you."

After checking his watch quickly, he stands up. "I should probably be heading down myself. Do you need anything else?"

"No, I'm fine. Thank you." I stand up, too, and start in the direction of the stairs. "I'll see you in the morning."

"Goodnight." He responds, turning and disappearing toward his room.

Brennan is definitely different than other men I've known. He isn't mean, but he isn't jolly either and it seems hard to get a read on him because he barely shows any emotion. I can tell there is so much sorrow in his heart and shake my head at the thought.

I decide to shower and read a bit before I fall asleep, so I climb into bed and settle in with my favorite book, which is so worn out from the amount of times it has been read. Maybe I'll browse Brennan's bookshelf in the loft one of these days to find something new. Change is good.

Chapter Five: The Office

By the time Monday rolls around, I am a mix of emotions. Sunday had been a lazy day around the house, getting to know the kids and getting more comfortable with my surroundings. However, today starts my big duties at Brennan's firm and I'm pretty anxious.

There is a lot to do, but I know I will be able to get it all done. I think I'm still just a bit intimidated by Brennan and the lifestyle to which I need to adapt.

I stand in the kitchen as I watch the kids eat their cereal, and prepare their lunches for the day. Turkey sandwiches and some chips for Sophia and Asher in their purple and green lunch packs, and a PB&J for Noah with some animal crackers in his monster lunchbox.

Brennan is in the office gathering his work things, which is the first place he went after preparing his coffee when he retreated from his room. He had said good morning to the kids and me, but it wasn't much of a greeting. I already wonder if he works himself way too much and I hope that isn't going to be a problem.

Once I finish my task, I check the clock on the stove which reads 7:15am. We are running right on time to get Sophia and the boys to the bus stop. I have time to make a quick bathroom break before Brennan finally comes out of his office ready to leave.

"Alright then, I'm going straight to the office while you get them on their buses" Brennan states without making eye contact as he pulls on his jacket and grabs his briefcase. "Are you okay with everything?"

"Yes, it's not a problem" I assure him "I'll be over to the office as soon as I'm done."

"Great" Brennan says as he kisses each of his kids on their foreheads and runs out the door. The kids clean up their breakfasts a few minutes later and we leave as well. The entire morning is very fast-paced, which makes me even more skeptical about the rest of my duties at the office.

I get the kids to their buses on time and pull into the parking garage near PPG Place around 8:45am. I hesitate before climbing out of my car and sit in silence for a few minutes.

I'm really nervous about this part of my job because it's a different atmosphere. It is one thing to be in a personal setting with Brennan, helping him at home with his kids, but it's different being in a professional setting with him, helping him in his career. A career I know nothing about, nonetheless.

I can't hide in my car forever, so I slowly walk myself to the office, taking deep breaths with each stride. It'll be okay, Ellie. Relax.

I enter the lobby, full of mumbles as lawyers talk with one another, already hard at work. I make my way through everyone and sneak into the kitchen to drop off my lunch and then head up to Brennan's office. Dakota waves at me with a huge grin as I pass her desk, and gives me a thumbs up. I'm thankful to have at least one familiar face in this new place.

When I walk into Brennan's office, he is on the phone and motions for me to sit on the couch and wait. I look around the office as I wait and realize how empty it is, considering how much time he spends here. There are no pictures on the wall or desk and the only furniture is Brennan's desk, the couch I'm sitting on, a few filing cabinets, and a large bookshelf to my left.

I can tell that Brennan likes to keep his work organized and separate from his personal life, which makes me even more nervous. I already know he's a different person at home, and I hope he's not too assertive at work. The last thing I want is to make him angry at his job. Maybe that's why the other nannies didn't work out.

"That's fine, Rich, just make sure the files get to me or I can't do anything for you." Brennan sighs with his eyes closed. "I'll call you later in the week to check in." He hangs up and turns to me.

"The kids got on the buses alright?" He asks, still tense.

"Everything went well" I respond with a nod. I don't want to waste any of his time so I quickly change the topic. "So, um, what can I help you with here?"

A faint smile appears on Brennan's face and he stands up.

"I appreciate your tenacity" He gestures to the multiple piles of folders and papers on the tops of the filing cabinets behind his desk. "Unfortunately, I'm a bit behind on filing my paperwork, so I'd really appreciate it if you could sort everything out by case and file it for me."

"Okay." I stand up and walk over to the folders. "Just file everything away."

I stare at everything for a few seconds, completely lost and not sure where to start. This is so embarrassing. How the heck do I file away legal papers?

"Ellen."

Brennan chuckles and I glance over at him to see a smirk on his face. He's laughing at me. I'm not sure whether to be embarrassed or amused by the situation, so I bite my bottom lip and look down at the floor.

"Don't look so nervous." He says as he joins me by the cabinets. "I'm going to have one of our paralegals walk you through everything and show you how things need to be organized."

"Oh, great," I let out a sigh of relief. "I was, uh, not sure where to start. This isn't my type of environment, I'm sorry."

"No worries" Brennan buttons his jacket and starts toward the door. "You'll catch on in no time. Come with me and I'll introduce you to everyone so you can get started."

We weave in and out of offices in the building where I meet the rest of Brennan's staff. Four of the offices belong to the other lawyers, Keith, Byron, Phillip, and Catherine. Byron and Phillip are older gentlemen, probably in their early 50s, and Keith is about my age in his late 20s. Catherine looks young as well, I'm guessing somewhere in her mid to late 30s.

One office is dedicated to the three law clerks who are working for credit toward their degrees. Chris, Mike, and Joe are all in their early 20s and have the appeal of college kids, spontaneous yet cordial.

Our last stop is the office where the paralegals work. Sarah and Brianna are at a regular level, while Lorelei is the senior paralegal as well as office administrator.

"Have you seen Lorelei?" Brennan asks after my introductions are finished.

"I think she ran down for some coffee". Sarah responds from behind her computer screen. Her blue eyes reflect the light from the screen and she smiles and nods at me before she returns to her work.

"Thank you," Brennan turns to leave the room and I follow. "I'll find her if you want to wait in – oh, never mind. There she is."

As we approach the door to Brennan's office, a young woman appears at the top of the stairs. For a moment, I feel like I'm in one of those movies where time slows down and the beautiful leading lady swings her hair back and forth. Lorelei is so pretty that I feel like I'm invisible as she smiles at Brennan.

"Looking for me, Ren?" She grins in all her confidence.

I take a moment to appreciate her flawless face with piercing, dark blue eyes that glow when she speaks. She tosses her wavy, auburn hair over her shoulder and extends a hand toward me.

"You must be Ellen." She introduces herself as I shake her hand. "It's so nice to meet you. I'm Lorelei James".

"Lory, I need you to help Ellen get settled into things today if you're not too busy." Brennan states, glancing at his watch. "I have to run down to the conference room for a quick meeting, but you two can get acquainted without me."

"Sure thing." Lorelei continues to smile as she watches him jog down the stairs. It doesn't take me long to realize that she's into Brennan, and I wait for her to come down from Cloud 9 and bring her attention back to me.

"So, Ellen, you're the new nanny, huh?" Lorelei starts into Brennan's office and places her coffee down on his desk like she owns the place. "You seem like a really nice girl, so I hope you stick around longer than the others."

What is that supposed to mean? I haven't even known the girl for two minutes and she's already insulting me. I've already decided I do not like this woman.

"Um, thanks." I respond, unsure of what I'm supposed to say to that. She certainly doesn't give a great first impression.

"Oh, no offence whatsoever!" Lorelei catches herself and puts a hand over her chest. "I just don't think the other ones were cut out for the job. But you. You seem like you've got what it takes."

"I hope you're right," I smile weakly, feeling even more out of my league than I did when I stepped into this building.

"Well, let's get started here," She claps her hands together and turns to the paperwork. I join her and we sort through everything as she explains the paperwork and how it gets filed away.

Brennan returns to the room and goes about his business while I continue to work with Lorelei on everything. Periodically she peaks over at him and I try not to notice how much she's trying to be noticed. It's pretty sad how she doesn't notice that he isn't into her. If this is how work is going to be all the time, I'm doomed.

Dakota insists on taking me to lunch instead of letting me eat what I brought from home, so we chat over sandwiches at the deli around the corner.

"How are you doing?" Dakota asks, studying my face. "I know it's a fast-paced environment, but I'm sure you're settling in nicely".

"The work is fairly easy, honestly." I admit, feeling much more at ease about my duties after all the help from Lorelei. "I'm just trying to ignore all the flirting".

"Flirting?" Dakota stops chewing and stares at me. "Who's flirting?"

I realize I probably should have kept quiet because Dakota loves gossip and digs it up any moment she gets. But, she's my best friend and I can't not talk to her about stuff like this.

"Um, Lorelei." I slowly take another bite of my sandwich and watch Dakota's expression shift from excitement to astonishment.

"Lorelei? And...Brennan?" She asks, completely at a loss for words.

"Well, he's not the one flirting". I explain. "You really haven't ever noticed the way she talks to him? Or that she checks him out just about every five seconds?"

"I'm not really around them a lot." Dakota says, wiping her mouth with a napkin. "I keep to myself most of the time, and I don't really have any reason to associate with any of the paralegals for more than a few minutes."

"Yeah, well, consider yourself lucky". I huff, staring down at my half-finished sandwich. "That girl is about as narcissistic as they come. And for good reason. She's a peacock, and I feel like a damn emu compared to her."

"Oh my god, Nelly!" Dakota laughs, covering her mouth to refrain from spitting her food all over me. "That is so far from the truth!"

"I just hope every day isn't like this." I laugh at myself "it's very distracting."

"You're gonna find that Brennan likes to work alone most of the time." Dakota says. "He doesn't usually work with any of the paralegals unless he's about to go on trial."

"Either way, I'm just gonna focus on me". I take a sip of my coke and smile. "I need to do my job and show Brennan I'm a hard worker. It makes me nervous that he's already been through a few nannies".

"Don't worry, girl." Dakota grins widely. "You got this."

I return from lunch to find Brennan on the phone again and Lorelei back in her own office. I tackle more of the filing cabinet and when two o'clock rolls around I leave to pick the kids up from school. On my drive, I smile to myself, satisfied with a great first day at work with Brennan. I'm not really sure why Lorelei's behavior bothered me so much, but I'm sure it's nothing.

***

My first week is over before I know it, and I've finally relaxed into the routine a bit better and feel much more comfortable with Brennan and the kids, as well as my duties at the office. The kids have been very welcoming and the house is beginning to feel more like home to me, which makes it easier to do my job. I'm passed the point of feeling like an intruder in someone else's home.

I wake up on Saturday to the sound of the boys giggling and sit up to stretch. I glance at the time and see that it's already nine and decide it's time to pull myself together for the day.

When I step out of my room, I find the boys playing a board game in the loft, while Sophia sits on one of the couches reading. I kneel down beside Asher and look at the blue and red pieces scattered around the board. It's been a long time since I've played a board game, and I love that these kids enjoy them.

"Ellen, play with us!" Noah cheers, happy as always, bringing a smile to my face. "You can be yellow!" He points to the yellow pieces in the box. Brennan had been right. The boys are a load of fun and I love that they already want to include me in their activities.

"I'll tell you what" I begin my proposition "After breakfast, I'll play the winner".

"Okay!" Both boys jump up and run down the stairs and I stand up to follow. I turn to look at Sophia who hasn't budged from the couch.

"Sophia, do you want to come eat?"

She looks at me with her shy expression and nods silently, placing her bookmark in her book and walking past me down the steps. Brennan is already on the couch downstairs reading the newspaper, so the kids sit down with him to watch some cartoons.

I whip up a batch of pancakes with bacon and eggs and we all sit down in the dining room to eat.

"Mmm." Asher hums with a mouthful of pancakes. "Dad, Ellen makes better pancakes than you".

He and Noah both giggle, and I smile as I glance over at Brennan. I'm still trying to figure him out, so it's moments like these that give me the chance to see what kind of person he is.

"Hey, my pancakes aren't that bad!" He throws his hand playfully over his heart and turns to his daughter for back up. "Tell 'em, Soph!"

Sophia shrugs and gives a small smile. "If you wanna call them pancakes."

Brennan nudges her shoulder and she lets out a small giggle. Her laugh is something I haven't heard a lot of since I arrived and I only hope that will change soon. She's a beautiful little girl, and I'd love to have some sort of relationship with her.

"I have to hand it to you, Ellen, you do make great pancakes." Brennan says to me from across the table. "And now these kids don't have to be subjected to my awful cooking". He winks at the boys with a big grin.

One thing I have learned is that Brennan shows a different side to himself when he's at home and it's great watching him interact with his children. He reminds me a lot of my dad sometimes. A hard exterior when it comes to work and business, but a softie when it comes to family.

I clean up after breakfast while Sophia, Asher, and Noah run upstairs to get dressed. I keep my promise and play a quick game with Asher before making a trip to the grocery store.

When I get back to the house, the kids are playing in the backyard while Brennan sits in the screened area on the deck, catching up on a few things for work. I quietly join him and sit down facing the yard so I can watch the kids. They're currently building a snowman and running around throwing snowballs at each other in the process.

"How are you doing?" Brennan asks suddenly, and I glance over to see him peaking at me from behind his laptop. "I think you've settled in nicely, and the kids seem to enjoy having you here."

"I think it's going very well so far." I smile. "And I enjoy being in their company, too. You've really got some wonderful children."

Brennan half-smiles and looks over at his kids running around the yard. I can tell he's got something on his mind, but I don't push him to tell me. It's still early in our acquaintanceship, and I want him to take his time with these things.

"I just wish Sophia would open up a bit." He admits as he continues to watch his daughter running around with her brothers. "She's been so different since Kayla passed away".

"I'm sure she'll get there." I assure him while I watch him. "It's a tough age for her to be dealing with that sort of loss, but she'll decide when she's ready to be more open around other people. This is an adjustment for all of you, but things will get better."

Brennan finally looks my way again and nods slightly. There is a hint of sadness in his eyes and I wish there were something I could say or do to make him feel better about this.

"I guess you're right. Only time will tell." He lets out a small sigh as he looks back down at his laptop and begins typing again.

I shift in my seat to watch Sophia and the boys finish up with their snowman. They're now wrapping a blue scarf around its neck and giggling as they shout out a bunch of potential names for their new friend.

"Frosty is too boring!" Asher chuckles. "How about Mr. Flurry Fancypants?"

"You're crazy". Sophia shoves him playfully and laughs. "Clearly, it should be Elsa Blueflake!"

"Chester Coldbutt!" Noah yells.

Sophia and Asher exchange a glance and break out into big smiles.

"It's perfect." Sophia hugs her little brother as he cheers and giggles at the name he has chosen.

As I watch their interactions, I know that is exactly what we all need. Time.

Chapter Six: The Valentine

Before I know it, we are already in the middle of February, and I'm spending my night baking and filling out valentines with the kids.

Noah's class is having a little party for Valentine's Day tomorrow, and the teacher wanted each kid to bring in something to eat. I guess Noah has been bragging about my awesome pancakes and promised to bring in cookies that were just as amazing. Now I need to make extra special cookies so I don't let him down. But, there's no pressure, right?

"Can I help with sprinkles?" Noah asks once he's done signing his name on his fishy valentines.

"Of course, you can." I carry the baking sheet full of heart-shaped cookies over to where the kids sit and grab the sprinkles for Noah.

"Be careful," Asher says from his seat beside Noah. "You don't wanna mess up Ellen's perfect cookies."

"I only wanna do some of them." Noah smiles as he mixes red and pink sprinkles over the white icing on two of the cookies. "She can do the others cause she's the best."

I smile to myself at Noah's comment and glance up at Brennan who has been silently watching Sophia and Asher fill out their valentines. He meets my gaze for a quick moment and smiles before looking back to his children.

I have to hand it to Brennan, he's had a great attitude towards Valentine's Day, and I give him a lot of credit. I'm sure this is a difficult day for him and yet he still manages to make it great for his kids. The more time I spend with him, the more I see his dedication to his family.

"All done, Daddy." Asher beams with pride as he looks at his dad, and Brennan smiles.

"Great job, bud." Brennan rubs Asher's back and looks over the valentines. "They look awesome. Now, go on upstairs and get yourself ready for bed."

I throw the prepped cookies into the oven and clean up the kitchen while Brennan gets the kids tucked in. I'm just pulling the cookies out of the oven to cool when he returns and sits back down at the island.

"Thank you for doing this." Brennan whispers and I turn to face him, leaning back against the counter. "I know it means a lot to Noah."

"I don't mind at all," I assure him. "I enjoyed helping him out, and I'm flattered he wanted me to cook for his class."

"Yeah, he really likes your food." Brennan smiles weakly and looks down while he plays with his hands. I can tell he's got a lot going on in his head and feel like I should try to help him in some way, but I'm unsure how.

"I think you should know that you're doing a great job." My words cause Brennan to stop and look back at me again. He seems a bit taken aback, yet still intrigued by what I have to say.

"I know this is probably a hard time for you, but I think you've done great staying strong for Sophia and the boys. And I know that hiring a nanny to help might make you feel like you can't do this on your own, but you're doing everything you can for your kids. That's what matters."

At first, Brennan just nods and looks down at the floor. His actions don't offend me because I understand how difficult it can be for him to think about his wife. He finally responds in a gentle voice.

"I appreciate that, Ellen."

He nods and meets my eyes with a grateful expression that reassures me that he isn't completely shut off from his emotions. Brennan may be tough to read, but I've come to learn that he will open up when he wants to.

We sit in silence for a few minutes before I realize that he's only staying awake for my sake.

"You look tired," I observe. "Why don't you get to bed? I'm just going to get these packed away once they've cooled and then I'm going to sleep."

Brennan nods in response and rises from his stool. "Thanks again. Goodnight."

"Night." I watch him carry himself to his room and then sigh once I'm fully alone.

I turn around and stare at the cookies on the tray in front of me. Brennan isn't the only one who is having a tough time with this holiday. I've had some pretty bad experiences that made Valentine's Day one of my least favorite days of the year.

***

"Happy Valentine's Day, Ellen!" Noah shouts as he runs down the stairs holding out a folded piece of pink construction paper. He hands me the handmade card once he reaches me in the kitchen and hugs my leg.

"Aww, thank you." I smile and look at the card.

The front is a jumbled mess of hearts and other designs with a message which reads 'Happy Valentine's Day, Ellen!' in a random combination of upper and lower-case letters. I open it to find a huge heart with Noah, Asher, and Sophia's signatures and a coupon for one free hug from each kid. Asher and Sophia join Noah at the island with smiles on their faces, and I finish observing my gift.

"This is really sweet of you guys, thank you," I speak to all of them and stand the card up in the center of the island on display.

The kids begin eating their breakfast and Brennan joins us in the kitchen for his usual morning routine of coffee and chatting with the kids. He smiles to himself once he notices the card on the island, but doesn't mention it at all.

"You look very pretty today, Soph." He says to Sophia, admiring her pink lacy shirt and red pants. "You should let Ellen do a braid in your hair. It's been a while, and you look so nice with a braid."

Sophia's gaze shifts to me, and she immediately looks down at her cereal once she realizes I'm looking at her.

"I don't wanna bother her." She mumbles low enough that I barely hear her.

"I would love to do your hair, Sophia," I say with a smile, and she looks at me again, but this time she seems welcoming. "That is, if you want me to."

"Okay." She gives me a small smile and follows me upstairs to my room where I throw her hair into a French braid. She doesn't speak while we are alone together, but the fact that she even accepted my help is enough for me.

"There we go!" Brennan beams as we return downstairs, pulling Sophia onto his lap and kissing her on the forehead. "Beautiful."

Brennan looks at me and mouths a 'thank you' before gathering his things to leave. I nod in response and continue to load the cookies into a nice Valentine's Day tin for Noah.

I drop the kids off for school and head to the office expecting it to be another normal day, but I am greeted by something completely different as I enter to lobby. There is an energetic atmosphere, and everyone seems a thousand times more animated than usual.

"Morning, Nelly!" Dakota beams once she sees me and I approach her desk with confusion written all over my face.

"Did I miss something?" I ask as I watch our coworkers chat merrily amongst themselves as they go about their daily routine.

"It's Valentine's Day, silly." Dakota chuckles, and I glance back at my best friend, wondering where the real Kody is.

"Yeah, I know that. But, why is everyone acting so differently?" I notice Dakota's attire – a nice, red, fitted dress – and shake my head. "And what was in the arrow Cupid shot at your butt?"

"You're crazy, but I love you." Dakota smiles and leans over her desk to whisper. "Honestly, I'm not sure why everyone gets so happy this time of year, and I know it's not your favorite day, but I just roll with it."

I shake my head and laugh a little as I realize that this is what normal people do on Valentine's Day. It's a festive day where people show their love, and I reflect on the fact that this day means nothing to me. It's actually the complete opposite for me.

"Right. Well, you enjoy yourself." I turn to head upstairs. "And I'll just be in my bubble of normalcy in Brennan's office."

Brennan is already on the phone when I enter the room, so I quietly go about my business. Whatever has gotten into everyone else, it didn't affect Brennan at all, and I was right. This is just as normal a day for him as it is for me.

A few hours later, Dakota and I are returning from lunch when I notice a rose on her desk. I'm about to ask about who it is from when we are interrupted by an approaching voice.

"Hey girls!" Lorelei waltzes over to Dakota's desk, rubbing her own, small rose around her neck like she's showing off.

"Hey, Lory." I smile in return even though I really don't want to. Although it's only been a few weeks, I've already decided that Lorelei is not the company I'd like to keep and I only get along with her for the sake of my job.

"Who is the rose from?" Dakota asks, playing along with Lorelei's game.

"Ren." Lorelei smiles as she smells the flower dramatically. Dakota rolls her eyes as she looks to me with a blunt expression. I feel myself getting angry at her constant shenanigans, but don't say anything. It's better that way.

"Brennan gave you that?" Dakota asks in a playful tone, and I can't help but feel like there's something I'm missing.

"Well, he didn't give it to me directly, but there was a tiny card with it on my desk this morning and –"

"'Thank you for all of your hard work. I appreciate all that you do. Happy V-Day – Brennan Grant'" Dakota interrupts Lorelei, reading her own card. She stares at Lorelei with a smirk as the smile is wiped away from the latter's face.

I glance at the company name on the back of Dakota's card, and the realization hits me.

"Oh, I've heard of this company," I say as I point to the card still in Dakota's hand. "We used to do something similar around Thanksgiving at the bakery. For every rose bought, the money goes to a charity of your choice."

"Well, it looks like our boss was very generous today," Dakota says, holding up the same rose from her desk that I was curious about. "That was really nice of him."

"Where's yours, Ellen?" Lorelei sneers at me with confidence, knowing the answer before I can even respond. "Looks like he wasn't feeling *that* gen –"

"Excuse me, ladies." Lorelei is interrupted once more by a delivery man holding a small bundle of three roses. "I have a delivery for, um."

He glances at the card in his hand and then turns his attention back to us.

"Ms. Mannis?"

"That's me," I say as I lift my hand to receive my gift. "Thank you."

I glance at the card and realize it's not the same company that Dakota and Lorelei got roses from. I also notice that the roses are velvet, as opposed to the real ones Brennan gave everyone else, and are a tiny bit bigger in size. Why would he get me three, velvet roses, instead of a real one like everyone else?

"Wait, there must be a mistake," I say, holding out the card and roses. "Are you sure this is for me?"

"Are you Ellen Mannis?" He asks with a small grin.

"Well, yes, but –"

"Then there's no mistake here." The man nods and then waves before he turns to leave. "Have a nice day, ladies."

I glance at Dakota briefly before she and Lorelei both peak over my shoulder at the card in my hand.

"'Thank you for taking a chance on my family. I appreciate everything you've done for my kids so far. Happy Valentine's Day. - Brennan'" Lorelei reads my card aloud and then sighs audibly. "Aww, how sweet. Good for you, Ellen. I told you you'd last longer than those other girls."

Lorelei walks away without another word, and I glare at her back as she disappears into the break room. She can be such a piece of work, but I don't let it bother me too much.

"Someone's jealous." Dakota laughs, and I can't help but join in for a second. She grabs the card from me and shakes her head in disbelief. "Seriously, though, he got you velvet roses that weren't for charity. That was really nice of him."

"Yeah, it was." I watch Brennan through the glass windows of the conference room where he's meeting with a few men. He's just full of surprises, I guess.

***

The rest of the day passes like normal, and the roses aren't brought up by either Brennan nor myself. I pick the kids up and listen to Noah excitedly recap his day and how much his class loved my cookies.

That night, once the kids are in bed, I sit at the island alone, rubbing my fingers along the petals of the velvet roses. I almost feel a little guilty that I didn't get something simple for Brennan now. I feel like I should put the roses somewhere, so I find a small glass that holds them perfectly and look for a place to display them.

As I'm placing the glass in the center of the island with my card from the kids, Brennan walks in from outside and stops when he sees the flowers. He doesn't seem mad, and it almost seems like satisfaction on his face.

"I, um, figured they should be somewhere they can be appreciated. I didn't want to just shove them in a drawer in my room."

I tuck some loose hair behind my ear nervously and bite my bottom lip. I feel awkward all of a sudden, and I suppose it's because it seems like I'm making myself at home in Brennan's kitchen.

"That's fine. They look nice there." Brennan smiles and then gestures to the flowers. "I would have gotten you a real one like I did everyone else, but I wanted to do something different for you to show my appreciation. And I figured the velvet would be nice so they'd last."

"No, it's great." I smile again and nod. "They're very nice roses. Very, um, festive. And I appreciate the gesture."

Brennan just watches me in amusement as I fumble over my words. Why am I suddenly acting like an idiot around him? I have always found him attractive, but that never made me act any different when I was with him. Now I feel so nervous and transparent, like he can see right through me.

"I guess I'm just not used to getting things on Valentine's Day." I rub my arm and look down at my feet. "My, uh, ex was never into that sort of stuff. It's not exactly my favorite day of the year."

"I see." Brennan nods with a weaker smile this time like he knows he touched on a tender subject. "Well, I'm glad you like them."

"I do, thank you," I say and glance at the time on the stove. "Well, I should probably get to sleep. I'll see you tomorrow."

"Goodnight, Ellen." Brennan grins, and I nod with a smile as I walk past him to go upstairs. What in the world has gotten into me? Snap out of it, Ellie.

Chapter Seven: The Past

The rest of the month flies by in the blink of an eye, and I can hardly remember where the time has gone. The boys have completely warmed up to me and, although Sophia still doesn't talk much, I can see that she's getting used to having me around as well.

Since Valentine's Day, Brennan has been much more open with me, and any awkwardness that was there in the beginning is now gone. Well, at least the 'stranger in a new home' awkwardness. I've still been acting like a total nutcase around him for some reason, and I'm not sure why.

It's a Friday afternoon at the end of March, and the kids are in the loft doing their homework while I'm in the kitchen getting things ready for dinner. As I pull out the meat from the refrigerator, my phone dings and I read a text from Brennan:

Hey, working late today so eat without me. See you all when I get home.

I sigh as I place my phone back down on the counter. It isn't the first time he has been home late, so I carry on like usual and begin to cook dinner. The children come down just as I'm prepping the ground beef for meatballs and sit at the island, watching me.

"Where's Daddy?" Noah has his face in his hand as he leans forward and examines what I'm doing.

"He just texted me a few minutes ago to say he's going to be late tonight." I shrug and watch as their faces drop from my news.

"Again?" Asher whines and plops his arms into his lap in frustration.

"Yes, so we are going to have to eat without him." I look at their sad little faces and try to think of a way to raise their spirits a bit. "But hey, if you guys help me clean up later, I think we can watch a movie. What do you say?"

That seems to do the trick because they all look at each other with small smirks and then nod at me excitedly. Over the last few weeks, I've really learned what motivates these kids and makes them happy. Let's just say, an animated movie usually does the trick.

"The bug movie!" Noah shouts with his fist in the air, and his siblings agree in unison.

"Alright, bugs it is," I laugh, rolling another meatball and placing it on the tray with the others. "But, like I said, only if you help me clean up after dinner."

"Done!"

"Okay!"

"Yay!"

They all keep me company while I cook and we chat about random things during our meal. I now know that a boy named Tommy in Noah's class picked his nose and ate it today. Not once, but three times. I also learn about the cool thing that Asher's science teacher showed them about clouds.

As promised, they help me clean up and then go upstairs to bathe before their movie. I set up the Blu-ray for when they come back down and get started on the dishes. By the time I'm done, they are all cuddled on the couch with their blankets watching their film.

Asher peers over at me while I dry my hands and waves me over. "Come watch with us, Ellen!"

I smile to myself as I hang the dish towel back on its hook and shut down the kitchen before walking over to the couch. When I get there, I see a space cleared for me between Noah and Sophia, and immediately settle in. I'm barely situated before Noah curls into my side and giggles, getting himself comfortable. Only a few minutes later, Sophia rests her head against my other shoulder, and I just smile to myself again. It's progress.

A while later, a gentle shake on my shoulder makes me open my eyes, and I realize that I fell asleep. The movie credits are rolling and Brennan stands in front of me with a frivolous grin. He's already in his sweatpants and t-shirt and crosses his arms as he watches me and the kids on the couch.

"Out cold," He chuckles.

"What?" I look down, taking in the kids sleeping all around me. "All of them?"

"All of them." He nods, still grinning, and I run my hand through Noah's thick hair as he sleeps peacefully on my lap.

Brennan gently picks Sophia up to bring her to bed while I remain on the couch with the boys. He comes back for Asher, and I follow him upstairs with Noah to tuck them in. I gently lay Noah down and kiss him on the forehead before following Brennan out to the hall.

"I can't believe we all fell asleep like that," I whisper as Brennan closes the bedroom door behind us. "They were so excited to watch that movie."

"I'm shocked, too. They don't usually fall asleep during movies" He says as we slowly walk down the hall, trying not to make too much noise. "I expected to come home to a madhouse, but I guess not."

We arrive back in the living room, and I gesture toward the kitchen. "There's a plate of spaghetti set aside for you to heat up if you're hungry."

"Great, I'm starving."

Brennan heats up his food and sits at the island eating while I put the movie away and shut down everything in the living room. When I'm finished, I join Brennan and lean against the island opposite him.

"I think I'm gonna get to sleep if you don't mind." I lift my hand to my mouth, covering the yawn that escapes.

"You know you don't have to ask, right?" Brennan asks with a smirk on his face, watching me intently.

I shrug and grin a little. "I do now. I just like to make sure everything is taken care of before I go to bed. And, I guess I feel a little guilty if I go to sleep before anyone else since this is my job."

"Well, you don't have to worry" He takes a small bite of his food. "Everything is perfectly fine. Go get some sleep, and I'll see you in the morning."

"Alright, alright. Goodnight."

We exchange smiles, and I head upstairs to shower and get some much-needed sleep. I feel strange going to bed so early on a Friday night, but I haven't been sleeping well lately, and I need to catch up on the lost sleep.

***

My eyes shoot open, and all I can see is darkness. I can't remember the dream that woke me, but my forehead is covered in a layer of sweat, and my heart is racing. I roll over and glance at the clock on the end table where the time is glowing green: 2:06am.

I turn the light on and sit up in bed, looking around the empty room and trying to gather my thoughts. Over the last few months, there have been times where I find it difficult to sleep at night, but I try not to think too much about it. I'm sure everyone deals with insomnia every now and then, right? Oh, who am I kidding?

I rub my left shoulder and sigh to myself. This has got to stop.

I know I'm not going to be able to fall back asleep right away, so I quietly go downstairs for a drink of water. Once I have my cup, I decide to relax in the sitting room and lounge in the window seat with my legs curled into my chest.

I rest my chin on my knees and stare out the window at the snow gently falling in the front yard. We haven't gotten a lot of snow this year, and I like to enjoy it while I can. The moonlight catches in the soft, white flakes as they make their journey to the ground and I think of my sister again.

When we were kids, we would always lay out a blanket in the living room at home and gossip about everything under the moon while we watched the snow fall. That was when we didn't have a care in the world. Back when life seemed so simple.

I close my eyes and let memories of the last few years fill my mind. How could I have been so stupid to throw away so many years? I could have done so much with my life, but instead, I got myself stuck in a terrible situation.

The sound of footsteps interrupts my thoughts, and I glance over to see Brennan entering the room, rubbing one of his eyes and letting out a quick yawn.

"I thought I heard something," He says as he puts his hands in the pockets of his sweatpants and looks at me through sleepy eyes. "Everything okay?"

"Yeah, I'm fine." I sit upright and hold my cup in my lap. "I just haven't been sleeping well lately and came down to clear my thoughts."

"How about some company, then?" Brennan asks before settling onto the loveseat next to me. I nod, and he just sits and watches me for a second, like he always does.

It seems strange that Brennan tends to watch me so much, but it doesn't bother me one bit. I know he's an observant man, and I assume he's just trying to understand me without quite asking outright. After all, he is a lawyer, and that's his forte. And, I'd be lying if I said I wasn't trying to understand him too.

"Penny for your thoughts?" He asks.

"The going rate is actually a dollar" I whisper lightheartedly.

I hear Brennan chuckle and meet his eyes, considering what I want to tell him. How much does he really need to know right now?

"My mind just gets running sometimes, thinking about the past. I shrug and look back out the window. I'm unsure whether I want to elaborate more on the subject. "Just stupid stuff, really."

"Anything to do with that?" Brennan's question causes me to look back at his face, and when I do, his gaze shifts to my shoulder and he nods toward it.

Busted.

I didn't think I'd be seeing him when I came down for my water, so I hadn't thought to cover up the scar that cuts across most of my shoulder. With it being winter, I have been lucky enough to not have to worry about covering it up around Brennan and the kids. I always sleep in a tank top, though, and would have slipped on a sweater had I known I would see him tonight.

I keep my eyes on Brennan and give him my best poker face.

"Maybe."

He nods slightly, keeping his eyes locked on mine.

"Can I ask what happened?" Brennan asks in a cool tone.

It's obvious that he doesn't want to pressure me into talking, but there is still the same curiosity in his voice that is always there.

"It's a long story," I reply "And it's in the past, so it doesn't matter now, anyway."

"The past always matters, especially when it leaves scars" He responds with distress.

I almost feel as if there's a hidden meaning to his words. I wonder if maybe there's something from his own past that left him scarred. We stare at each other for a few seconds before he realizes what he has said.

"Of course, you don't have to tell me. I completely understand if you're not ready for that yet. I'm sorry if I overstepped my boundaries."

That's the thing. He didn't overstep any boundaries. Something inside of me wants to tell him. He hasn't been fully open with me yet, but a part of me wants to talk to him about everything. The problem is, my story is still so fresh in my mind that I have no idea where to even begin.

"No," I brush my hand gently over my scar "No, I want to tell you."

I decide it's best to start at the very beginning and I let out a small sigh to clear my mind. I straighten out, so I'm sitting with my back to the window, and close my eyes.

"When I was in my senior year of college, I met this guy at a bar." I begin my tale, gripping the cup in my hands for moral support. "Typical boy meets girl scenario. He was incredible. Very handsome, lots of fun, and it didn't take long for me to fall hard."

I speak slowly as I recall the past events, trying not to let my emotions get the best of me.

"Well, not even a month into the relationship we were living together, and within the year we were married," I shake my head at my own stupidity. "Things moved so fast that they're pretty much a blur to me now."

"Things were going great. We seemed to have a perfect life, and I didn't think things could get any better. And I was right because a few years into the marriage, things began to fall apart."

I take a break to gather my thoughts, but Brennan doesn't rush me. Instead, he sits silently in his seat, waiting for me to continue at my own pace.

"He started to drink more and more, which made him very aggressive, and it got to the point where we were fighting all the time."

Here comes the hard part.

"It wasn't long before he started getting physical during our fights and for whatever reason, I still wanted to see the good in him. He was in there somewhere, the man I fell in love with. No matter how much he hit and abused me, I held hope that things could get better again."

I glance up at Brennan for the first time since I started my story and his face is expressionless as he intently takes in every detail. I can tell he knows where the story is going, but he still just listens in silence.

"I let the abuse go on for almost two years, even after some serious incidents. Well, one night, almost a year ago, I decided that I had had enough. We were having a huge argument and he –"

I close my eyes again and feel a lump forming in my throat. My eyes are stinging, but I refuse to cry. Not again. The memories are so fresh, but I refuse to let them get to me.

"He shoved me."

Another quick glance at Brennan tells me he's still paying close attention.

"It was so hard that I went crashing through our glass shower door and got some deep gashes in a few areas. I had to be rushed to the hospital, but I was out within a week."

I keep my eyes glued to my cup and slow my talking to avoid a crack in my voice. The events are still hard to think about and as the memories resurface, so does the pain.

"That's the personal matter that made you move from Philly to here," Brennan states quietly, causing me to glance up at him again. I nod in response and continue with my story.

"The whole thing was an eye opener, and before I moved back here, I told him I wanted a divorce in exchange for me not pressing charges, and he agreed to it. I found a place here and tried to get back on my feet while the process happened. Everything has finally been settled, and the divorce was finalized a few months before I started working for you. Now I just want to leave him, and everything that happened, behind me."

A few moments go by as Brennan and I sit in silence but, as I look at him, I see sadness in the blue eyes looking back at me. I know that he feels my pain as he shakes his head and looks back at my scar.

"I'm so sorry, Ellen," His voice is only a whisper "You don't deserve any of that, and it's a good thing you got out when you did."

All I can manage is another small nod. He moves from his seat to kneel in front of me and gently lays a hand on mine in my lap.

"You're safe now."

Brennan pulls me into a hug and I close my eyes, feeling a single, warm tear slide down my cheek. For the longest time, that was all I wanted. Safety. It took a while to finally feel normal again and now, more than ever, life seems to be full of light again.

As I pull out of the hug, I wipe my cheek and take a deep breath to shake the numbness away. I'm not going to let it get to me again. I had my time to cope and I'm much stronger now because of it.

"Thank you" I take one last sip of my water and sigh.

Brennan watches me carefully, and I get the impression that, for whatever reason, he cares about my situation. He cares about me. He's usually very reserved, but right now I feel like he understands me.

"I should probably try to get more sleep before the kids wake up" I break the silence.

Brennan stands up as I do and we both make our way back into the kitchen. I place my cup in the sink and turn around, leaning against the counter with my arms crossed. It isn't cold in the house, but I have chills and a bad feeling in my stomach. Will the pain that comes with the memories ever go away?

"I hope you get more sleep," Brennan says as he slowly makes his way back toward his room with his hands tucked in his pockets again "Night."

"Brennan?" I stop him just as he reaches the hall. He turns back to face me, and a small smile appears on his face.

"Please, call me Ren," He says "It's what my friends and family call me."

I smile in response to his statement and look down at the floor. He considers me a friend, and that makes me feel a little better than I felt a few minutes ago.

"I just wanted to thank you for listening. I'm sorry I didn't tell you sooner, I –" I take a deep breath. "I'm not proud of my past and try to avoid it as much as possible."

"Don't be sorry, Ellen" He shakes his head "I completely understand. I know how it feels to have things you'd rather not think about."

There's sincerity in the way he says it, and I know that he truly does understand. We may have different stories, but we both know the pain that comes from our pasts, and it's clear we are both still trying to figure out how to deal with it.

"You can call me Ellie," I offer with a smile "I prefer it to my full name."

"Okay, Ellie." Brennan smiles at me and nods his head "Goodnight."

"Goodnight," I watch him walk away and stand alone in the kitchen for a few minutes, wondering how I am ever going to get back to sleep with everything on my mind.

Chapter Eight: The Party

Sunday was back to normal, and we decided to make it a lazy day for all of us. Aside from Brennan getting on his laptop for a little while to do some work while the kids ran around, we didn't do a whole lot. I love days like that.

The following morning, Sophia is the first person to join me in the kitchen with her backpack strung across her shoulder and headphones in her ears.

She takes a seat at the island, and I give her a nod, knowing she won't hear me if I say good morning. I slide her lunch money in front of her and give her a bowl and spoon for her cereal. She peers up at me through her bangs and one side of her lips curves up.

"Thank you," She says in her mouse-like voice, bringing a smile to my lips. I'm really glad to hear her talking more, even if it is only a little at a time. She's been slowly opening up to me more, and it makes me feel like I must be doing something right.

"You're welcome" I say before walking back to the opposite counter to finish up with Noah's lunch.

Brennan walks into the kitchen in full work mode, straightening his tie and buttoning up his jacket.

"Good morning" He grins, and I can see that the lazy day has rejuvenated him and he is back-to-business Brennan. I think our little heart to heart over the weekend helped, too, because he seems much more laid back around me now.

"Good morning. Your coffee is ready to go" I point to the travel mug sitting by his briefcase on the counter as I load up Noah's lunchbox.

"Thank you. You're amazing" He takes a quick sip, and I just watch him, astonished by his words.

I don't think he realizes what he said because he goes about drinking his coffee. It hadn't taken me long to catch on to how he prepared it – two sugars and a little half and half – and I try to have it ready for him during the week now. I look at the clock and realize we have to leave soon, so I call up to the boys.

"Asher, Noah, hurry up. We don't want to be late." I yell to the balcony and not even a minute later the boys are sitting at the island with their sister, chowing down on their breakfast.

The rest of the morning goes like normal, with me dropping the kids off and jumping into my duties at the office. By the time lunch rolls around I'm starving, and I realize it probably wasn't the smartest idea to eat nothing more than a granola bar for breakfast.

As I settle down at one of the tables in the break room, I decide to call my mother to check in. It's been a while since we spoke and I feel awful about it.

"Is his house huge? What am I saying? Of course, it is!" Mom keeps loading me with questions.

In reality, it feels like a one-sided conversation, but I won't complain. It's great to hear her voice. She sounds happy, and I'm just glad she isn't lecturing me about a million other things.

"It really is a beautiful house" I admit "I love the job so far."

That's the understatement of the year. The house is more than amazing, and I'm lucky to be able to call it home, if only for a little while. As if reading my mind, Mom asks the same question I've been wondering since I started the job.

"Do you know how long you'll be there?"

"I'm actually not sure yet. We haven't talked about it"

I really do wish I knew how long I'd be staying with Brennan and the kids. Hopefully, he gives me enough notice to find another job before I have to leave, when the time comes. I hear my mother sigh through the phone.

"Well, will he at least give you Saturday off to spend time with us and celebrate?"

I quickly glance at the calendar by the microwave and slap my forehead. With this new living arrangement and getting settled into a different routine, it had completely slipped my mind that my birthday is coming up this Friday.

"I'm not sure, Mom," I reply, hoping she won't freak out about this.

This is the first time in years that I'm in town for my birthday and have the opportunity to spend it with my family, but I'm not sure it's gonna happen. I know she wants to celebrate with me, but this job is important.

"I think you should at least ask him, sweetie. We'd really like to see you."

I relax in my seat a little, thankful she sounds calm and not agitated. She tends to make a big deal out of the smallest things sometimes, but thankfully this isn't one of them.

"Okay, I will. But if it doesn't happen, it's not the end of the world," I laugh "I'm 29. It's not like when I was 12."

I hear footsteps approaching and within a few seconds, Brennan strides in with his lunch from the coffee shop down the block, which I thought he'd be eating there. He doesn't normally stay at the office for lunch.

"Mom, let me talk to you later, okay?" I try to get her off the phone, but she keeps yapping "Yes, I know. I'll ask him. I'll talk to you later! Love you, bye."

I hang up the phone and glance up at Brennan.

"Ask who, what?" He asks with a smirk and I bite my bottom lip as I think of a response.

"Oh, it's about this weekend" I wave it off like it's nothing and change the subject, "I thought you were eating out for lunch like you always do."

"I figured I'd bring something here and keep you company. Not sure if you've noticed, but you tend to eat alone a lot," Brennan responds as he adjusts the buttons on his jacket and takes a seat across from me.

"Dakota likes to go out for lunch, and I just prefer to stay here."

I glance around the room and realize how lonely it really seems when I eat by myself.

"I guess I also just feel out of place sometimes. I'm not exactly the type of person who belongs in a law firm," I chuckle to myself.

"I think you fit in just fine," He grins, eyeing me warmly. "Don't be so quick to push yourself aside, Ellie."

Brennan takes a bite of his sandwich and looks at my lunch, which I haven't even touched yet. I take this as a hint and unwrap my own sandwich to take a bite. For some reason, although we eat every meal together at home, this feels weird to me. I'm strangely nervous.

"So, what's going on this weekend?" He asks in between bites.

"Oh." I didn't plan on asking him now. "You don't have to worry about that now. We can talk about it later."

Brennan pats his face with a napkin "I really don't mind. Now is okay."

I should have known he'd be stubborn about this. I shouldn't have said anything at all.

"Okay." I look down at my sandwich and think about how to explain. "It's my birthday on Friday, and my parents wanted to see if I could go see them to celebrate at some point this weekend."

I watch Brennan for a reaction, and he just nods while he chews. I decide to continue.

"I know it's only been a couple months and is kind of soon to be asking for the time off, but my mom wanted me to bring it up anyway."

Brennan just watches me while he chews and I can tell he's deep in thought. I feel stupid for even asking now, and can feel myself starting to turn red.

"Why don't you invite them to the house on Saturday?" He finally asks.

"What?" I can't help my surprised tone, but I wasn't expecting a response like that. "I don't want to put you out. Really, it's not a big deal. I can always make up for it another time."

"It's not putting me out at all. I really don't mind. Plus, I think the kids would enjoy a little get-together at the house."

I just stare at him, amazed that he is even offering to do something like this for me. And yet, I'm a bit nervous for him to meet my family. I don't need anyone getting the wrong impression.

"Um, okay."

"Okay," he smiles "And I obviously won't make you work that day. They can come in the afternoon, and I will barbeque, and then they can leave when they want. Is it just your parents?"

"Well, my sister and her fiancé would be coming too, actually. If that's okay, of course."

I really can't believe where this conversation has gone. It was very generous for Brennan to open his home for my family and I can't help but admire him for the gesture. He's certainly full of surprises, and I am grateful that he has turned out to be such a nice guy. Especially after the first impression he had given me during the interview. I admit that I had prepared myself for the worst.

"I look forward to meeting them all," he smiles as he finishes his food "I can even invite a few people from here if you'd like. Turn it into a little party."

"That sounds nice." I agree. "Thank you, Ren. This means a lot to me".

"My pleasure," he says and smiles at me with his mouth full. I smile to myself and look away. I'm always happy to see his goofball side every now and then.

His phone buzzes, and he pulls it out to check it quickly. At that moment, Dakota walks in and stops the moment she sees Brennan sitting with me. She shoots me a questioning gaze just as he tucks his phone away and turns to her with a smile.

"Perfect timing, Dakota." He stands to throw his garbage away, and Dakota stands there like she's waiting for him to give her something to do. "As you are well aware, Friday is Ellie's birthday. I am having her family over to my house on Saturday to celebrate, and you are welcome to join us."

"Okay!" She seems confused and excited at the same time. "If there's a party, I'll be there. Thanks for the invitation."

"Of course. What's a birthday party without her best friend, right?" Brennan smiles at both of us and then walks toward the hallway. "I'll see you in my office, Ellie."

Once he's gone, Dakota rushes over and plops down in the seat Brennan left vacant.

"A party at Brennan's?" She gushes, unable to contain her excitement. "How did *that* happen?"

Dakota laughs as I stand up to throw out my garbage. I dampen a paper towel and wipe my hands and face off and turn back to my best friend.

"That wasn't my intention at all, but I'll take it." I shrug and lean against the counter with a smile, recalling the events that just occurred. "I just told him my family wanted to see me this weekend for my birthday and he recommended a party at the house. It was really nice of him."

"I'll say!" Dakota smiles, shaking her head. "Very surprising. I can't wait!"

I can't either, to be honest. It's going to be nice having everyone together. I imagine the day in my head as Dakota and I leave the kitchen to go about the rest of our day before I leave to get the kids home.

***

The rest of the day seems to fly by, and before I know it, Brennan, the kids and I are all eating in the dining room, talking about the day. Brennan and I listen to the kids as they recap their days, in which we learn that Tommy in Noah's class ate a bug on the playground, and some girl in Sophia's class was planning a birthday party soon. Once Brennan has heard everything, and we are just about done eating, he brings up the plans for Saturday.

"So, kids, what do you think of having a little party this weekend?" He cuts a final piece of his steak as he speaks and I watch their little faces light up at the idea.

"A party?" Noah shouts in excitement "I love parties!"

It is incredible how this kid has an enthusiasm for every little thing, and I can't help but chuckle to myself at his vivacity.

"What's the party for?" Sophia asks, and I can see that even she is enlivened by the thought of a party. This just makes me even more excited for the weekend.

Brennan looks at me and then at Sophia. "Well, Ellie's birthday is on Friday, so we are going to have her family and some friends over on Saturday to celebrate."

Asher instantly shifts his gaze to look at me with his signature grin. "It's your birthday? How old are you gonna be?"

"Ash, it's not polite to ask people that," Brennan says and lifts his cup to take a sip. I don't mind the question, though.

"It's okay." I smile and lean forward as if I'm about to tell a secret, but speak loud enough for everyone to hear. "I'll be 29."

"Cool!" Asher seems impressed, and I giggle. "You're almost as old as Daddy. He's 34. Such an old fart!"

Brennan chokes a bit on his drink, and it makes me laugh even harder. When he catches his breath again, he looks at me with a warm expression and begins laughing with me. For a moment, the kids just watch us laugh and then giggle along.

"Thank you for that, Asher." Brennan jokes and looks back down at his empty plate. "Kids, I think it's bath time."

Sophia and the boys follow orders and run upstairs as their giggles echo throughout the house. I shake my head in amusement as I stand up.

"Your kids are amazing, let me tell you."

I still have a smile on my face while I gather some of the plates and walk into the kitchen. Brennan follows behind with the rest and places them in the sink for me.

"They make me very happy." He says, and I notice that he's still smiling, too, as he walks back into the dining room to clear the rest of the table.

"I can see that," I say when he returns. "You're a great dad, and those kids love you so much."

Brennan grins at me, and then we proceed to clean up the dishes before heading upstairs to tuck the kids in together.

While Brennan puts Sophia to sleep, I tuck Asher and Noah in. They ask me to read a little story to them, so we huddle together on the bottom bunk and I read them one of their favorite books.

When I'm finished reading, Asher throws himself into my arms and hugs me tightly before climbing up to the top bunk. I kiss Noah on the forehead and stand up to leave, but before I get to the door, he quietly calls my name.

"Ellie?" I hear his whisper and turn back to him.

"Yes, Noah?" I kneel beside him and look at his face, which is glowing from the illumination of their nightlight. He's such a beautiful little boy.

"Don't ever leave us, okay?" He says, and I smile faintly, running my fingers through his long hair. I have no idea how to respond, so I choose my words wisely.

"I'm not going anywhere right now. Get some sleep, sweetie." I kiss him again and walk out into the hall where I find Brennan waiting against the wall in between the bedroom doors.

I'm not sure if he heard what Noah said, but if he did, he doesn't show it.

"I figured I'd wait to say goodnight before I head back down." He says with his hands in his pockets.

He's still in his work clothes, and I can tell he is more than ready to turn in for the night.

"I really can't tell you how much it means to me that the kids are so open with you. It's nice to see them this happy."

"I'm just glad they like me," I admit as I slowly make my way toward my bedroom. "I was nervous they would hate me or something"

I laugh a little and look down at the floor.

"Well, that's clearly far from the truth" Brennan smiles. "Goodnight, Ellie."

"Goodnight." I step into my room and close the door behind me.

As I get myself ready for bed, I think about the day and how immensely thrilled I am that things are going so well. It makes me sort of sad that I am only here indefinitely and I wonder, as always, if I should back off from the kids a bit before any of us get too attached. It already hurts to even think about leaving them, and Noah's words tonight did not help.

I also think about Brennan and how close we've gotten since I started. It worries me a little because he's a great guy and I sometimes feel like there might be something more there. Anytime I think I feel anything slightly affectionate, I shake the idea away and carry on. After all, he's my boss, and that sort of thing just can't happen between us.

Before falling asleep, I decide to read for a little while and sit in the lounge chair by the window. It's still chilly outside, but the breeze feels nice, and I kneel by the window, gazing at the moon reflecting on the half-melted pond. Nature always seems to soothe me, no matter the situation.

I hear mumbling from below but see nothing when I look down. I assume Brennan must have his window open too, and is on the phone with someone. I can't make out what he's saying, but I do catch a name. He's talking to someone named Ruth, and I find myself jealous. I'm not in any position to feel this way, but hearing him speak to another woman makes my heart ache a little bit.

Chapter Nine: The Question

The next day, I wake up before everyone else like usual and get a start on my morning duties. I set up the coffee machine, pull out bowls, spoons, and cereal for the kids, and begin making Noah's lunch. I'm just mixing Brennan's cup of coffee when he dashes in from his room, talking to someone on his cell.

"Yes, I understand. I'll be there as soon as possible, Byron." He ends the call and takes the mug I'm holding out for him. "Thank you. The kids aren't up yet?" He asks as he looks around the empty room.

"I heard them talking so I know they're awake, they just haven't come down yet." I examine Brennan as I speak and can tell something is wrong. "Everything okay?"

He looks back at me with a confused look, as if he didn't fully comprehend my question. Then the realization hits him.

"Oh, yeah, it's fine. I just have to leave for work earlier than usual to help take care of some things." He runs his hand through his hair, and that's when I know he's already frustrated.

"Do you need me to come in today?" I ask, even though it's my day off. "I don't mind coming if you need the extra help."

"No, that's fine." He says, not meeting my eyes. "I'm fine."

Brennan seems like he's shutting me out again, and it makes me feel a bit crestfallen. I walk into the living room without saying another word to him and call for the kids to come down and eat. They're barely seated at the island when Brennan gives them all kisses and says goodbye for the day.

"Someone's in a bad mood," Asher says after Brennan disappears to the garage.

"No, he's just having a busy morning," I tell them, though I'm not so sure I'm convinced either.

He seemed so different this morning, and I wonder if everything is okay at the office.

"He's always busy," Sophia mumbles while she pours some berry cereal into her bowl.

I lean on the island across from the kids and examine their glum little faces. It breaks my heart to see them so upset.

"Let me ask you guys something. Do you know how much your daddy loves you?"

All three of them nod, and I continue.

"Good, because I know that you are everything to him and make him very, very happy. I know he seems busy all of the time, but he works so much so that he can take care of the three of you. And that's why I'm here now. So that I can help him out a bit. I promise that you are the thing that keeps him going each day."

They all begin to smile when I finish my little speech and Noah sits up in his seat and speaks with a mouthful of food.

"I love Daddy!"

"I know you do," I laugh and tousle his hair. "Now eat up, silly. We have to get you all to school."

***

I have a normal day while the kids are gone, catching up on laundry and other chores around the house. When they come home, we tackle homework before they put in a movie to watch before Brennan gets home. When he walks in the door around six o'clock, we aren't too sure what to expect, so the kids just watch their movie while I quietly cook dinner.

"Hey." He says as he enters the room.

"Hey." I respond as I continue stirring the rice in the frying pan.

I don't look up, and I don't say anything else because I'm not even sure what's on my mind. I'm afraid I might offend him if I say the wrong thing, so it's best to just stay silent.

"How are the kids?"

In my peripheral view, I see Brennan loosen his tie and glance over at where they sit in the living room. I finally look at him and notice how exhausted he looks. He looks like he just survived a hurricane and I wonder what happened at work and why he didn't want my help.

"You should go talk to them. I think this morning kind of threw them off."

He sighs and rubs his forehead. The bags under his eyes seem to be growing by the second, and I can tell it's been a long day for him.

"I'm sorry about this morning," He says. "Things just get thrown at me sometimes, and I get a bit overwhelmed."

"I understand." I watch him as I speak. "But they don't, and they can tell when you're angry. It confuses them. If you feel the need to apologize, it's them you need to talk to."

I realize how harsh the words sound once they've left my mouth, but I want him to see the effect he has on his children. I immediately shut up and carry on with dinner.

"You're right," Brennan simply nods and walks out of the kitchen to join his kids, leaving me alone to cook.

I don't hear what he tells them, but whatever it is it cheers them up because, not soon after he joins them, I hear them giggling and happy again. I watch them and smile to myself, pleased with the way he handled the situation.

He may let work get to him sometimes, but he knows his limit between work and home, and he knows how to keep a good relationship with his kids. I still just wish he would let me help him when he gets so stressed. After all, that's what he hired me for.

We sit down to dinner, and I'm happy to see that everyone seems to be in much better spirits as they all talk and laugh about random things. We go about the rest of our night, and once the kids are asleep, I join Brennan out on the deck where he's working on his laptop. Shocker.

"Don't you ever just relax when you're home?" I joke as I sit down at the table, though it's not really a joke. Sometimes I wonder if Brennan works himself too much.

He looks up from the screen and shakes his head with a sigh. "Not really. I guess now you see why I needed a nanny."

"I do," I agree, "But I also see that they still need their dad."

Brennan's expression grows pensive as he takes in my words. He closes his laptop and holds it in his lap as he listens to me.

"I understand how much you have on your plate, and you do such a great job handling it all most of the time," I say, "But after seeing them so upset this morning, I think your kids just wish they had some more time with you."

"I know, and I want that too." He says, looking at the floor. "I don't like putting work before my family, and I've been trying very hard to fix that this past year."

I look down at my hands in my lap and begin picking at my nail beds. Seriously, it's a terrible habit. I need to stop. I just feel weird having this kind of conversation with Brennan because I don't want him thinking I'm telling him how to father his kids. I just want him to know the truth.

"For the record, this morning wasn't entirely about work." He finally says, breaking the silence.

I glance up and see his eyes still glued to me. He's watching me intently, like he's got some internal battle preventing him from letting me in. I wish I knew what was on his mind, but I'm not a mind reader. His expression makes me reflect on the previous night and anything I may have done to upset him, but I can't think of anything. In fact, it was a great night with the kids, and I had enjoyed myself.

"I hope it's wasn't something I said or did."

"Absolutely not," He shakes his head, and I let out a small sigh of relief. "I just barely got any sleep last night. For some reason, I was very restless and I kept tossing and turning."

I'm surprised by his honesty and have no idea how to respond. Brennan doesn't usually get incredibly personal with me, and I wonder what's causing him to act like this. A part of me hopes he'll keep going and tell me what's on his mind.

"I'm sorry to hear that," I say, "Are you alright?"

"Just, a lot on my mind lately." He sighs, looking down again.

I want to help him, but I'm not sure if he wants me to. I observe his face, trying to get a clue as to what he is feeling, but he doesn't show any emotion. He is always a closed book, and it's practically impossible to get an idea of what's going on in his head most of the time.

"Do you want to talk about it?" I offer, knowing perfectly well that he'll probably refuse.

"It's nothing, really" The tone in his voice isn't very convincing, and I'm a bit curious, but of course I won't push him.

All I can do is nod and smile, like I normally do when there isn't much to say.

"Well, if you ever want to talk, I'm all ears."

Brennan watches me with contemplation as if there is more he wants to say, but he's holding back. Suddenly, he rises and walks behind me to lean on the railing of the deck. He stands there for a little while, deep in thought, while I sit quietly at the table. Somehow, the silence isn't uncomfortable, and I seem to enjoy his company whether or not we are talking.

He finally speaks after a few minutes. "How do you do it?"

I spin around in my seat and glance up at him, but he is still looking out toward the pond, shadowed in darkness. He's trying to communicate with me, and I feel the excitement rush through me.

"How do I do what?" I have no idea what he is referring to and watch him intently while I wait for a response. He doesn't look at me, but he turns his head so I can hear him speak.

"The kids." He pauses. "I don't get how you won them over so quickly. They've barely known you three months, but they're already so fascinated by you. I can see a change in them and, I just –"

He stops talking for a second and turns his body to face me fully. He gazes at me with admiration, and my heart skips a beat. What is going on?

"I just never heard Noah say something like that to anyone before."

And there it is. Brennan had heard Noah's comment to me last night at bedtime.

"Oh," I can't manage to say anything else because I have no words.

What am I supposed to say to that? I had been hoping to keep that to myself because I didn't know how Brennan would react. Would he think I'm getting too close with them? Maybe that's what has been on his mind. He wants me to back off. Oh, I really hope he's not going to terminate me.

He walks back to his seat and slides the chair a little closer, so he's sitting right in front of me, looking into my eyes. My pulse races as I worry about Brennan's reaction to my encounter with his son.

"I wasn't trying to spy," He admits, "I just wanted to see how the boys were with you when I'm not around, and it just seemed like the opportune moment. I watched you read them their story and kiss them goodnight and when Noah said that, I had no idea what to think."

His eyes burn into mine as he explains himself and I feel heat rush to my face in a quick flash. Hopefully, he doesn't notice.

"If you want me to back off a bit, I can do that." I finally find my words. "I know there's a line I should probably draw because this is just a job, and I don't want us all getting too attached because I'll have to leave eventually, but I just don't want to have a bad relationship with them."

Great, I'm rambling now.

"Goodness, no." Brennan shakes his head. "I want you to have a good relationship with them, too. It just amazes me how they've warmed up to you after such a short amount of time."

He sighs and watches me with disbelief.

"I'm not going to lie, I was expecting to be in search of a new nanny at this point. The others just didn't click so well with the kids and didn't last long at all. I was afraid the same would happen with you."

I silently list to Brennan, thankful he's not angry with me. He looks down at his hands as he speaks and his expression changes to display a hint of pain.

"You've just got a way with them that brings them back to who they used to be, back before they lost their mother. It's honestly very refreshing for me to see."

Brennan meets my eyes again, and I can see sadness as he watches me. My heart aches to see him like that, and I look away to prevent from giving myself away. Whatever silly feelings I've had lately are irrelevant, and the important thing is that I take care of this family like I was hired to do.

"I'm not sure how long you were planning on staying with us, but I hope that you stick around for a while. This is the happiest I've seen them in so long, and I'd hate for that to be taken away from them again. At least, not so soon."

For the first time since I started this job, Brennan mentions my potential dismissal. I wasn't sure how long he needed a nanny for when I took the job, but I didn't care at the time. I just wanted to help him, and now I can't help but wonder how long I can do this before I'm in over my head.

"I will be here as long as you need me, Ren." I smile in assurance. "Honestly, with everything I've been through over the last few years, this is the happiest I've been in a while too. I have no intention of leaving before you relieve me of duty."

Brennan smiles and nods. "I'm glad. Thank you, Ellie."

"No need to thank me. I told you on day one, I'm happy to help."

We stare at each other for a few seconds, and then I feel myself start to blush again. I need to be careful of the way I act when I'm around Brennan. Giving into these feelings will certainly be what pushes me too far, and I need to be here for the kids. Besides, I know these emotions are only one-sided, and that a relationship is the last thing on Brennan's mind right now.

I lift my hand to brush my face, trying to hide my rosy cheeks, and stand up. "Well, I'm gonna get to bed."

"I am, too." Brennan pulls his laptop back onto his lap. "Right after I finish this statement."

"Okay, workaholic." I chuckle and walk toward the door, placing a hand on his shoulder as I pass.

Brennan places a hand over mine and smiles up at me. "Thanks again for the talk, Ellie. Sleep well. Goodnight."

I nod in response, and he removes his hand, allowing me to leave. When I reach the door, I look over my shoulder at him quickly before stepping inside. I still feel like there is something he isn't telling me, but in time I'm sure he will come around. Tonight was progress, and these baby steps are what will keep things right.

Chapter Ten: The Birthday

On the morning of my birthday, the kids surprise me with handmade birthday cards, much like the Valentine's Day card they gave me. Work is normal, but a bunch of people give me warm wishes, and a few cards, and I'm happy to see that they thought of me.

After dinner, Brennan and the kids have a small cake prepared, and we enjoy a movie together before bed. I couldn't ask for a better day surrounded by people I've come to care about.

I wake up on Saturday morning in good spirits and slowly get myself ready since I'm up early. I slip on a dark blue, cap sleeve dress that flows to my knees, and step into a nice pair of black flats. The dress had been a gift from my mom, and I haven't had a reason to wear it yet, so this seems like a good occasion. It's not dressy, but it's better than my usual jeans and t-shirt.

After pulling my hair into a simple side bun, I decide to go downstairs and get breakfast started. I tiptoe down the hall, so I don't wake the kids and smell something burning as I walk down the steps. I quicken my pace, nervous that we left something on the night before and hoping to not find the house burning down.

When I reach the kitchen, I find Brennan standing at the stove wrestling with a pan of bacon. I watch in amusement as he curses to himself and tries to fix the food.

"Need some help?" I giggle, and he turns around, startled by my entrance.

He instantly stops what he's doing and lets his eyes wander the length of my body, taking in my appearance. His gaze makes my heart beat faster, but I ignore the feeling and admire his outfit, which is different than anything I've seen him in before.

Apparently, I'm not the only one who had the idea to dress up because Brennan is dressed in tan khakis and a black button down with the sleeves rolled up. This is a nice medium between the business attire he wears for work, and his casual wear at home. His dark hair is combed neatly as it is most days, and he looks very handsome.

He looks back down at the pan in his hand and grins. "Yes, please." He pleads, and I join him at the stove, looking down at the blackened strips on the skillet.

"How about we start over and I do the cooking?" I smirk as he steps away from the stove with his hands extended as if to say 'after you.'

"I told you I'm not a good cook," He huffs. "I just wanted to help out more today."

I watch him as I clean off the skillet and can't help but smile at his demeanor. He looks like a kid who just discovered the truth about Santa Claus. I'm flattered that he feels so bad about not being able to give me a full day off.

"I really appreciate that, but you can help later. That is, as long as you actually know how to use that grill outside." I joke, and he nudges my shoulder playfully.

"Very funny," he quips "I'm great with the grill. The stove? Not so much."

Brennan puts his hands in his pockets and leans against the counter as he watches me cook.

"You look nice, by the way." He says, and I glance up at him with a smile.

There's a tenderness in the way he's looking at me, and it's a look I've noticed more frequently the last few days. I bite my lip and glance back down at the food before I do something stupid.

"Thanks. I figured I'd do more than the normal casual wear today. I see you had the same idea." I state, flipping over a piece of bacon.

"I like to look nice when I have company, especially those I haven't met before."

"Well, mission accomplished."

I continue to cook, hoping it will be a distraction, but Brennan continues to watch me. After a few minutes, to my relief, he goes up to wake the kids and get them ready for the day.

We all eat breakfast, and afterwards Brennan cleans up while I play a quick game with the boys in the loft while Sophia watches. At around 12:30 pm, the doorbell rings.

I open the door and greet my family as Brennan approaches from behind me.

"Mr. and Mrs. Mannis, it's very nice to meet you." Brennan holds out his hand and Dad gives it a firm shake.

Mom shakes her head and throws her hands up in protest before shaking Brennan's hand.

"Please, call me Linda." She is grinning from ear to ear while she looks around the house in awe. "You have a beautiful home, Brennan. Thank you for having us over."

"My pleasure, entirely. I'm glad you could make it." He shifts his attention to my sister and holds out his hand once more. "And you must be Clarissa and Gareth. Congratulations on your engagement."

Clarissa's face lights up with her megawatt smile while Gareth shakes Brennan's hand. "Thank you, very much."

Once all of the introductions are done in the foyer, we lead my family into the living room to meet the kids. Sophia is her quiet self, but still polite, whereas the boys are hyper as usual and talking to everyone.

Over the next hour, Dakota and some other people from work arrive, and we all finally end up outside where everyone scatters around the deck and patio, chatting amongst themselves. Sophia and the boys eventually head over to the jungle gym to play while Brennan, Gareth, and my dad hang out by the grill.

My mom leans over and lays a hand on my knee, smiling like she has been since they arrived.

"They all see great, sweetie. Are you enjoying the job?"

"It's amazing," I admit. "The kids are wonderful, and I love spending time with them."

"Daddy ain't too bad, either," Clarissa mumbles just loud enough for us to hear.

I playfully roll my eyes at her comment and continue. "Brennan has been great so far, and very professional, so keep your panties on."

Mom ignores our little exchange and continues about the job, thankfully. "So, does it ever get awkward at all? You know, being in someone else's house all the time?"

"No, actually." I shrug. "They were so welcoming when I got here, and I've pretty much adapted to their routine, so things just feel normal. Plus, I'm at work with Brennan most of the time anyway, so it's not like I'm stuck here all day doing nothing."

"That's great," Mom says, taking a sip from her glass of water and looking around the yard. "I'm really happy for you, Ellen."

I sigh and look at her and my sister. "It's going to be weird when I have to leave."

Before either of them can respond, the guys arrive with the food. The burgers smell delicious, and I can't wait to dig in. I'm especially looking forward to seeing Brennan's cooking skills.

"Come and eat, everyone!" Brennan calls out as he brings the burgers over to the food table and within a few minutes, everyone has been served, and we chat while we eat.

"Well, you are definitely much better with the grill than the stove." I mock Brennan after one bite of my juicy burger. Probably the best home-made burger I've ever tasted, no offence to my dad.

Dad and a few of the men from work laugh and Brennan looks at me from across the lounge area with a lopsided smile.

"Not much of a chef, huh?" Dad teases.

"Not really." Brennan laughs at himself. "That was my wife's thing. And now, Ellie has brought the joys of great cooking back into the house." He nods in my direction with a thankful smile.

"I love her pancakes!" Noah chimes in, making the rest of us laugh.

"To Ellie's pancakes." Brennan smiles and raises his glass. "And to the last year of your 20's. May it be the best one yet. Happy birthday."

"Happy Birthday, Ellie!" The rest of our guests all cheer in unison, causing me to laugh out loud.

I meet Brennan's eyes again and nod in appreciation. He winks before starting up a conversation with the guys from work and my heart skips a beat. I wish that would stop happening.

I revel in the moment as I watch different conversations tossed around amongst everyone. It's so great to see people from different areas of my life getting along so well.

I run to the bathroom quickly and when I return, I look around at the various groups scattered around. Mom, Clarissa, and Dakota are chatting, and I catch a bit of their conversation as I make my way over to my dad, who sits near the steps drinking a beer.

"So, have you made any more big decisions for the wedding?" I hear Dakota ask my sister as I plop down next to my dad.

"Actually, yes! I was just telling Nelly the other day." Clarissa smiles. "We finally booked our venue, and I'm really excited!"

I almost forgot that she mentioned it and I'm reminded that I need to give Brennan some notice about time off for that weekend. Thankfully it's far enough out that I don't feel bad asking for the time.

"Oh my gosh, that's gonna be so beautiful, Clary!" Dakota beams as she looks through the pictures Clarissa is showing her, clearly excited for the big day. Give her a reason to party, and she's ready to go.

"Right? Next big choice is dresses, so I'll call you once I get the time to take you all out shopping!" Clarissa catches my eye and smiles while she continues talking to Dakota and Mom.

Dad wraps his arm around my shoulder and hugs me close.

"You've got a nice little situation here, baby girl." I look into his blue-green eyes and see the sincerity in them. "I should apologize for freaking out about the job. I can see you're doing very well here and Brennan and his family are wonderful."

"You don't have to apologize for anything." I shake my head. "You were just looking out for me, and I appreciate it. I know what it probably looked like and I haven't exactly given you a reason to trust me when it comes to the men in my life."

"That's not why I do it, Ellie." Dad sighs. "No matter what happened with that idiot, you're my daughter and I will always make sure you're protected. Always."

I lay my head on his shoulder, and he kisses my forehead. I can't help my smile at his words. He may not be my real father, but he has always treated me like his real daughter, and I love that. He's given me 20 years of amazing memories, and I've enjoyed our connection.

I glance over at Brennan, who is talking to Keith, Mike, and Lorelei – of course. She has been practically glued to his side since she got here. After a moment, Brennan looks in my direction and smiles before returning his attention to his conversation. I smile to myself again, satisfied with the day so far.

As promised, Brennan won't let me lift a single finger, and he has the kids help him clean up before we move our little party into the living room. All of our work guests leave, with the exception of Dakota and Lorelei.

While the adults are sitting around chatting, I notice the kids huddled together on the floor with bored expressions on each of their faces. To relieve them of their boredom, I decide to liven things up and make a recommendation to Asher.

"How about we make this fun, huh?" I whisper to him and his siblings. "I would love to see you guys dance."

Asher's face lights up the moment I finish my sentence, and he looks over to his dad, who heard my comment and gives his nod of approval. Asher jumps up and sets up the gaming console, drawing attention from everyone else who begin to quiet down. He looks to Sophia to see if she's going to join him, but she sits down on the couch beside Brennan.

"You go first. Do your favorite" She speaks in a hushed tone, just loud enough for a few of us to hear, and smiles sincerely at her brother.

As the song begins, Noah skips over to where I sit on the floor and plops down on my lap, giggling as always. I rock him to the beat of the music, and he starts clapping along while Asher dances. I glance up at my mom who watches me with a blissful smile, and at this moment, I feel completely elated.

Next, Sophia joins Asher and they both dance to one of the duets. As I watch, I am impressed by her dancing, and I can tell she really enjoys it. All of her shyness seems to wash away as she lets loose through the music and has a great time with her brother.

Once they're finished, Asher looks around at the adults and asks who's next, to which we all panic. Everyone points to someone else in the room, hoping to get out of dancing, and we all burst into laughter.

"How about you, Lory?" Dakota challenges playfully, clearly testing her.

"Oh, no, no." Lorelei objects with a wave of her hand. "This is not my scene."

Asher's face drops a little, breaking my heart. I can tell I'm going to have to save the game, so I stand up and fix my dress.

"Oh, what the heck," I say, laughing as I reach out for the third remote, which Sophia gleefully hands to me.

"There we go, let's get the birthday gal up there!" Dad cheers.

I skim through the songs with Asher and Dakota calls out when she recognizes a song from our childhood. "That one! I love that song!" Asher laughs as he selects the song and he, Sophia and I get into position.

"I'm warning you all now, this won't be pretty!" I announce as the music starts.

My terrible dancing doesn't deceive me, and I mess up countless times, but I don't care because it's fun. Asher and Sophia continue to get perfect ratings, and they both keep cracking up throughout the entire song. When we finish, I turn and take a fake bow while everyone applauds.

"Alright, Clary and Kody, get your butts up here!" I pull my sister and best friend off the couch and get them to dance to another song with me.

We haven't been this goofy since we were kids, and I'm thoroughly enjoying it. Normally, I'd feel a bit self-conscious about looking dumb in front of everyone, especially Brennan, but tonight I don't even care.

Everyone else gets a chance to dance to a song, and it makes for a lot of laughs and jokes. The best is probably when my mom and dad take a turn, because I'm fairly certain they had no clue what they were doing. I'm not even sure my dad's remote was turned on.

The only person who doesn't dance is Lorelei, who remains on the couch watching with a scowl. I don't pay her any mind, though, because I want to enjoy this night with my family and friends. If she thinks she's going to rain on my parade, she's got another thing coming.

Once eight o'clock rolls around, we decide to end the night, and the kids say their goodbyes and run upstairs to get cleaned up. Brennan walks over to me and lays a hand on my arm.

"Why don't you say goodbye and I'll get the kids to bed." He smiles and says his goodbyes before retreating upstairs.

I walk my family out to their car to say goodbye and tell them I'll see them soon. I'm not sure if I'll see them before the wedding, but I know it's something they need to hear. I'm so grateful for this amazing day Brennan planned for me.

***

On Monday, it's back to normal, and I arrive at the office around nine o'clock. Brennan seems to be in a great mood, and I'm happy to see him this way, especially at work. He gathers everyone for a late morning meeting before lunch to check in on everything.

"Ellie, you can head up to the office. I'll just be a few more minutes." He says to me after he wraps up the meeting and everyone dismisses.

I do as he says and start filing more paperwork once I'm upstairs. Not even a minute later, I hear the door open and turn to see Lorelei standing in the doorway, arms crossed and the same scowl on her face that was there on Saturday evening.

"I know what you're doing, and it's not going to work." She sneers.

Chapter Eleven: The Paralegal

"I'm sorry?" I ask as I stare at Lorelei, who glares at me with so much disgust you'd think I were expired milk. What could I have possibly done to piss her off this much?

"Don't act dumb, *Ellie.*" She says angrily, applying mocking emphasis to my name. "I watched you on Saturday, and I know what you're trying to do with Ren, but it isn't going to happen."

"Why don't you just get to the point and tell me exactly what it is I'm doing, Lorelei?" I snap, annoyed that she's confronting me at work. "Because I have no idea what you're talking about."

She closes the door, leaving it slightly ajar, and then inches closer toward me with her arms still crossed.

"I see you getting all cozy with Ren and his kids, trying to make yourself part of the family." She says. "In case I didn't make it clear enough for you by now, Brennan is my domain."

I am almost dumfounded by Lorelei's comment and my eyebrows raise in surprise. One thing they don't tell you about adulthood, is that the high school drama follows you long after you've graduated.

"Seriously?" I laugh. "Is he aware of that? Because I'm pretty sure he doesn't feel the same way."

Lorelei's face drops a bit, and I can tell I just added fuel to the fire. Good. She deserves it if she really thinks I'm playing this game with her.

"I don't have to explain myself to you, Lorelei. I am just doing my job."

I cross my own arms, making a point that I'm not someone she wants to mess with. This is such childish behavior, and I expected more from someone of her stature.

"Exactly." She snarls. "Your job is the nanny, Ellen. Nothing more."

I look down at the floor as I let her words sink in, knowing fully well that I'm giving her the upper hand here. While what she says is true, it still hurts to have it thrown in my face like that. Why does she even think I want more from this situation? I have never done anything to give her, or anyone else for that matter, the impression that I wanted this to be more than a job. Did I?

"That's what I thought." Lorelei regains her confidence and points a finger at me. "You think you've got those little brats wrapped around your finger, but it won't last. You can just stop trying now. Disappear like the other nannies."

The moment the word 'brats' leaves Lorelei's mouth, I feel the anger rush through my body. My hands turn to fists on my sides, and it takes everything I have to not yell at her, or punch her, for that matter. I know better, though, so I take a deep breath and keep my composure as I stare daggers at this hateful woman.

"Lorelei, those *brats* are the greatest kids I've ever met. How dare you speak of them so appallingly. They've got great hearts, and they mean the world to Brennan." I growl through gritted teeth. "You might want to straighten out your priorities if you really want a chance with him."

"I don't need to straighten anything out, Ellie." Lorelei snaps. "I just need you to stay out of my way. You don't want to know what happens when you cross me. Got it?"

"Whatever, Lorelei," I respond casually, though my body is still slightly shaky from my adrenaline rush. "I don't have time for this right now. Do what you want."

"Good." A mischievous smile appears on Lorelei's face, and just as I'm about to ask her to leave, the door opens.

"Ellie, could you do me a favor and –" Brennan walks in, looking at a piece of paper, and stops when he sees Lorelei. "Oh, hello Lorelei. Did you need something?"

"Sorry, Ren." Lorelei coos with a soft tone. She's so fake it's not even funny. "I just wanted to tell Ellie what a wonderful time I had on Saturday and that we should get together again soon."

"I see." Brennan nods and offers a halfhearted smile. "Well, I've got a few things I need Ellie to do right now, so."

"Of course! No problem. We can talk later." Lorelei smiles and walks toward the door.

She shoots me one last glare before she disappears out of sight and when I look back to Brennan, he's watching me curiously. I can tell he knows something it up, and I'm sure my expression probably doesn't help. He stares at me, perplexed, and I wonder if he heard our conversation. And if he did, how much.

"You needed me to do something?" I try to change the topic to prevent this from getting awkward.

"Um, never mind." Brennan glances down at the paper for a split second and then presses it against is chest before meeting my eyes again. "Why don't you go home early?"

"I'm sorry, what?" I am taken aback, and I know something is wrong. "Are you sure?"

"I'm sure." He nods without emotion, and I feel a pit form in my stomach. He doesn't want me here all of a sudden. He must be mad at me. We were having such a great morning. How did it come to this?

"Did I do something wrong?" I ask, trying to get to the bottom of this now. I hate confrontation, and the idea of him being upset with me leaves a bad taste in my mouth. "I'm sorry if I –"

"No, Ellie." Brennan walks over to his desk and sits down. "It's just slow today, and you should get out of here and enjoy some of the day before you pick the kids up. Just go."

"Okay," I whisper and back away toward the door.

Brennan looks back down at his paperwork without another word, and I step out of the office, closing the door behind me. I look down the hall and see Lorelei standing in the doorway of her office, smiling at me with her arms crossed. What is her problem?

I say goodbye to Dakota on my way out and call my mom once I'm outside. I ask her to meet me for lunch and walk over to the fountain in the square before I leave. How did this happen? I know how I've been feeling about Brennan lately, but I don't think I've ever made it obvious before.

I glance back at the office and see Brennan standing in the window of his office looking in my direction. He turns around, and I see another figure by his side. It looks like Lorelei, and I'm immediately filled with despair. That girl doesn't waste any time. I throw my purse over my shoulder and make my way toward my car. I definitely need this lunch with my mom.

We meet at a restaurant near our halfway point and sit near the window with our soups and salads.

"So, to what do I owe this pleasure?" Mom asks, opening her packet of crackers.

"I, uh, just have a lot on my mind today." I sigh and swirl my spoon around my soup. "Do you think I'm in over my head?"

"What?" Mom stops moving and looks at me. "Honey, is this about your job?"

"I –" I lay my spoon down and sit back in my chair, finally meeting my mom's eyes. "I just don't know if I can tell when enough is enough."

"Ellen, talk to me." Mom rubs my arm. "What's on your mind?"

I sigh and shake my head in agitation. Why is this so hard to talk about? Especially to my mom, of all people. I'm just not sure she would understand, and I don't want her judging me.

"I knew this job would get personal, but I just didn't think I'd become so close with them all." As I look at my mom, her gentle eyes put me at ease, like always, and I find it easier to speak again. "What happens when I'm not needed anymore? I've come to care about those kids so much, and I think it's going to be so hard leaving them when the time comes."

"Why is this coming up now?" Mom asks. "You've known from the beginning this was the case, sweetie. Has Brennan said something about letting you go?"

"Not at all." I shake my head and break a piece off my bread roll. "I just think I'm getting too comfortable and maybe I need to back off a bit."

"I wouldn't do that if I were you." Mom states and I immediately look at her again. She's giving me the look that makes it all seem so simple and obviously plain. "Don't do that to the kids. The best thing you can do is continue to give them all that you've got and just prepare yourself for what the future holds."

"You think so?" I ask hopefully.

"I know so. I saw the way those kids interact with you, and I think you need to keep doing what you're doing. They need this happiness in their lives right now."

I smile at my mother's words because I know she's right. We may not always see eye to eye, but she sure knows how to make me feel better about everything when I'm feeling down. It's what I've been saying since the beginning. Those kids need me and I'm going to do everything I can to make them happy for as long as I'm with them.

"Thank you, Mom." I grab her hand over the table. "You're absolutely right."

***

I arrive back home with the kids a little while later, and we go about our afternoon routine of homework and a game or two in the loft. As I'm about to follow the boys downstairs to set up a movie before dinner, Sophia grabs my arm.

"Um, Ellie?" She whispers softly. "Can I talk to you for a second?"

"Of course." We both walk back over to the couch and I sit down facing her. She looks so nervous. "What's up, sweetie?"

"I just wanted some advice about something." She bites her lip and looks down at her lap, fiddling with her thumbs. "There's this thing at school, and everyone is doing it, and I kind of wanted to do it too."

"Well, what kind of thing is it?" I ask, trying not to jump to conclusions. I'm sure she wouldn't be involved in anything bad, but I know how some kids are these days. Maybe I should have her talk to her father.

"It's, uh, the school play." She meets my eyes as she answers and I can't help but smile.

"That sounds awesome!" I exclaim. "You should do it!"

"Really?" Sophia smiles bashfully. "Because all of my friends are doing it and I think it could be fun."

"Absolutely!" I agree enthusiastically. "You're a very talented young lady, and I think this would be a fun adventure for you and your friends."

"But I've never really acted before." She sits back against the couch. "Some of my friends have done the school plays before, and they can sing and dance and all that."

"You dance." I think back to the night of the party.

"Me? D-dance?" Sophia stammers and shakes her head. "N-no, I'm not a good dancer. I just do that for fun."

I shake my head and smile at her modesty. She really doesn't know the talent she's got.

"You are an amazing dancer, Soph." I place a hand on her shoulder. "I've watched you play that dancing game with your brothers, and I can see your passion when you move."

Sophia rubs her neck and blushes. "I do love to dance, but I think it's gonna take more than that to get in the play."

"Sure, it requires other talents, too, but I know you can do this!" I say. "You can be shy sometimes, but if this is something you really want to do, you'll forget about everything the moment you're on that stage performing."

"You think so?" She beams.

I immediately think back to my conversation with my mother earlier, when I asked the same thing. I finally realize that Sophia came to me for comfort just like I had with my mother, and exhilaration courses through my veins.

"I know so." I mimic my mother's words as I smile at Sophia. "Just you and your friends having fun putting on a show. You'll have a lot of fun, and trust me, it could always be way worse. I was in a school play when I was young and it wasn't very exciting. I played a tree in the background of one of the scenes and just had to stand there like this for the whole 20 minutes."

I hold out my arms awkwardly to show her my stance and she lets out the loudest laugh, taking me by surprise. I've never made her truly laugh before, and it's such a gratifying feeling.

"Seriously, I was only seven! I shouldn't have stood that way for that long. I thought I'd be stuck like that forever afterwards."

Sophia laughs even harder, falling backward on the couch, and before I know it, we are both laughing together. It's such a great moment, and I'm glad she came to me for advice.

"What's so funny?" A voice says from the top of the stairs. Sophia and I both look over to see Brennan standing against the bannister with his hands in his pockets.

"Daddy!" Sophia jumps up and runs over to hug her father. "I'm gonna audition for the school play this year! Ellie said I'd be great!"

"Did she?" He glances up at me for a second and then returns his eyes to Sophia. "That sounds really fun. I can't wait to see it."

"Can I help you cook dinner?" Sophia looks back my way and waits for a reply. My mouth drops for a split second and I'm momentarily at a loss for words.

"Oh, um, of course you can." I smile even though I'm completely dumbfounded by the request. "I'll meet you down there."

"Okay!" Sophia skips down the stairs, leaving Brennan and me alone.

"I'm not sure what just happened," Brennan gazes at me in shock. "But thank you. I haven't seen her this animated in a long time."

I nod in response, unsure of how to act after everything that happened at work earlier today. Brennan rubs his neck anxiously with a slight frown. Well, this is awkward.

"Look, about earlier – "

"Daddy!" Asher calls from downstairs, interrupting Brennan. "Can you help us with our movie?"

Brennan nods at me and then silently retreats downstairs, where I follow to meet Sophia in the kitchen. After Sophia and I get dinner made, we gather around the table to eat. Brennan hasn't said anything else to me, but I'm not going to push it. Instead, I let him speak with Sophia and the boys about their day.

"So, I wanted to talk to you guys about something," Brennan says after finishing up his pasta. "About your visit to Nana and Poppy's."

"Oh, no!" Asher whines, dramatically dropping his fork on his plate. "We are still going, right?"

"Of course, you are, Ash." Brennan sighs. "I would never take that away from you guys. But this year will be different."

"Different how?" Sophia tilts her head in curiosity. I just sit and listen, curious myself as to where this is going.

"Well, this year I'll be going with you," Brennan states, looking around at his kids for their reactions.

"Yay, Daddy!" Noah claps and a huge smile appears on his siblings' faces.

"Wait!" Sophia leans toward Brennan. "For the whole month?"

"For the whole month." Brennan nods with a small smile and the children all erupt into cheers.

I watch Brennan anxiously, wondering what this means for the office and me. Is he seriously going away for a whole month?

"What about Ellie?" Asher asks, turning his gaze back to me.

Brennan meets my eyes, and I look down at my plate.

"Well, I've already spoken with Nana, and she said Ellie is welcome to join us if she wants to." I look back up at Brennan, and he nods with a sincere smile.

"Yay!" Noah claps again. "Come with us, Ellie!"

"You can take some time to think about it," Brennan says to me. "But just know that we would love to have you with us."

I nod in acknowledgment and smile in response.

"That being said, I think it's close to bedtime." Brennan looks at the kids. "Go get yourselves cleaned up and we'll be up to say goodnight."

The kids don't hesitate and run upstairs giggling about their impending trip. I stand up to grab the plates and Brennan places a hand over mine.

"Please sit with me, Ellie." He pleads, and I slowly sit back down in the seat that Asher left vacant.

Brennan looks at me, silent for a few seconds before opening his mouth to speak again. He seems so distant, just like he had at his office earlier, and I'm very nervous about it. Is he going to let me go? I'm not sure if I'm ready for this yet.

I look down at the table with a thousand thoughts rushing through my brain. Where am I going to live if this is over? What will I do about a job? How am I going to just get on with life as if I never met these wonderful kids?

Brennan drags me out of my panic with four words.

"I fired Lorelei today."

Chapter Twelve: The Nightmare

"You... what?" I gape at Brennan, stunned by his news. Was this my fault? I didn't mean for her to get in trouble with everything.

"This afternoon after you left, I called Lorelei into my office and had a long talk with her," Brennan explains, looking down at the table.

I remember seeing the both of them in the window and now realize why she was there. I had been upset by her presence in his office, and it turns out there was more to the story. I really need to not jump to conclusions.

"In the end, I had to let her go because –" He trails off and I remain silent, letting him finish. "Well, because I can't employ someone who acts like a child and meddles in my personal life. Someone who speaks negatively about my kids and calls them brats in my own office."

My heart sinks into my stomach and a sense of guilt washes over me. I'm not sure how long he was standing outside the door, but Brennan had heard more than enough of my conversation with Lorelei. I am now ashamed at the way I handled the entire situation.

"Ren, I am so, so –" I begin to apologize but Brennan meets my eyes again, and I can't finish my words.

He shakes his head.

"Please don't apologize. It's not your fault." He says. "I've known about Lorelei's affections for a long time, but I guess I just hoped her career was more important to her than this infatuation."

I drop my gaze to the table and listen as Brennan speaks, feeling completely awful for my actions. This was never my intention at all. Of course, I wanted Lorelei to act like an adult and leave Brennan be, but I never wanted to jeopardize her career.

"I've learned to just ignore the signals she sent out, and that was going okay," Brennan sighs and shakes his head again, rubbing the bridge of his nose. "But hearing her speak of my kids like that and then threaten you was the last straw. I just can't do that anymore."

"I didn't mean for you to lose one of your best employees, Brennan." I shake my head. "I didn't want this to happen."

"I will find someone just as good to replace her." Brennan nods as we lock eyes again. "I'm glad today happened, Ellie. Not that you had to endure that argument, but that you were able to expose her for who she is. You defended my children and for that, I am eternally grateful."

I nod and look over toward the stairs in the foyer, listening to the children still giggling upstairs. I had to defend them today. I can't even imagine how someone can look at those kids and not see what I see. They are so spirited, and I can't imagine never knowing them.

"I meant what I said. They really are the greatest kids I've ever known," I whisper as I listen to the laughter. "They're kind, and caring, and humble, and they bring so much joy into my life. I don't understand how someone can speak of them like that. You've done an amazing job with them, Ren."

"Thank you." Brennan follows my gaze toward the stairs. "I know I probably shouldn't run away with them for a month-long vacation, especially after I just fired one of my most valued employees. But, I think this is just something we need right now. My kids need me, and everyone else will be able to handle the firm until I return.

"If I were to stay behind, would you like me to stay with Dakota while you're gone?"

I ask the question that's been on my mind since the moment he mentioned the trip. I'm not sure how comfortable he is with me staying alone in his house without him here.

"You're welcome to stay here, Ellie." He gazes at me again with hopeful eyes. "But I have to be honest, I'd really like it if you came on the trip with us.

I look away and open my mouth to reply, but Brennan lays a hand on mine again.

"Just think about it, okay?"

I nod without saying a word and then stand up to clear the table while Brennan goes upstairs to say goodnight. He retreats to his office while I read the boys a quick story and say goodnight to Sophia.

When I return downstairs, I can see the light still on in the office and slowly walk over to it. I hear Brennan mumbling, clearly on the phone, and I don't want to disturb him, though I feel I should check on him before bed.

I gently knock on the door, and the mumbling stops. A few seconds later the door opens, and Brennan gestures for me to come in as he tucks his phone back in his pocket. I've still never been in this room since Brennan told me not to worry about it. It's beautiful, and nothing like his work office.

The moment I enter the room, I am greeted by a small, gray couch with an end table on both sides and a bookshelf on the wall perpendicular. A round, blue area rug sits in front of them, and large photographs are hung on the walls all around the room. A beautiful mahogany L-shaped desk with hutch sits in the far corner near the window, and two small filing cabinets sit in the adjacent corner.

As I take in my surroundings, I can see why Brennan told me not to bother with this room. The desk is an absolute mess with piles upon piles of papers and folders, and the bookshelf is a shamble of law books and other novels. I'm not sure how Brennan finds anything in here, but if it works for him, who cares?

Once I'm done admiring the room, I realize Brennan has taken a seat on the couch and has been silently watching me.

"These pictures are beautiful." I make small talk, trying to lighten the mood. I step closer to a canvas of a snowy landscape. "Who's the photographer?"

"Kayla." Brennan stands back up and joins me by the picture.

"Your wife?" I gawk at him, and he nods in return. "She was so talented. These are seriously incredible." I gaze at the light reflecting on the icy trees and snowy hills.

"This one was from our honeymoon in Aspen." He smiles at the photo. "She always saw the beauty in the world and wanted to remember it, so she decided the best way to do that was to photograph it."

I shift my gaze from the picture to Brennan while he still stares at the canvas, a sense of sorrow on his face. He doesn't talk about her much, but I can understand that he is still mourning.

"I wish I could have known her." I look back at the other pictures on the wall. "She sounds like the most amazing woman."

"She was." Brennan finally returns to the couch again, mumbling under his breath. "And she was taken too soon. It should have been me in that car, not her."

I watch him as he walks away, stunned by his words. He can't possibly think that. What happened to Kayla was a complete accident and that wasn't his fault.

Once he's seated again, Brennan looks at me and realizes that I heard what he said. He attempts to shift the focus of our conversation.

"I think you two would have gotten along very well." He says sincerely.

"Oh yeah?" I ask, joining him on the couch. "Why do you say that?"

"Because she had the same enthusiasm for life that you have. And she had a gentle soul like you." He watches me as he relays this information and I feel myself starting to blush. "You both care for others more than yourself, and you're the only other person I think would defend my kids through anything."

"Brennan…" I start, and he sits forward, placing a hand on my knee. A spark flies through my body at his touch, but I ignore it.

"I want you to know, Ellie, that I mean it when I say that I appreciate everything you've done for my family. More than you know."

He stares into my eyes with complete reverence and I realize now that it was the same emotion on his face at the office earlier. At the time I thought he was mad at me, but he was actually thankful I defended his kids.

"I know today seems like it was hectic and abysmal, but I wouldn't change a thing about it." He says calmly, "I see things clearly now, and I can move forward from here."

I'm getting so many mixed feelings from Brennan's words, and I have no idea what to think. This entire day has been one emotional rollercoaster and I can't seem to process anything properly right now.

"I'm glad you feel that way, Ren." I hold his hand that's been resting on my knee. "I care about your children very much, and I'll do anything to make sure they're taken care of. I know the past two years have not been easy for you, but you're doing a great job with them. Those kids deserve better than what Lorelei said about them, and I think you did the right thing today."

"I think so, too." Brennan nods, and we sit in silence for a moment, still holding hands.

I look down, and we release each other, both a little flustered and unsure what to do next.

"Thank you for the talk." Brennan smiles. "I think I needed it."

"Happy to oblige." I stand and walk toward the door. "Are you okay now? Because I'm going to get to bed, but I want to make sure you're okay first."

"I'm great." He smiles and follows me out of the room. "And I should probably get to sleep as well. Thanks again."

"Sleep well," I say once we've reached the living room. "Goodnight."

"You too," Brennan whispers, remaining in his spot as he watches me leave.

***

Lorelei stalks toward me, but I can't seem to move. We are in a dimly lit room that looks like Brennan's home office, but there's something different about it. It's empty. There's nothing but the two of us, and she walks up to me with her mischievous, devious grin.

"You're nothing, Ellie." She says as she grabs my face with one hand. "You're just the nanny. Nothing more."

She shoves my face away and laughs maniacally as her appearance begins to shift into another person. A second later, I'm staring into Jake's face.

"You're nothing." His voice echoes in the darkness, and he disappears.

It's completely black now, and all I can hear are Jake and Lorelei's voices echoing the same word.

"Nothing. Nothing. Nothing."

Suddenly, my hair is pulled back, and I feel breathing on my neck.

"You're nothing," Jake whispers into my ear and then shoves me forward.

Time seems to slow as I fly into a glass door, shards flying in every direction. I open my mouth to scream, but nothing comes out. I'm completely helpless.

"Ellie! Ellie!" I hear my name and jump back to consciousness, realizing that I am screaming out loud.

I open my eyes and see Brennan sitting on the edge of my bed next to me, holding my arms in his hands to steady me. I immediately grab my scarred shoulder and look around the room, panting and trying to gather my thoughts.

"Ellie." He says calmly, brushing my damp hair out of my face.

I roll onto my side, facing away from Brennan, and begin to cry into my hands. I haven't had a nightmare like that in months, and I feel like I've taken a thousand steps in the wrong direction. My nightmares used to pop up when something bad or stressful happened, so I guess the incident with Lorelei sparked this one.

"Is she okay, Daddy?" I hear Sophia ask from the doorway, and I feel even worse knowing that I woke the kids up.

I cover my face with my hands and silently sob into them as Brennan responds to Sophia.

"Everything is okay, sweetie." Brennan remains calm. "You and your brothers go back to sleep. Ellie just had a bad dream. It's okay."

I hear them comply and mumble to each other as they walk back into the hall toward their rooms. They probably think I'm crazy. How could I let this happen? I can't let Brennan think I'm incapable of caring for his kids. Or worse, that I'm mentally unstable.

"Ellie?" Brennan whispers. I feel him rest his hand gently on my back, but the contact still makes me flinch. "It's just me. It's okay."

I gather all my strength and push myself to sit up. I hesitate at first, but then I look over at Brennan, who is staring at me with lamentation. I feel the tears come again and he pulls me into a hug, where I melt in his embrace. My shaking body begins to mollify, and I bury my face into his shoulder while he strokes my back.

"I'm sorry." I manage to say with a cracked voice. "This won't happen again."

"Do you want to talk about it?" He asks, still hugging me. I sit quietly for a moment, deciding if I want to say anything about it.

"My injury." I finally sigh. "The pain all over again, but worse. And he's there."

I decide to leave the part about Lorelei out because he doesn't need to worry about that.

"Well, he's not here." Brennan stops rubbing my back and pulls out of our embrace, looking deep into my eyes. "You're safe from him now."

I nod anxiously. "You should get back to bed. I didn't mean to wake you."

"It's alright." He runs a hand down my arm, giving me goosebumps. "Are you okay?"

"I'm okay." I lie as I wipe the tears from my face. I just need to be alone.

"I'll see you in the morning, then."

Brennan's expression is pensive as he slowly rises and exits the room, leaving me in my damp clothes. I take a quick shower and check the time, seeing that it is only 12:43 am. I climb back into bed and stare at the ceiling until my exhaustion takes over one more.

I wake in the morning still feeling timid and afraid, but I get ready and face the day, staying strong like I need to. Brennan is already awake when I enter the kitchen and a sense of guilt washes over me once more.

"Hey, you feeling better?" He looks up from his phone and watches me.

"I am." I lie again, forcing a smile while I open the fridge to start on lunch for Noah. I realize that it's already made, sitting on the counter. "You made Noah's lunch?"

"I did." Brennan continues to watch me curiously. "I wanted to give you a little break. Why don't you stay home today?"

I close my eyes as the frustration hits me. This is exactly what I didn't want. I don't want Brennan to treat me differently because I have a few bad dreams here and there.

"With all due respect, Ren, I think getting out of the house will be good for me today." I close the fridge and lean against the counter beside it. "I know how to face the world after a bad night like that."

"Of course, you do." Brennan smiles faintly and nods. "You're a strong woman. It was just a recommendation. But, as long as you're okay, it's fine."

"Thank you." I sigh and take a seat next to him at the island. "I don't want you to think I'm unhinged or anything."

I stare at the grooves in the marble, fully aware that Brennan is still watching me. I just want things to go back to normal.

"I don't think that, Ellie. We're all entitled to a nightmare once in a while. Things will start to get better again."

"I guess you're right," I say, still refusing to meet his eyes.

Thankfully, I don't have to avoid him for long because the kids enter the kitchen about a minute later.

"Are you okay, Ellie?" Noah walks around the island and throws his arms around me.

"I'm much better now." I smile, returning the hug. "Thank you."

Brennan and I both stand to allow the kids to sit at the island for breakfast. After they've prepared their bowls of cereal, Asher looks at me.

"So, what happened?" He asks through a mouthful of food.

"Ash, don't be rude," Brennan responds immediately, leaning against the counter opposite the island, giving his son a stern look. "I'm sure Ellie doesn't want to talk about it."

"It's okay, Brennan." I give him a look that says I've got this figured out and he watches me curiously as I lean against the counter and look Asher in the eyes.

"You see, I tend to have these weird dreams where dinosaurs surround me." Asher's eyes widen in astonishment. "Most of the time they're happy dreams, but sometimes I'm being chased. And this time? Well, it was a T-Rex, so it was really scary."

"Wow." He says with a huge smile. "You're so brave!"

Sophia chuckles, and I look back at Brennan who is watching me with a thankful smile. He nods in appreciation, and I smile back. Having this support from Brennan and his kids will make it a lot easier for things to feel normal again.

Chapter Thirteen: The Decision

"What do you think of this one, Nelly?" Clarissa snaps me out of my daze, holding out a spaghetti strap gown with a fitted bodice.

It has been almost three weeks since Lorelei was fired and things are back to normal for the most part. Brennan is still working to find a replacement and get ready for his trip with the kids in a few weeks.

Today is the day Clarissa wanted to pick out the dresses for the wedding, but I'm not really in the mood to be surrounded by all the girls. So, instead, I met her a few hours earlier so we could shop just us and Mom.

"Um, not loving it." I shrug and lean back against the couch my mother and I are sitting on. Clarissa hangs the dress back up on a rack and sits down next to me, grabbing my hands in hers.

"Okay, what's up?" She asks, batting her eyelashes and giving me the sympathetic look she always does when she's trying to be supportive. "I know you too well, sis, and right now something is definitely on your mind."

"It's a long story, really." I sigh and stand up to skim through some dresses myself.

I've been acting a bit glum since I showed up at the bridal shop and am feeling guilty. I shouldn't be making this about my problems. My sister is getting married and I'm acting like a lovesick teenager.

"And besides, today is about you and the wedding, not me."

"Nelly, you know that's not true." Clarissa steps up beside me and tilts her head in confusion. "We can talk about anything you want, no matter what we're doing."

I grab the first dress I can get my hands on and hold it up between us to change the topic.

"I'm going to try this one." I smile briefly and disappear into one of the dressing rooms.

I hadn't gotten a good look at the dress when I grabbed it, and now I realize that it's strapless, which is something Clarissa agreed I wouldn't wear because I don't want my shoulder exposed. I slip the dress on anyway and step out to show my mom and sister.

"Honey, that's strapless. I thought you didn't want your shoulder showing?" Mom says as she approaches me to examine the dress.

"I guess I didn't notice when I grabbed it." I shake my head and look down to fix the bottom of the dress. Talk about giving myself away. You don't know how to be subtle, Ellie.

"Seriously, Ellen, what's wrong," Clarissa asks again, and she crosses her arms.

She only uses my full name in serious situations, so I know she's starting to worry.

"You're not yourself today, and I hate seeing you like this."

"Is it about the job?" Mom chimes in, which doesn't help the situation. "I know we talked about it a few weeks ago, and if something has come up, you know you can talk to us about it."

"I got Lorelei fired from the firm." I blurt out and my mother and sister gape at me in silence.

"What?" Mom continues to stare, and I look back down at the dress I'm standing in.

I didn't exactly want to be in a formal gown when I had this conversation, but it came up and I can't back out now. I have to finish the story.

"Brennan overheard an argument I had with her the Monday after my birthday party, and he fired her after he let me go home for the day." I walk back over to the couch and carefully sit down, trying not to wrinkle the dress.

"Wow, that's crazy." Clarissa joins me and shakes her head. "Why were you arguing?"

"It's a long story." I look down at my lap, ashamed of myself once more for everything that happened with Lorelei.

Mom stops looking at dresses and turns to face us on the couch. "Wait, you said the Monday after the party? This happened before we met for lunch?"

"I called you for lunch right after it happened." I peer up at my mother. "I didn't want to be alone after everything."

"I wish you would have told me." Mom kneels in front of me and takes my hands in hers. "You can come to me with anything."

She smiles compassionately, and that is what always makes me feel better. At this moment, I miss being able to go to her with my problems. Then again, this isn't just a scraped knee or teenage boy problem. I have screwed up a part of someone's life, and I have no idea how to handle that.

"I guess I wasn't ready to deal with it at the time." I sigh. "Lorelei has always been into Brennan, and I've known it since the moment I met her. She thought I was getting in the way of her chance to be with him. Said I needed to back off and stay out of her way, but I'm just doing my job."

"Maybe she just felt insecure." Clarissa chimes in. "I'd be intimidated if someone as amazing as you were in the picture, too!" She smirks and bumps my shoulder, letting out a small giggle.

"I just feel bad. I didn't want to mess anything up, and then I went and made Brennan lose one of his best employees."

I stand up and decide to get out of the dress because it is uncomfortable. When I return from the dressing room, Mom and Clarissa are back to skimming through the dresses.

"I still don't understand something," Clarissa says, holding out a cap sleeved gown to examine it. She decides she doesn't like it and sneers at it as she hangs it back on the rack. "Why would Brennan fire Lorelei because she thought you were trying to steal him?"

"Well, there's more to it," I admit, looking through dresses again myself. "She said some mean things about the kids. She called them brats and basically said they're not a priority."

"That'll do it." Mom chuckles. "You can't be with someone who hates your children. If Eamon hadn't loved you two from the start, I probably wouldn't have been able to stay with him. Brennan's a smart guy for getting rid of her. He doesn't need that negativity distracting him from what's important to him. And shame on her for acting so childish."

"I didn't like her anyway." Clarissa laughs, and I roll my eyes with a smirk.

My sister can be so blunt sometimes, and it amazes me. I continue to look through the dresses and find one I think is nice.

"What do you think of this?" I hold out the dress to show my mom and sister.

It's a one-shoulder, floor length gown with a lacy bodice and lace flutter sleeve that would cover my scar perfectly. It's very pretty, yet still simple enough to not take away from Clarissa.

"Ooh, I like that!" Clarissa swoons. "Try it on!"

I barely have the dress fully on when I decide how much I love it. It's very comfortable and covers my scar nicely, just like I had thought it would. I emerge from the dressing room to see my mom and sister smiling from ear to ear.

"Sold!" Mom cheers and walks over to examine it. "You look beautiful in this, Ellen. I think it's perfect."

"And it will look amazing in the burgundy color I chose for you." Clarissa beans and stares at every inch of the dress.

"Wait, burgundy?" I ask. "I thought you were going with plum for the bridesmaids?"

"I am." She smiles. "But I want my maid of honor to stand out from the others, so I chose a slightly different color. I might go with another one shoulder dress for them, too, though. I love the style. This one is nice!" She says, grabbing another lacy, one-shoulder dress. "I'll see what the girls think!"

"I agree, it's very elegant." Mom smiles at my sister then looks back at me. "Do you like this one? It's comfortable and everything?"

"It's perfect," I assure her with a smile and go back to change into my clothes.

Before I leave, Clarissa wants to show me her dress, so she goes to try it on when I get back from the changing room. I sit down on the couch with my mom and let out a sigh.

"Things seem different after everything happened with Lorelei and I can't tell if I'm just thinking too much into it." I lean forward and play with my thumbs.

I have been a nervous wreck since that day, and I can't quite get a handle on it. Nothing with Brennan feels the same, and I'm worried about what that could mean.

"Ellen, everything will be fine." Mom strokes my back gently. "This wasn't your fault, and it's almost good that you were there or else Brennan wouldn't have found out how she really felt. If that relationship had blossomed, he would have been trapped."

"I guess you're right. But, I can't help but feel completely responsible. It hasn't even been a half a year on the job, and I've already managed to screw up something this big."

"Everything happens for a reason, hunny. It's cliché, but it's true." Mom comforts me. "As I said, Brennan needed you around to see the big picture."

I gaze into her eyes and know she's right. If I hadn't been there, Brennan wouldn't have seen the true Lorelei and who knows where that could have gone.

"Thanks, Mom." I lean in and hug her, happy that I have a family who knows how to console me when things get hectic.

After seeing the gorgeous, strapless gown made of lace that Clarissa has chosen, I part ways with her and my mom to head back home.

I walk into an empty, silent house and eventually find everyone out back, enjoying the beautiful, spring day. Brennan and the kids are all in the pool, splashing around when I walk onto the deck. I watch them play for a while until they notice me standing there.

"You're back!" Noah cheers as he squirms around in his little floaties.

"Come swim with us!" Sophia calls from where she sits on the edge of the pool by the fountain.

"I was enjoying watching you all," I reply with a grin. "I don't want to interrupt!"

"Nonsense," Brennan laughs as he swims to the edge of the pool nearest to where I am. "We just got in a few minutes ago, so come on in."

"If you all insist." I laugh and head upstairs to change into my swimsuit.

It's been a while since I swam, so I'm glad to see that my old, pink one-piece still fits. It's the only one I have so I would have been out of luck if it hadn't.

When I get back outside, the kids are playing catch with a water ball while Brennan sits on the edge of the pool with his feet in. He glances at me as I approach and his eyes rake over my body, making my heart skip a beat. He doesn't take his eyes off me until I sit down next to him.

"How was dress shopping?" He asks, gently kicking his feet around in the cool water.

"I could lie and say it was extremely thrilling, but it was pretty boring." I joke.

He doesn't need to know the details of my trip, especially since he was the topic of conversation for most of it.

"I see." He nods in one big motion. "Doesn't seem like it would be fun. Then again, I am a man." He smirks as his eyes meet mine again and I can't help but smile.

"Ellie, catch!" Asher yells, and before I can register what is happening, the water ball hits my chest, causing water to splash out all over me. Brennan covers his mouth to refrain from laughing, and the kids are a mix of giggles. I stand up and back away from the pool a little.

"Oh, you are gonna get it!" I laugh and jump in, landing a few inches from where the kids are gathered.

The cold water is a shock to my body, but it feels great on this warm day. When I resurface, the kids are swimming away, and I chase them until I finally get a hold of Asher. He laughs as I tickle him and splash him with water. A large wave of water hits me from behind and I realize that Brennan has joined us.

Noah paddles his way through the water to get to me and wraps his arms around my neck, giggling. He notices the scar on my shoulder and gently runs his hand over it.

"What happened to you, Ellie?" He asks with a pout. "You have a boo-boo."

His innocent little face makes my heart melt as he waits for my explanation.

"Yeah, I do. I had a little accident a while ago and got a big cut, but the doctors helped it get better. Don't worry, it doesn't hurt anymore. I promise." I smile at him in reassurance and he smiles again.

"Good. I'll just kiss it to make sure!" He says and places a quick kiss on the tip of my scar. "All better."

I hug him and glance over at Brennan who has been admiring our exchange. We share a brief smile and then continue playing with the kids until it's time for dinner.

After we eat, Brennan and I get the kids to sleep and clean up the house a bit. I decide to go back outside for a bit while Brennan works on his laptop in the living room.

I sit on the edge of the pool again with my feet in the water, watching the water ripple from the fountain. I let my mind wander and reflect on everything that I've done over the last few years. Time has a funny way of changing things so much.

"You okay out here?" Brennan's voice startles me, and I turn to see him standing a few feet behind me.

"Hey, yeah, I'm good." I turn back to the water and tilt my head to the side. "Just enjoying some fresh air before bed."

Brennan sits down beside me, and we both watch the water trickle in the pool for a bit before he finally says something I had been anticipating.

"I was wondering if you've decided about the trip yet."

I knew he would ask sooner or later. It has been a few weeks since he mentioned it and I'm sure he needs to get arrangements figured out if I'll be joining them for the month.

"I don't want to rush your decision, but hurry up with an answer, will ya?" He chortles, and I glance at him with a smirk.

He keeps laughing, and I don't even think before shoving him into the pool, fully clothed. When he resurfaces, he wipes his face and gapes at me for a split second before we both burst out laughing.

"I'm so sorry, but it was just so tempting," I say between laughs, and he swims over to the edge and looks up at me affectionately.

"I'm sure it was." He continues to smile, and then he sighs. "Honestly, though, you don't have to give me an answer now, I just –"

"Yes." I interrupt him, and he gives me a sideways glance.

"Yes, what?" He asks playfully.

"Yes, I'll come with you guys," I say, wondering if that's really the best decision.

I know I want to go, but with everything that happened with Lorelei, and what I've been feeling about Brennan, I still wonder if maybe I should just stay here.

"Really?" Brennan asks in the most hopeful tone. I nod, and his smile grows wider. "Good, I'm glad. The kids will be psyched to have you there."

"Good, because they're the reason I'm going." I smile and Brennan moves a little closer to me, grabbing my hand in his.

"Is that so?" He jeers just before pulling me into the water with him. I squeal as I hit the cold water, and when I resurface, I playfully smack his chest.

"Jerk," I say as I slick my wet hair back.

Brennan remains close to me in the water. Much closer than he probably should, and we fall silent for a moment. The pool lights shine up and reflect on our faces, just enough for me to appreciate his features. His eyes burn into mine and I almost forget how to breath for a second. Why does he do this to me?

I notice his white shirt clinging to his body and can't help but stare, even though I'm fully aware of the fact that he's still watching me. I immediately regret my decision to shove him into the pool and realize that I need to get out of this situation before I do something stupid.

"It's getting late," I whisper as I look back toward the house. "I think we should call it a night."

"You're right."

A dejected Brennan swims toward the ladder and climbs out, and I follow. I wrap a towel around myself and ring out my hair, trying my best not to stare at Brennan. He looks so good right now, and I know I shouldn't be thinking like this.

"So, I'll see you in the morning then," Brennan speaks up first and then makes his way inside. "Thanks for the extra swim. Goodnight" He smiles at me before closing the door.

I sit down on the deck steps and let out a huge sigh as I run my hands across my slicked back hair. I bury my face in my towel and focus on deep breaths before I hyperventilate. What is wrong with me? I think about what I told my mom earlier. Things really have been different the past few weeks, and I have no idea what to think or feel anymore.

My emotions are a roller coaster, and I don't want to ruin anything else. It's probably best if I just keep to myself and do my job like usual. That way, things stay the same, and nothing else can change or go wrong.

Chapter Fourteen: The Play

The night of the school play arrives in no time, and Brennan and I arrive at the school early with the kids so Sophia and Asher can get ready. From the moment Sophia came home from school with the news that she got the lead role in *Annie*, we've all been very excited to see her in action. Asher had decided to join his sister at auditions and, although it's not a big part, he landed the role of the dog, Sandy. He's thrilled about it.

"Alright you two," Brennan kisses his kids on their foreheads. "Break a leg!"

"Thanks, Daddy" Sophia smiles and grabs Asher's hand before running down the hallway toward the chorus room.

"It's amazing, isn't it?" Brennan says as he watches them disappear from sight. "She doesn't look the least bit nervous."

He's right about that. Ever since Sophia earned the lead role and began rehearsals, she has really come out of her shell, and it's a beautiful sight to see. I guess she just needed the right thing to come along and help her find herself again.

"I'm proud of her." I respond with a smile, and Brennan meets my eyes. "She's got a lot of confidence, and I think this show has been helping her express it a bit more."

"Thank you for convincing her to do this." Brennan smiles at me as he picks Noah up. "I don't think she would have done this on her own."

"She would have, it just would have taken her longer to convince herself." I look around at all of the families beginning to file in and nod toward the auditorium doors. "We should probably get inside if we want good seats."

"Good idea."

Brennan leads the way and we manage to grab great seats in the front row, almost center stage. It's the perfect spot to see everything up close and personal.

While we wait for the show to start, I skim the program I grabbed at the door and read through, smiling when I come across Sophia and Asher's names in the casting list. They're not my kids, but I'm proud to see them doing something so fun and exciting.

The room gradually gets louder as people fill the seats around us and families talk excitedly amongst themselves. The atmosphere is enthusiastic and I can tell everyone is looking forward to this show. Clary and I never got into theater when we were younger, but we used to attend shows in support of some of our friends. I have to say, those turnouts were never quite this impressive.

"Brennan?" A soft voice calls from a few seats down, and Brennan and I both look to find the source.

A petite, blonde woman smiles at us and gets out of her seat to come and greet us. I've never seen her before, but I don't usually see the parents of Sophia or the boys' friends.

"Hi, Emily. It's good to see you." Brennan stands up to hug her quickly. "Is Julie in the play, too?"

"Yes, she's one of the orphans. I don't remember which one." Emily smiles and then her face becomes serious. "I haven't seen you around in a while, and I wanted to make sure you're doing alright."

She runs a hand down his arm and a knot forms in my stomach. This is the first time I've really seen someone from Brennan's personal life interact with him, and I find myself incredibly jealous. Emily is gorgeous, and just what Brennan would be looking for if he were ready to move on.

"Thank you, we've been doing well." Brennan smiles in appreciation. "I'm sorry I haven't been around much this school year, but work has been very busy. Our nanny, Ellen, has been helping with everything for the kids the past few months."

"It's so nice to meet you, Ellen." Emily extends a hand in greeting and I shake it with a grin.

"You, too." I nod and her attention is instantly turned back to Brennan. Who cares about the lame nanny, right?

"It was so good to see you, Brennan." She rubs his arm again, still smiling. "If you ever need anything, don't hesitate to call, okay? You know that I understand what you're going through, and I'm always around if you need to talk."

"Thank you, I appreciate that." Brennan nods and returns to his seat next to me. "Enjoy the show."

I watch after Emily as she heads back to her seat where another child, about Asher's age, sits waiting for her. I glance at Brennan and he looks at me with curiosity. I can tell he knows what I'm thinking.

"She lost her husband a few years ago. He was a Marine, deployed in Iraq." Brennan explains and I look back over at Emily and her daughter, imagining how hard that must have been. She and Brennan share the same strength that I admire, and I give her a lot of credit.

Some people are so good at keeping their lives private, so that you'd never know what they've been through. Emily and her daughter both look so happy, and you'd never believe they lost their husband and father not long ago. That's the sort of thing that motivates me to bury my own past and move on with life.

The lights dim on and off a few times, alerting everyone that the show will be starting soon. Noah claps and glances up at Brennan with a big smile.

"Yay! It's starting!" He cheers and I giggle to myself. Always the enthusiast.

The principal of the school takes center stage and welcomes everyone, outlining the rules during the performance. Audience members are allowed to take pictures and videos, as long as the flash is turned off to prevent from disturbing the cast. However, the school has a photographer who will be providing photos for any parents who want them.

Once she has finished her speech, the curtain rises, revealing the opening scene of the play. The lights dim and I smile with anticipation.

The character named Molly awakens from a bad dream, and soon a bunch of little girls are bickering on the stage. Sophia joins in and I can't stop the smile that appears on my face.

She looks adorable in her shaggy clothes, short red hair, and locket around her neck. Brennan had allowed her to use temporary red dye in her hair for the role so she wouldn't have to wear a wig.

I hear Brennan gasp and his hand lands on my thigh, giving it a quick squeeze. I can sense his excitement and it makes me smile even more.

"Look at her." He whispers loud enough for me to hear and I smile as I rest my hand over his in acknowledgement.

Brennan holds my hand as the play resumes, and his thumb gently brushes over my knuckles, which I think he's doing subconsciously. I glance up at him while Sophia sings her first song, *Maybe*, and his eyes are glued to her. His smile remains on his face as he watches his daughter, and a euphoric sensation overcomes me as I read the adoration in his expression.

I don't think I'll ever get over how happy it makes me to see Brennan caring for his children the way he does. It's so attractive when a man loves his kids that much, and I feel myself blush as I look back at

Sophia on stage. I feel guilty for having these thoughts and am almost thankful when Brennan releases my hand to applaud once Sophia has finished singing.

When it's time for Asher to make his appearance, I get the camera on my phone ready so I can record him and Sophia while she sings *Tomorrow*. I knew she was talented, especially after seeing her dance, but I had no idea she sang, too. She's doing amazingly, and I am so glad she decided to do the show.

The rest of the show is wonderful and once it's over, the entire auditorium gives the cast a standing ovation. Sophia and Asher stand with their fellow castmates with bright smiles as they take their bows, and as the kids begin to file toward their families, Asher runs over and tackles Brennan.

"Daddy, that was so much fun!" Asher yells with glee.

"You guys did so great!" Brennan beams with pride as he releases Asher and lifts Sophia into a huge bear hug. "I am so proud of you both. Great show."

"Thanks, Daddy." Sophia smiles and then looks at me. "Thanks for talking me into it, Ellie."

"You're more than welcome, Soph." I smile. "I knew you were talented, but that performance was something else. Simply amazing, sweetie."

"I have to go say goodbye to Julie and the others! I'll be quick." Sophia runs off to find her friends and I feel Noah tugging on the bottom of my dress.

"Ellie, I have to pee." He says and points toward the exit.

"Okay, let's make it quick." I say and turn to Brennan, who is talking to Asher. "Brennan, I'm gonna run Noah to the bathroom. I'll meet you guys in the hallway."

"Okay, thanks." Brennan responds and turns back to Asher. "Let's go find your sister."

Noah skips as we walk hand in hand to the bathroom. He sings to himself and I smile as we pass through the crowd.

Once he has finished, we exit the bathroom into the overcrowded hallway, filled with families chatting with one another. I search around for Brennan and the kids, and see them down the hall a bit. As we get closer, I realize that Asher and Sophia are talking to a few girls and their parents, while Brennan speaks to Emily a few feet away.

For a brief moment, the jealousy returns as I watch Brennan and Emily. I shake the feeling off immediately and walk over to Sophia and Asher, still holding Noah's hand.

"Hey, Ellie!" Sophia smiles once I reach them and drags me by my other hand. "These are my friends, Julie, Hannah, and Ashley."

"Hi, girls. It's nice to meet you." I nod to each of them with a smile. "You did great in the show."

"Thanks!" They all reply in unison, and I glance up at their mothers who are all staring at me.

"I don't think we've met." One of the moms says to me. "I didn't realize Brennan was seeing anyone."

"Oh, we're not –" I stumble over my words. "I'm just the nanny." I extend my hand with a smile. "Ellen Mannis. It's nice to meet you."

I shake each of their hands as they introduce themselves – Kate, Amy, and Rachel – and plaster on a big smile, though I feel crappy inside.

Why do I hate introducing myself as 'just the nanny'? It's my job, and that is what I am.

I glance briefly over at Brennan and see him laughing with Emily, causing my jealousy to take over again. What is wrong with me tonight? I have no right to be upset because he's my boss and this is just a temporary situation.

If anything, Brennan deserves someone like Emily. They've known each other for a long time, and they've both been through a similar ordeal. I shake the thoughts from my head and chat with the other moms while the kids laugh and talk about the show.

After what feels like an eternity later, Brennan joins us and smiles at everyone.

"I see you've met the girls' moms." Brennan says and Kate and the others smile and nod.

"Yes, we were wondering who the mystery woman was with you tonight." Rachel smiles and then tosses me a quick wink.

Um, what?

"Yes, Ellie's been a very helpful addition at home." Brennan smiles, nodding in my direction.

Kate and the others eye the two of us and I can tell they think there is more going on here. I nervously tuck some hair behind my ear and look away. I feel like a bug under a microscope.

"Ellie, I'm tired." Noah tugs on my dress again and rubs his eye with his free hand. Saved by the bell.

"We should be getting home." Brennan says so Sophia and Asher hear, and they hug their friends and join my side. "It was nice seeing you, ladies. Until next time."

We say our goodbyes, and I feel them all watching us as we walk away. Once we're settled in the car, I relax a bit like a weight has been lifted off my shoulders. I felt like I was a part of an interrogation with those other moms. They're not kidding when they say moms like to gossip. As we pull out of the parking lot, I turn around to look at the kids.

"You guys seriously rocked it up there tonight." I grin and Sophia and Asher both smile and high five each other.

"I wholeheartedly agree." Brennan says, keeping his eyes on the road, but still grinning from ear to ear. "I couldn't be prouder."

I watch as Sophia smiles bashfully and looks out the window as we drive the rest of the way home in silence.

Once we arrive home, the kids immediately head upstairs to clean up and get ready for bed while Brennan and I hang out in the kitchen. We sit in silence, and I'm not really sure what to say. He's been a bit quiet since we left the school.

"Tonight must have been exciting for you," I say, quietly, trying to strike up some kind of conversation. "It's not every day your daughter is the lead in the school play."

"It was amazing." Brennan grins for a split second and then his smile fades, like something else has come to mind. "I, uh, I'm sorry about earlier."

I blush a little, wondering if he's referring to when he held my hand during the first musical number. I had kind of hoped we would forget about it and move on. I know it didn't mean anything, and it was all in the excitement of the moment.

"For what?" I ask, not sure what else to say.

"I didn't mean to get so caught up talking to Emily." He responds and I nod once in acknowledgement. A part of me is thankful he wasn't apologizing for holding my hand. If I'm being honest, I liked it. But, I wouldn't tell him that.

"You don't have to be sorry about that." I say, "She seems really nice, and it's great that you have someone who knows what you're going through."

"You know what I'm going through," Brennan replies, analyzing my face as he always does when we have a serious conversation.

"Of course, I do," I nod. "But our experiences are different. I had to leave someone. I didn't lose him. Emily understands what it's like to be in your shoes, and that can make a big difference."

"Yeah, she understands that aspect of my life, but I don't know. It's not the same talking to her. Plus, I think she wants there to be more between us." He admits and I raise my eyebrows in shock. I can't believe he's talking to me about this.

"Oh. I see." I whisper. "And how do you feel about that?"

Once the question leaves my mouth, I instantly regret it. I'm not sure I want to know the answer at all, and I wish I could just end this conversation. But, I will be supportive because that's just who I am. I'm a good friend.

"Honestly?" Brennan looks deep into my eyes and I sense a bit of hesitation in his gaze.

There is definitely something he wants to tell me, but he's holding back. What is on your mind, Brennan Grant?

"You can tell me anything, Brennan." I find myself caught up in the moment, and I'm saying things before I can even think them. Shut up, Ellie.

"I just don't see it." He sighs, breaking eye contact with me and I glance down at the floor. "I know I'm allowed to move on with my life, but Emily just doesn't seem to be a part of that equation."

"Well, I'm sure the kids would approve." I sigh, meeting Brennan's eyes again. "After all, her daughter is one of Sophia's best friends, and all of the kids are close with that family. They wouldn't resent you if you ever decided to pursue anything with Emily."

"I know they wouldn't." Brennan continues to stare at me while he speaks. "But the kids will just have to approve of someone else when the time comes. I'll know when it feels right."

His eyes burn into mine and I'm having a hard time reading him again. There are many times when Brennan says one thing, but I get the sense that he means something else. This is one of those moments, but I won't let myself think like that because it's not what we need right now. Things are fine just the way they are between Brennan and me, and I can't ruin that now. There's too much at stake.

Chapter Fifteen: The Vacation

Once school finally lets out, I enjoy the start of summer vacation with the kids. With them home all the time, I don't work at the office with Brennan, and that means less time with him and more time with the kids. This is the best thing for me right now, especially since my feelings have been out of control and I need to focus on what's important: my job.

After the school play, Brennan and I never mentioned Emily, and it was as if the entire conversation had never happened that night. Brennan will move on when he's ready, and when that time comes, I'm sure the kids and I will know.

Our trip to the Poconos quickly approaches, and on the morning of July 1, Brennan and I wake up early to get everything together in the Suburban before waking the kids and getting on the road.

I've been having mixed feelings about the trip since the moment I told Brennan I would definitely accompany them because somehow it feels wrong for me to join them on their vacation. The kids were really excited when they found out, though, so as long as they want me there, I'm going to make the best of this visit.

I look forward to meeting Brennan's parents and seeing the kids enjoy their time with their grandparents. Plus, it's a break for me since Brennan will be able to dedicate all his time to Sophia and the boys. In a way, it's a little vacation for me as well as Brennan and his family.

I use our five-hour drive to calm my nerves and relax a bit before we arrive at his parents' house on Lake Wallenpaupack. It has been a few years since I was in the Poconos, so it's nice to see all the sights again as we drive through.

By noon, we pull into the grand driveway of a gorgeous log home right on the water. I step out of the car and gaze around at the house, which is just as big as Brennan's. For some reason, I was expecting something small and simple from his parents, but this is far from that.

The exterior is a mix of log and stone that gives off an elegant, yet country, vibe. The two-car garage is separated from the house by a huge, wrap-around porch that stretches from the front door around the left side of the house to the back. I haven't even seen the inside of the house, and I'm already very impressed.

After I help Noah out of the car, he and his siblings run toward the couple who has just walked out of the front door. Brennan and I follow behind to greet his parents.

"Mom, Dad, it's great to see you." Brennan hugs them when we reach them and places a hand on my back to bring me forward for introductions. "This is Ellen. Ellie, these are my parents, Anna and William."

Brennan's parents are around the same age as my parents, but look completely different. Although she doesn't look quite as young as my mom, Anna definitely does not look like she's in her 50s. She is a petite woman with shoulder length, brown hair and bright, blue eyes that pop. Brennan's eyes.

William has some features similar to Eamon, like his broad shoulders and height, but it's the snow-white hair that sets him apart from the dark-haired man I'm used to. Eamon also has a ton of wrinkles in the corners of his eyes from years of laughter, which are barely present on William's face. He's a stern man, I can already tell.

"Oh, Ellie." Anna pulls me into a hug. "It's so nice to finally meet you, sweetie. Brennan has told us so much about you and how well you've been taking care of my grandchildren."

"Well, they make it very easy," I admit with a smile once we pull out of the hug. "They're amazing kids."

"They are, aren't they?" Anna responds like a true grandmother. "Well, let me get you all set up inside, and we can chit chat later!"

The kids run right past us as we walk through the door and I take in the beauty of the house as we pass through.

We enter the foyer, which opens to a small sitting room on the right before leading to a hallway that leads back toward the living room. The sitting room is about the size of Brennan's, with two small couches and three giant bookcases filled with more books than I've ever seen outside of a library.

I follow Anna down the hall and into the open living room which has tall, vaulted ceilings with wooden beams. I am greeted by a beautiful view of Lake Wallenpaupack through the tall windows, much like the ones in Brennan's house, that surround the fireplace. There's a staircase on the right wall that either goes up to the second level or down to the basement, and the bathroom door sits right next to it.

On the opposite side of the room is the dining room, and wrapping around the wall to the left brings us into the grand kitchen, which seems completely remodeled with stainless steel appliances and granite countertops.

There is a lot of country appeal to the house, but it still has its modern touches. It's a perfect place for a small family.

Anna shows the way up the stairs to the open loft that overlooks the rest of the house and leads to three bedrooms. One belongs to the boys and has two twin-sized beds, while another belongs to Sophia and has a full-sized bed. Both bedrooms are filled with toys that I assume are kept for when the kids are here to visit. This is their home away from home.

The last bedroom upstairs was originally meant to be the master bedroom, but Anna and William decided to put up a wall in the basement to convert half the area to their master suite. This room is now used as a guest room.

"Now, Brennan usually stays in this room, but I'm going to set him up on the pull-out couch in the sitting room downstairs so you can sleep in here," Anna explains as we enter the room, which is about the size of Brennan's bedroom back home.

"Oh, you don't have to do that." I object. "Brennan can stay in here, and I'll take the couch. I don't mind at all."

"Too late." Brennan waltzes into the room with my bags and places them on the bed. "You're staying in here. I'll be fine downstairs."

"Yes, you will." Anna snickers and winks at Brennan before looking back at me. "I'll let you get settled in, and I'll be downstairs if you need anything."

She places a hand on Brennan's cheek and smiles. In one gesture, I see how much he means to his mother.

"Oh, and your sister will be by this weekend to see you all," Anna adds before leaving the room.

I had no idea Brennan even had a sister. He never mentioned it. I wonder what she's like. I snap out of my daze and look down at my bags on the bed.

"Are you sure about this?" I ask when we are alone. "I really don't mind staying downstairs. This is your room."

Brennan puts his hands on my shoulders and chuckles. "And while you're here, it's your room. Got it?" I nod gently, and he walks back to the door.

"I didn't know you had a sister," I call to him before he leaves.

Brennan turns in the doorway and smirks. "You never asked."

I laugh in response and watch him leave. I'm not sure what's gotten into him, but I like the fun, spunky attitude he's been showing lately. It's a complete change from the intimidating man I met the day of the interview.

As I finish unpacking my bags, Sophia comes into my room, already dressed in a bathing suit and pullover. These kids seriously don't waste any time.

"We're going to go down to the dock if you want to come." She offers, hugging her towel as she watches me put the last of my clothes in the dresser.

She has changed so much since I met her, but she still has some shy tendencies every so often.

"You guys go ahead. I'll be down in a bit." I smile and watch as she skips out of the room and runs downstairs with her brothers.

I walk into the loft and listen to their giggles as they run onto the back deck and down the stairs that bring them to the vast backyard. There, Brennan is waiting for them and chases them down the pathway that leads straight to the water, where I can see a small dock with a boat.

The entire house is simply amazing, and I think back to when Clarissa and I used to take weekend trips out here with some friends. I used to see huge houses like this and wonder who lived in them. Well, now I have my answer.

I make my way downstairs and peek at each of the pictures hanging on the wall as I go. There are lots of photos of Sophia, Asher, and Noah, as well as pictures of a younger Brennan and a girl I assume is his sister.

When I get to the bottom of the stairs, I get caught up looking at a Christmas picture of Brennan, Kayla, and the kids. They are all dressed festively and sit in front of a giant Christmas tree by a fireplace. The picture was taken here.

"Beautiful, wasn't she?" Anna walks up beside me, startling me for a second. I wonder how long she had been watching me.

"She's gorgeous," I admit, turning my attention back to the photo. "I've actually never seen a picture of her before now."

I gaze at the woman looking back at me. Her short, dirty blonde hair is a perfect match to Sophia's and has a gentle curl to it. She has big, brown eyes like the boys and a smile that fills me with joy. The whole family looks so happy, and for a second it breaks my heart to think that they no longer have her.

"That doesn't surprise me," Anna responds to my statement. "Brennan was so lost when she passed, and he beat himself up about it for a long time afterward. I think he found that leaving it alone was best to help him move on."

I see Anna's point, but I don't think I agree. I have things from my past that I don't want to be reminded of, but those are different. I can only imagine how hard it was for Brennan to lose the woman he loved and raise their children on his own, but I feel like her memory should live on. He shouldn't beat himself up over it.

"I'm sorry you all lost her." I turn back to Anna who is also looking at the picture. "From what Brennan has said, I can tell she was a wonderful person."

"She was beautiful inside and out, and made Brennan very happy." She says, leaving the sentence open like there is more to it. "But he has done a great job with the children, given the circumstances."

Anna finally looks back at me with a content expression. "I'm very glad they have you, now." She takes my hand in hers. "It's the first time I've seen them all truly happy since everything happened."

That doesn't seem possible to me because it's been over two and a half years since Kayla passed. Surely something has made them all happy since then.

"You seem to be taking good care of them, and I can't thank you enough." Anna smiles again. "I've noticed a change in them since you showed up. Especially Brennan."

"I do what I can." I return a smile and glance out the window toward the lake. "They make me very happy, too."

The kids are playing in the water as Brennan sits on the edge of the dock, kicking water at them. Of course, I am glad I have become a part of their lives. They make me feel like I'm worth something, and I don't feel as lost as I did before I started this job.

"Well, William was going to barbeque soon, so I'd better get everything prepped before I'm rushing to do it later." Anna chuckles and releases my hand to head toward the kitchen.

"Anything I can help with?" I ask.

"You're sweet." She grins. "I'm okay, though. Why don't you join them outside? I know you're usually doing everything, but this is your vacation, too."

Anna winks as she disappears into the kitchen, leaving me standing by the window. I step out onto the deck and take in the fresh air, slowly breathing in the musky, pine smell as it fills my nose. After a minute, I head down the steps and take the path toward the water, taking in my surroundings as I walk.

There's a fire pit with wooden benches surrounding it at the edge of the patio where the lawn begins, and on the other side of the property, closer to the forest, is an old gazebo with a small swing inside.

Closer to the dock there are two picnic tables under a huge oak tree right where the sand begins, and some lawn chairs sit just near the water. I stride onto the dock and take a seat beside Brennan.

"Hey there." He smiles. "Get everything set up for yourself?"

"Yup, everything is great." I nod and kick my flip flops off to dip my feet in the water. "Your parents' house is just as gorgeous as yours in its own way."

Brennan looks back at the house. "Yeah, I love it here. And so do the kids."

His expression changes a bit, and I sense some sadness in his voice as he continues.

"Honestly, it almost hurts to be back here again."

"You haven't been here since the accident? But, I thought the kids come here every summer?"

"They do, but my dad met up with me halfway the past two years to pick them up so it would be easier for me." He explains. "The last time I was here was the Christmas before Kay passed."

He looks down at his lap, and I think back to the picture I saw earlier. That was taken the last time Brennan was here, and I feel a pit form in my stomach as I think about the pain he must feel being back here. I don't want to dig into the subject any further, so I sit quietly while he takes a moment.

"I can't avoid this place forever, so I decided this trip was something we needed." He glances up at me, and a faint smile appears on his face. "The memories are great, but there are always new ones to be made."

I smile at his words. I'm flattered that he decided to include me in those memories.

"I'm sorry. I seem to always throw my problems at you." He sighs. "It's just nice to have someone who listens."

"You don't have to apologize," I assure him. And I mean it. "I'm all ears whenever you need to talk about things."

He nods. "And I appreciate that." He looks at his kids playing and then out at the rest of the huge lake that sits in front of us. "Sometimes I enjoy adult conversation. There's just so much I can't talk to the kids about."

"That's understandable." I nod, gently kicking my feet around in the water. "It's important for you to talk about those things. It's bad to keep it bottled up. I mean it when I say I'm here for you."

Brennan peers at me and smiles, discreetly placing his hand on mine. "Thank you."

I blush at the feeling of his hand on mine, but the moment is washed away when we hear shouting from the direction of the house.

"There you all are!" A woman's voice calls from behind us.

Brennan and I turn simultaneously, and I see a tall brunette making her way down the path in our direction.

Chapter Sixteen: The Sister

"Ruth!" Brennan stands up and rushes over to greet the woman who has made her way down from the house.

Ruth? So, this is the woman he was talking to on the phone a few weeks ago. I follow behind, and it isn't until I'm a few feet away that I realize how much she looks like Brennan. She could be his twin the similarity is that perfect. This must be his sister, and I feel stupid now for being jealous when I heard him on the phone with her.

"I thought you were coming by this weekend?" Brennan says, wrapping Ruth in a bear hug and patting her back.

"Yeah, well, I heard you were coming in today, and I couldn't wait to see you, so I decided to stop by for a bit." Ruth smiles and then looks over at me. "I think you're being a little rude, here, Ren. Who is the lovely lady?"

"Of course, I'm sorry." Brennan places his hand on my arm to guide me closer to them. "This is our nanny, Ellen. Ellen, this is my older sister, Ruth."

"Ellie is fine. It's so nice to meet you, Ruth." I smile and extend my hand to shake, but instead, she throws her arms around me.

"Please, Ellie, the pleasure is all mine." She steps back and grins at me. "It's nice to meet the woman who has been keeping my little brother out of trouble." She winks at Brennan, and he laughs.

"Auntie Ruth!" Asher cheers from the water and the kids all run over to grab their towels and then practically trample Ruth to the ground with hugs.

"There are my little rascals!" She kisses them a thousand times each and then turns her attention back to Brennan and me.

"FYI, I'll be stealing these kiddos for a day or two while you're here." She smiles and starts goofing around with the boys as we all make our way back up to the house.

"Ah, perfect timing," William says as we reach the top step on the deck. "I just finished the burgers and dogs."

He holds up a plate full of food and makes his way inside.

"Yay, food!" Noah cheers.

"I'm starving!" Asher yells.

"Boys." Sophia rolls her eyes, and Ruth wraps an arm around her shoulder, guiding her inside to follow the boys.

Brennan and I are last to follow, and we all gather around the dining room table.

"Looks great, Dad." Ruth rubs her hands together as she grabs a plate and begins to collect her food.

Once we are all seated and eating, Ruth decides to bombard me with questions to get to know me better. Normally, I'd feel a little intimidated, but Brennan's family makes everything feel so natural.

"I think it's very admirable of you to give up everything to help my little brother, Ellie." She pats her face with a napkin and smiles at me from across the table. "And from what I hear, you've been nothing short of amazing."

"Thank you." I nod and grin. "I'm very happy to help, and it wasn't a problem at all. I've recently been going through some big life changes, so Brennan caught me at just the right time."

I glance at Brennan, who smiles and nods, acknowledging the meaning in my words. He understands me now, and I appreciate that so much. I'll spare his family the details, though.

"Well, thank goodness for that." Ruth pops a potato chip in her mouth. "I think you are just what they needed."

"Or he could have moved back home after everything so we could help with the kids," William mumbles low enough that I almost don't catch his comment.

"Dad, not now." Brennan shoots his father a stern look to which William lifts his hands in defeat.

I can sense a bit of tension between the two but try to ignore it and stay positive. It's probably nothing.

"So, Ruth, are you living back here now?" Brennan changes the subject.

"I am." She sighs. "I think I just need to stay grounded for a little while."

I assume Brennan notices the confusion on my face, so he explains what Ruth meant.

"Ruth is a travel blogger, so she's usually all over the place." He says.

I nod in response and glance back to Ruth. Traveling is something I've always wanted to do.

"That sounds so exciting!" I say with genuine enthusiasm. "I'm sure you've been to some great places."

"Amazing places." Ruth swoons, placing her hands over her heart in endearment. "The world is a beautiful place, and I love to explore new locations."

"I would love that, too." My smile falters a bit. "I haven't had the opportunities to travel over the last few years, but I hope to sometime in the future."

"What were you doing before you started with Brennan?" Ruth asks.

"Well, I was working at a bakery when I interviewed with him, but before that, I had a great job at a daycare for a few years. I had to leave due to some, uh, complications."

"Busy girl! I can see why you haven't had much time to travel." Ruth nods. "I hope you can get where you want soon because the world really is spectacular."

I nod and look down at my plate. Me, too. I guess it doesn't help that I was stuck with a man who never did a nice thing for me in his life. He never wanted to go out and see the world. He was content with staying home, drinking, and losing his temper.

I feel something on my knee and realize that Brennan has placed a reassuring hand there to comfort me. He knows why I haven't traveled, and I can feel the apology in his gesture. The regret I felt just seconds ago is washed away, and I pull myself back into the moment.

"Auntie Ruthie, play a game with us!" Noah tugs on Ruth's shirt, and she chuckles. She pinches his cheek, making him smile.

"Sure thing, little man." She stands up and places hers and the kids' plates in the sink and follows them to the stairs. "I'll catch you all later."

She salutes us as she disappears into the loft, and I can't help but laugh.

"She's great," I say once she's out of sight.

"She's a sweetheart." Anna beams with pride. "A bit crazy, but she's got a big heart and we love her."

Despite her objections, I help Anna clean up after our meal while Brennan and his father retreat to the deck. We chat about random things, and I can't help but love the woman. She's so gentle and kind, and she fills me with serenity when she speaks. It's like being with my own mother.

I show Anna and Ruth the videos from the school play and they both gush over how cute Sophia and Asher were in their respective roles. I wish they could have been there to see it in person because it was fantastic, but Anna seems to appreciate the video footage.

Later on, Ruth helps me put the kids to bed early and then we meet with Brennan and Anna in the living room. William has already escaped to the bedroom for the night, heading down the moment he was done talking with Brennan.

A few glasses of wine later, I am starting to truly see Ruth's crazy side as she giggles randomly and becomes blunt about everything under the sun.

"Goodness, Ellie." She grabs my face and moves my cheeks around like she's trying to see if I'm real or not. "You are just so pretty."

I giggle and just play along. "Thank you, Ruth. You're pretty, too."

"No, I'm super serious." She looks over at Brennan with my face still in her hands. "Isn't she pretty, Brennan?"

Brennan watches us in amusement, and I silently plead for some assistance while his sister waits for a response.

"Yes, she's very pretty." He says quietly, and I feel myself blush under Ruth's grasp. "I don't think she's interested though, Ruth." He laughs, and Ruth finally releases my face.

"That's not what I meant, ya jerk." She throws her shoe at Brennan, and I can't help but laugh out loud.

Brennan chuckles and meets my eyes again for a second before speaking to Ruth.

"How's that boyfriend of yours, anyway?" He asks.

"That moron can burn in the deepest fires of Hell." Ruth blurts out and then laughs hysterically.

I glance over at Brennan and Anna who both seem just as shocked by her words as I am.

"What are you going on about?" Anna sits forward and places her glass on the table, not taking her eyes off her daughter. "You said he moved back here with you."

"Yeah, well, I lied." Ruth sighs and rubs her temple. "I found him in bed with some blonde bimbo when I came back from my trip to Scotland, so I packed up and left his ass."

"That fucking prick," Brennan growls, and I am shocked by his words.

I don't think I've ever heard Brennan say the F-word before in the time I've known him.

"Brennan, watch your mouth." Anna smacks him on the arm, and a small smile creeps across my face.

Even in his thirties, Anna talks to him like her little boy.

"Sorry." Brennan apologizes and meets my eyes with a mischievous smirk. He must be amused by the same thought as me. "I'm sorry to hear that, Ruth."

"It's whatever." She mumbles. "At least I found out instead of living a lie."

We all nod in agreement and then Ruth turns to me again.

"Don't get yourself tied down because men suck." She says seriously. If she only knew. "Well, except my baby brother here. He's a good guy. You can do whatever you want with him."

My eyebrows shoot up in astonishment, and I am completely flabbergasted. Did she really just say that to me? Brennan immediately stands up, clearly just as surprised as me, and rests a hand gently on his sister's shoulder.

"Alright, crazy." He takes her arm and lifts her off the couch. "I think you've had enough for tonight."

"Aw, don't be embarrassed, Ren." She giggles as she wraps her arms around Brennan's neck to hug him. "You are a good guy, and Ellie is a good girl and –"

"Okay, okay." Brennan cuts her off and looks back at me with apologetic eyes. "Say goodnight to everyone."

"Goodnight, my beauties." Ruth waves and blows us kisses as Brennan drags her out of the room.

I bite my bottom lip and look at Anna who is watching me with a content grin.

"Sorry about that." Anna chuckles. "She gets a little intense when she drinks."

"That's perfectly alright." I smile in assurance. "At least she's a happy drunk."

I glance down at the floor, and my smile vanishes. I've spent so much time around an angry drunk that I've gotten to the point where I don't even pay attention to the happy ones. Honestly, it's almost comforting to be around that kind. I think it's a safety thing. The happy ones don't want to smack me or yell in my face.

"You okay, sweetie?" Anna's voice pulls me back to reality, and I notice that she is now standing.

"Oh, yeah, sorry." I stand and fidget with my fingers. "I'm just tired, so I'm going to head upstairs."

"That's fine." She smiles and pulls me into a tight hug. When she pulls back, she holds both of my hands in hers. "I'm so glad you came along on this trip with Brennan."

"Me too." I smile and nod. "I'm glad I got to meet you all."

"Sleep well, dear." Anna pats my shoulder and turns down the hall Brennan and Ruth disappeared down.

Once in my room, I change into something comfortable and lay down on the bed, staring at the ceiling. I can't seem to fall asleep because all I can think about is Ruth's words. No matter how hard I try, I can't seem to shake these feeling for Brennan. I can't ruin this job. The kids need me, and I don't want anything to get in the way of that. I need to pull myself together.

***

A few days go by, and we spend it enjoying the outdoors and hanging out around the house. The kids enjoy a few boat rides out in the lake and s'mores around the fire pit in the evenings. Nothing is brought up about the night Ruth got drunk, and things are fairly normal except the tension I still sense between Brennan and William.

The afternoon of the Fourth of July, I help Anna with lunch while Brennan, Ruth and the kids play frisbee in the yard. We have plans to watch fireworks over the lake from the high school property, so we are just relaxing until then.

At around seven o'clock we decide to leave so we can get good parking and just hang out before the show starts. Brennan and I drive with the kids while Ruth drives with their parents.

"Wow, it's busy this year," Brennan says as we climb out of the car. "I don't think I've ever seen this many people here before."

"Well, let's make sure we stick together," I say to the kids as I help them out of the back seat. "Don't want any of you getting lost."

Noah and Asher hold my hands and Sophia holds Brennan's as we walk along the lot to meet up with the others. We make our way to the field where families have already started gathering and take a seat in the grass. There's a lot of people, much more than I expected to see in such a smaller populated area like Wallenpaupack.

We joke around and play with the kids while we wait for the fireworks, and I'm really enjoying myself. Brennan's family has been very welcoming, and I forget any regret I had on coming along on the trip.

Sophia strikes up a game of tag with her brothers, and I sit with Brennan watching them.

"You two have very beautiful children." An elderly lady comments as she walks by, admiring the kids.

"Oh, I –" I begin to object, but Brennan cuts me off.

"Thank you, ma'am." He nods at the lady with a smile, and she walks away grinning.

Brennan turns back to me and laughs.

"What she doesn't know won't hurt her." He winks, and I smile in return.

"If you say so," I say as I look back at the kids running around.

I can't believe someone thought they were mine. I wish they were, and I'd be proud to be their mom. But motherhood just isn't for me.

"You okay?" Brennan leans closer to keep our conversation private.

"Definitely," I whisper, trying to sound convincing. He doesn't buy it though and narrows his eyes, looking at me skeptically. "Really, I'm fine. Just a lot on my mind."

"If you say so." He repeats my statement from earlier and shrugs.

I shove his shoulder, and we both laugh. I don't know what it is, but I enjoy his company immensely. For a split second, I think about how different he is when he's not worrying about work. He's fun and spirited, and it's just more appealing than the Brennan I've come to know. That's why I'm worried that maybe I've already done what I promised myself I wouldn't. Maybe I'm already in over my head.

Chapter Seventeen: The Confrontation

The firework show is beautiful, and the kids absolutely love it. Noah sits in my lap and points every time he sees one he loves. I hug him close and enjoy this moment while it lasts.

The crowd of people breaks into a gush of applause and whistles after the finale and people begin retreating to their cars. We all stand up and get ready to leave as well, but then I feel Noah tugging on my arm.

"I have to pee!" He whispers and does a little dance trying to hold it in.

I would ask if he can hold it until we get home since it's only a few minutes' drive, but who am I kidding?

"Okay, let me see where the potty is." I look around and notice a port-o-potty over by the building. I grab Brennan's arm to get his attention. "I'm going to run Noah to the potty quick, and we will meet you at the car."

"Okay." He nods and leads Sophia and Asher toward the parking lot.

Noah skips along toward the bathroom, holding my hand and going on about how cool the fireworks were. The enthusiasm from this child never ceases to amaze me.

"I love the green ones!" He cheers. "They're the best!"

"Oh yeah?" I ask cheerfully. "Why is that?"

"Because green is my favorite color, silly!" He giggles and skips some more.

"Ah, I see." I grin and open the door to the potty. "I like green, too."

Noah does his business, and then we step out of the potty. We begin walking back to the car, but he stops me a few steps away from the building.

"Ellie?" He asks, gazing up into my face.

"What's up, bud?" I kneel so I can look into his eyes and he just smiles at me.

"I just wanted to say thank you." He pats my shoulder compassionately, and my face breaks into a huge smile. He is just too cute.

"Thank me for what?"

"Just everything." He kisses my forehead, and my heart melts. I adore this child so much.

"Well, you are very welcome." I smile and stand up, offering him my hand again. "Now let's go. Your daddy probably thinks the potty gobbled us up."

Noah giggles as he skips alongside me again. After shuffling through the last few people making their way to the parking lot, we finally reach the car, but Brennan isn't there. Instead, Ruth steps out of the front seat and walks up to us.

"Brennan is talking to my parents." She looks worried, and I immediately look around the parking lot for them. "Let me get Noah buckled in so you can go look for him."

I nod and walk in the direction of Anna and William's car, a little nervous about the talk they're having. I know things have been tense between Brennan and his father, and with the look on Ruth's face, I'm not sure this is a good talk.

I finally reach their car but stop short when I hear the raised voices coming from their direction. I stand behind a truck I'm next to and listen to what they're saying.

"You've been acting like this ever since we got here and I think it would be nice for you to spend some time with your grandkids while you have the chance." Brennan's voice is stern, and I don't think I like where this conversation is going.

"That wouldn't have been a problem if you had just come home like we told you to." William murmurs with anger in his tone.

It's exactly like the comment he made at dinner the other night, but there is more hostility this time.

"We are not doing that now, Dad." Brennan hisses. "Today of all days, really? You couldn't just enjoy the holiday with your family?"

"You never want to talk about it. You could have come home, and we could have helped you with everything. You could have worked for me and –."

"Dad, just stop." Brennan cuts him off angrily. "I've told you a thousand times I am not coming back here. I have myself established in Pittsburgh, and that is our home now."

"So, you just decide to go off and hire some stranger to take care of your kids instead of accepting a little help from your parents?" William snaps. "You're so stubborn, Brennan."

I feel shame wash over me as I take in William's words. I obviously didn't know Brennan when he hired me, but I've gotten close with him and the kids since then. Is that all William sees me as? The stranger living with his son?

"Will..." Anna sighs.

"No, you're just as bad." William spits. "You're always defending him. Don't you want to see your grandchildren? Didn't you want him to come home after his wife died?"

I can't believe what I'm hearing. He is really attacking Anna for this too? Since we arrived, I haven't heard him speak to her like that, and it makes me a little angry.

"I just want him to do what's best for him and his kids, Will." Anna defends herself, a slight pain in her voice as she speaks.

I just want to wrap her in a hug.

"Apparently nanny hopping is the best option," William says. "He could have saved all the money he's been paying these women for the kids' future. Didn't you think about that, Brennan?"

I can't stand to listen to this anymore and decide that I need to stop eavesdropping. I step around the car and into plain sight, and they all turn to look at me. I can see the anger written on William and Brennan's faces.

"And here she is," William exclaims. "Tell me, Ellen, just how much is my dear son paying you to live with him in luxury and take care of my grandchildren?"

My heart sinks a little, and I feel my adrenaline start to rush. With just a few words, Brennan's father has made me feel like a worthless person, mooching off a respectable man and his family. I don't even do this for the money. Even from the beginning this was about helping Brennan, and now I do it for the kids.

"Don't you dare talk to her like that!" Brennan growls with his hands forming into fists. "She has done nothing wrong, so leave her out of it."

"William, I can't believe you." Anna wails and immediately walks over to me and wraps me in a comforting hug. "What the hell has gotten into you?"

"Go ahead and take her side, too." William huffs as he glares in our direction. "I'm done with this shit, Ann."

"Yeah, well, so am I." She yells, and at that moment, I'm glad that there aren't any people around us to hear this exchange. "I think you should stay somewhere else tonight."

"Gladly," William mumbles before climbing into his car and starting it. Brennan, Anna and I stand in silence as we watch him pull away and drive off.

"Anna, I'm so sorry," I say once I realize what just happened.

What have I done?

"This is not your fault, Ellie." She rubs my arm. "Please don't apologize."

"We should get going." Brennan approaches us and leads us both back to his car where Ruth and the kids are still waiting. His face is emotionless, and an emptiness fills my stomach.

The car ride home is completely silent, and I let the whole scene replay in my mind again and again. Although Anna said it isn't, I can't help but feel like this is mostly my fault. After all, the argument was centered around the fact that Brennan hired a nanny instead of moving back home after Kayla passed. William saw me as a barrier, holding Brennan back, and I don't see how this isn't my fault.

I sit between Asher and Noah, watching Brennan's face in the rear-view mirror as he drives. He looks tired. It's like seeing him after a long and exhausting day at work, and that makes me feel even more guilty. This day has done a complete 360, going from amazing to depressing.

The minute we walk in the door, Ruth and I bring the kids upstairs to get bathed and ready for bed while Brennan and Anna talk in the sitting room. Thankfully, the kids are still their cheerful selves, and they relieve a bit of my stress with their giggles and games.

Afterwards, Ruth and I sit in the loft while Sophia and the boys play a bit before bed.

"So, it was bad, then." She sighs after I explain the events in the parking lot. "I've seen them argue before, but this sounds like it's getting to be the last straw."

"I didn't know they had problems." I frown, looking down at my lap. "The last few days they've just seemed so... normal."

"Trust me, they've got a lot of problems." Ruth shakes her head in frustration. "They've been arguing about so much since Brennan and I were little. I don't even remember a time when they were perfect."

"I'm sorry to hear that." I look up at Ruth, and her expression seems indifferent.

"It happens." She shrugs. "And it kind of brought Ren and me closer. But I've known this was coming for a long time."

I consider her words for a moment and think about the exchange between William and Anna. They just seemed so fed up with each other, and I can't believe I hadn't noticed it sooner.

"Be honest with me. Do you think Brennan made a mistake hiring me?" I ask the question that has been burning in my mind since we left the high school.

I need to know if everyone else feels the same way William does.

"Absolutely not." Ruth looks at me with complete respect and shifts herself to fully face me on the couch. "Don't beat yourself up over this, Ellie. Trust me, this was inevitable."

"But —" I start to speak, but Ruth closes my mouth.

"Brennan is a grown man with his own family that he needs to look out for. Could he have moved back here after he lost Kay? Of course. But that wasn't what he wanted, and regardless of whether my father agreed with that choice, he should have respected Brennan's wishes."

I nod in agreement and look back down at my hands. I can't help but dig at my nailbeds. My mind is all over the place.

"I think that Brennan did a great thing hiring a nanny to help with the kids because I know he couldn't do this on his own. And I'm so glad that you turned out to be such a peach because it really is just what he needs. He needs that positivity at home so he can move forward with his life. Coming back here would have been like taking one step forward and two steps back."

I register what Ruth is saying and know that she is right. What good would it have done Brennan to move back here after everything happened? He needed to move on, and he did everything he could to make sure he kept things running like normal, especially for the kids.

"Don't let my dad get to you." Ruth places a hand on my knee and gives it a light squeeze. "He can be a real asshole sometimes, and this isn't about you at all."

"Thanks, Ruth." I glance back at her and smile. "I appreciate everything."

"Anytime." She nods.

We both just listen to the kids playing in the bedroom, and my heart becomes uneasy for a second. I don't know what I've done to deserve these people in my life, but I am very thankful I've got them, even if our time together is limited.

"Well, I better get going." Ruth stands up and goes to say goodnight to the kids before hugging me. "I'll see you guys in a few days."

"Okay, drive safe."

I wave to her as she makes her way down the stairs and I listen for the front door to know that she has left. I look at the huge clock above the fireplace in the living room and realize I should get the kids to bed. I know they'll want to say goodnight to Brennan, though, so I make my way downstairs to see how he's doing.

As I make my way down the hallway, I can hear the soft mumbles of Brennan and Anna still talking in the sitting room. I stop for a second, considering my options. I hate to let the kids go to bed without saying goodnight to their dad, but I also don't want to interrupt.

I decide to listen in a bit and enter when the time is right.

Chapter Eighteen: The Split

I quietly inch a little closer so I can hear what Anna and Brennan are saying. I hate to eavesdrop, but I can't think of another way to get Brennan's attention. And now, I wait.

"It's not like that, Mom," Brennan whispers.

I didn't hear what Anna said, but he seems a bit flustered.

"If you say so." Anna jeers and sighs. "Just do me a favor, sweetie, and don't turn out like your father." There is a short silence before she continues. "That man cares far too much about his job and image, and it has blinded him from what is most important."

I nod to myself, agreeing with Anna's words. I knew immediately upon meeting him that William was too concerned with his reputation.

"Family always comes first, Brennan." She continues, and I lean against the wall while I listen. "Sophia, Asher, and Noah should always be your priority. Don't take them for granted. I'd hate to see a repeat of your relationship with your father."

"That will never happen," Brennan responds immediately. "While I care about my job, I care about my kids more, and they will always take precedence. I know what happened in the past, and I'm learning from it."

"Good, I'm glad." I hear Anna stand up and I slowly back away toward the living room.

There goes my opportunity to get Brennan's attention.

"I'm just glad you have Ellie to help keep you on track." Anna chuckles.

"Mom..." Brennan sighs again, and I turn around to go back upstairs with the kids.

When I reach the balcony, I hear giggles still coming from the boys' room, so I peek in and watch them. Asher and Noah are pretending to be knights while Sophia is their princess. One thing I've come to admire about her is that she always plays along with her brothers, even if the activities are a bit juvenile for her.

I lean against the doorframe for a second and enjoy the show. Asher pretends to ride on his valiant steed while Noah draws his sword.

"We must protect the castle from the fire breathing dragon!" Asher cries as he jumps up onto the bed. He finally notices me and points in my direction. "And there's the dragon! Save the princess!"

I put my hands up like I'm going to attack and slowly stalk into the room.

"I'm feeling very ferocious today!" I lock my eyes on Noah. "And I think. I'm. Going. To… Get you!"

I grab Noah and start tickling him, and he bursts into a fit of giggles.

"Oh, no!" Asher laughs as he runs over to us. "We are no match for the dragon!"

He pokes me in the side with his toy sword, and I turn and grab him too, tickling him and growling.

"So much for saving the princess!" Sophia chuckles and joins in on the tickle fest, hugging Noah and laughing.

Once we finish tickling the boys, we all just lay around the floor, panting and trying to catch our breath. In the corner of my eye, I notice a figure in the doorway and look over to see Brennan smiling.

"Wonderful show." He starts clapping. "You fought valiantly, boys."

He chuckles, and the boys both stand up and take a fake bow.

"The dragon got us, Daddy!" Noah giggles and hugs Brennan's leg.

"I saw!" Brennan smiles wider and kneels. "You'll get the dragon next time, bud. But right now, I think it's time for bed."

"Aww, okay." Asher sighs and starts cleaning up his toys.

Sophia and Noah help and then Sophia goes to her room while we tuck the boys in. Once they're all asleep, Brennan and I take a stroll outside.

"So, how are you doing?" I ask, watching my feet as I walk along the cobblestones.

"I'm alright." Brennan shoves his hands in his pockets and shrugs. "Not exactly how I thought this vacation would go, but such is life, I guess."

"I'm really sorry about everything." I apologize for what feels like the hundredth time.

"It's not your fault." He looks out at the lake in front of us. "It was bound to happen eventually. My father has his priorities all mixed up."

We reach the dock, and I sit in the sand. Brennan joins me, and we are silent for a few moments while we both watch the water rippling against the shore. It's a warm night, and I hang my head to the side, breathing in the fresh, musky air. Some fireworks are still going off in the distance, and their booms fill the silence.

"How long have you known something was wrong with your parents?" I ask Brennan, giving him the opportunity to open up a bit. I want him to know that I'm here for him.

"A few years, I guess." He shrugs, leaning back on his hands. "My father has always been way too invested in his work. I've seen that since I was a kid, and that's why I didn't want to stay here and work for him. I branched his firm out into Pittsburgh, and that made him angry, but I couldn't become him." He pauses for a second. "There was a time when I didn't realize how similar I was becoming, and I have tried very hard to change that since then."

I turn to look at him, silently taking in his words. I can't imagine him being anything like William. Brennan has this gentleness to him, and I know how much his kids mean to him. I can't see him letting anything get in the way of that, especially after what just happened with Lorelei.

"But for the last few years, my parents have just seemed more distant than usual." He continues his explanation. "Each visit has become more and more difficult to bear because they've changed so much and make it obvious every time I see them. So, I saw this coming."

His words reflect what Ruth said earlier, and it makes me sad. I can't imagine growing up with parents who clearly didn't want to be together.

"It must be hard." I look back out at the dark water softly dancing in the night. "To watch your parents just grow apart. And to know the reason why."

"You're lucky you don't have to know." He says. "Your parents still look so happy together after all this time. Good for them."

I can't help but smile at his words.

"What?" He notices my expression and turns his body to face me.

"Eamon isn't my real dad." I shake my head and chuckle.

"Wait, what?" Confusion takes over Brennan's face, and I keep smiling.

"Well, I mean he's been in my life since I was eight years old, but he's not my biological father," I explain. "My real dad died from his job as a firefighter, and my mom met Eamon a few years later. They haven't been married for as long as your parents, but I see what you mean. They are very happy together, and I am lucky not to have to endure what you're going through now."

"I never would have thought Eamon was your stepfather." Brennan shakes his head with a small smile. "I mean, aside from the Irish accent, you two are so close, and you have his last name."

"Blood or not, he's been my father for twenty years, and we've developed quite the father-daughter bond." I sigh, thinking about how great life has been with a father figure like Eamon. "And my mother had Eamon legally adopt us, and changed us his surname so he knew that he was our father."

"That's really nice." Brennan watches me, and I look down at the sand around my feet. After a moment of silence, I speak again.

"I think you and Kayla would have lasted like my parents." I pick up some sand and let it fall through my fingers.

"Why do you say that?" I can sense Brennan's curious gaze on me. "You didn't even know her."

"No, I didn't," I say, glancing up at him again. "But I have heard the way you describe her, and I know you two had a real connection. I don't know if true love exists. But, if it does, you and Kayla were the definition of it."

Brennan doesn't say anything but stares at me with an expression I can't quite explain. He seems very engrossed in my statement, and curious, as if he didn't know why I would say these things about a woman I never met. He's trying to read me like he always does.

"The wrong people tend to end up together sometimes, and I know that from personal experience. But, I also think that other times, we get these rare occurrences when two people couldn't be more perfect for each other."

I continue talking, still mixing sand between my hands.

"I think it's completely unfair that you were one of those few, lucky people, and that you got it taken away from you. What I wouldn't give to have someone talk about me the way that you talk about her." I sigh. "It was never like that with my ex."

"Ellie," Brennan whispers and closes his eyes.

"I'm sorry if I crossed any boundaries." I shake the sand off my hands. "I just wanted to tell you that I know you'd never end up like your father. You've got a big heart, and I know you'd never let anything, even your job, come between you and your kids."

Brennan gapes at me with his mouth slightly open, as if I've completely surprised him. He sits there, speechless and unable to respond. I'm sure at this point he knows that I heard some of his conversation with his mom earlier, and he seems rather nervous about that.

"It's getting pretty late, and it's been a long day." I slowly stand up, offering a hand out for him. "We should get some sleep."

"Yes." Brennan finally says, taking my hand and standing up.

He stands close to me, still holding my hand and gazing into my eyes. I feel myself blush and I look down at the ground, pulling my hand away. Damn it, Ren, stop that.

We walk back up to the house in complete silence. No sound but the wind through the trees and crickets in the distance. We part ways at the foot of the stairs, and I throw myself onto the bed once I reach my room. I cry a little to myself, reflecting on this crazy day.

I'm up early the next morning and head downstairs for some fresh air. As I walk down the steps, I hear Anna talking to someone and slow down, wondering if I should just turn around. I realize it's Brennan she's talking to, and I don't want to interrupt again, so I sneak down hoping to get out the door without them noticing.

My hand is on the handle of the sliding glass door when I hear the mumbling stop.

"Good morning, Ellie." Anna sings from the kitchen, and I look over to see her and Brennan staring at me.

"Hey." I awkwardly wave, tucking my other arm nervously behind my back. "I just wanted some fresh air, and I was just trying not to disturb you."

"Don't worry about it." Brennan stands and places his mug in the sink. "I'll join you."

My heartrate increases, and my smile disappears. I'm not sure I'm ready to talk to Brennan yet after last night. I know I was blunt, and I kind of regret everything I said at this point.

"I'm going to get started on breakfast, so don't be too long," Anna smirks, eyeing Brennan.

I'm not sure what that's all about, but I just ignore it.

Brennan and I step out onto the deck and take a seat at the table. I look out over the yard and admire the beauty of the morning, taking a deep breath. I remain silent, giving Brennan the opportunity to talk if he wants to.

"Ellie." He mumbles. I look at him, and he's looking out at the lake as well. "I appreciate what you said last night."

"You do?" I silently sigh in relief, glad that he's not mad. "I tend to ramble sometimes, and I was nervous you'd be a bit mad at me," I admit.

"Absolutely not." He meets my gaze for the first time, and I can see the tenderness in his eyes. "You said nothing but nice things about my wife and me. So, thank you."

"Well, you're welcome." I nod and look back out over at the lake again, assuming we are finished with that part of our conversation.

"I, um, realize I don't talk about her enough, especially with the kids." Brennan rubs his neck and shakes his head. "But it's just hard. I was in a really bad place after we lost her, and I don't think I'll ever forgive myself for what happened, but I've had a lot of time to reflect on it."

I turn to face him and listen as he says this. I'm at a loss for words because I never thought he'd feel comfortable enough to openly discuss this with me. He's never said anything about Kayla's death, so I'm flattered he feels confident enough to tell me about it.

"I understand how hard it must be for you." I shift my entire body, so I'm fully facing him. "So, don't feel like you have to talk about it. You lost someone very important to you, and I can appreciate how heartbroken that must make you."

I look down briefly before meeting his eyes again. I'm trying to pick my words carefully, so that I don't overwhelm Brennan with this topic.

"As for Sophia and the boys, just remember that they are still young. They've got their whole lives to hear about how amazing she was, so don't feel bad that you can't talk to them about it yet. It's going to take some time, and the important thing is that they've got you here for them right now."

"And you." Brennan smiles weakly at me. "I really can't thank you enough for all that you've done for us so far. I think I'd be pretty lost if I didn't have you around."

"I'm happy to be here and help you in whatever way you need." I grin. "Those kids deserve the best."

"Speaking of." I follow Brennan's gaze inside where I see the kids running across the living room toward the kitchen.

I stand to go in and look back at Brennan. "Do you want a few minutes alone?"

"No." he smiles at me and rises from his chair. "But Ellie?" I turn around again to look at him. "I'm sorry about what my dad said. I hope you know that you're not the problem."

"I did for a little while, but I'm okay now." I smile and turn to enter the house. He follows me, and we join the kids and Anna in the kitchen.

"Everyone sleep well?" Brennan asks, sitting down at the table and pulling Noah onto his lap.

"Yeah!" Asher says excitedly. "What are we doing today, Daddy?"

"Oh, lots of stuff." Brennan pronounces to the kids. "The rest of this trip is going to be filled with lots of fun and excitement. I promise."

And Brennan keeps his promise. The rest of the month goes by in a flash an all I can remember is the laughter and joy from the kids as they spend some much-needed quality time with their father. Ruth came around a lot, and Brennan and I even had a few days to ourselves while she took them out.

William and Anna officially separated, but Will came around a lot to be with his grandchildren at least. The visits weren't exactly thrilling, but the kids definitely needed that special time with him.

On the last day of the trip, Brennan and I have loaded the vehicle while the kids say goodbye to Anna and Ruth. Once they're all buckled in and ready to go, I say my goodbyes as well.

Ruth squeezes me so tight I can hardly breathe, and Anna hugs me for a good whole minute before finally releasing me.

"Thank you for taking care of my grandbabies." She says with tears in her eyes. "I will come visit you all very soon."

She kisses my cheek and then hugs Brennan. She whispers something in his ear, and his eyes shoot over to me. I'm not sure what she said, but he blushes a little.

"Goodbye, Mom." He coughs as she releases him and we make our way to the car again. "Love you!" He waves just before climbing into the driver's side.

And just like that, we are on our way back home. The kids fall asleep about halfway through the trip, so Brennan and I just chat and listen to music. It was a great trip, but now it's back to reality. And reality means backing off a bit.

Anna and Ruth were so welcoming that I felt like a part of the family this past month, but I know that is not the case. I'm just the nanny and to have to remember that.

Chapter Nineteen: The Realization

Once home, we settle back into our normal routine, and before I know it, August has come and gone, and the kids are back at school. This means that I'm back at the office with Brennan and surprisingly, I have been looking forward to it.

While I loved every minute home with the kids over their vacation, it's nice to get out of the house more and see other people. People I can have adult conversations with. The rest of the summer after the visit to Lake Wallenpaupack was very laid back with me and the kids at home or the park, so a little change is just what I need right now.

It's been a week since I returned to the office, and I decide to grab a quick breakfast with Dakota before work one day. I haven't had a lot of time with her since I got back, so we catch up on everything that has happened in the last two months.

"It seriously sounds like you had an amazing trip." Dakota smiles from beside.

The weather is so nice today, so we are sitting on the ground near the fountain in the square at PPG place. People are looking at us strangely as they pass, but it doesn't bother me. I'm enjoying the weather while I can.

"It was nice" I nod in agreement and smile to myself. "His mother is such a sweetheart and his sister is about as crazy as you."

"Hey, I'm gonna take that as a compliment." She laughs with a mouthful of food.

I shake my head and chuckle. She's so classy sometimes.

"Of course." I take a bite of my bagel. "It was totally meant to be one."

I glance around at the other people who had the same idea as us to sit outdoors today. With fall quickly approaching, everyone seems to want to enjoy the warmth and the sunshine while it lasts before the snow comes.

"Sucks about his dad, though," Dakota adds, wiping her face. "Guy sounds like a total jerk, so I'm sure Brennan and the rest of them will be better off without him."

"Yeah, well, Brennan has been handling it very well, considering."

I peek up at the empty window to Brennan's office and think about his attitude the past month. You would never think the man just had a falling out with his dad because he's been his happy, normal self with the kids and me. His mood at work has even been spirited, as well.

"And that's the way it should be," Dakota says. "He doesn't need more stress on his plate right now, especially with the workload that just got thrown at him."

"Speaking of," I gather up my garbage and stuff it in the bag our food came in. "Brennan finally has a new contender for Lorelei's position, and they're coming for an interview today."

"Ugh, thank god!" Dakota cries in excitement and throws her garbage in the bag with mine. "Seriously, the last three sucked!"

"Agreed."

I think about the few people Brennan had hired over the summer. They all seemed amazing during the interview process, but it just didn't work out with any of them in the end. One of them was a completely lazy, never getting anything done. Another couldn't seem to comprehend the job and her duties at all no matter how hard she tried. And the last one barely showed up for work at all. So, needless to say, we are all hoping the next one works out.

"I hope he's hot." Dakota blurts out nonchalantly.

"Kody!" I smack her arm, and she bursts out laughing.

"What?" She keeps laughing. "We need some new eye candy!"

"And if it's a woman?" I ask teasingly with a raised eyebrow.

"Well, then I hope she's hot too!" She sticks her tongue out, and I pinch her arm.

"You're insane."

"Yeah, well, not all of us get to be around the gorgeous boss all day long." She teases, and I shoot her a glare in return. "I'm just saying, you guys are always together."

"That would be because I'm his assistant, crazy."

I look away, trying not to think about Brennan because Dakota is right. He is very good looking, and every woman who has met him is well aware of that fact. And if I'm honest with myself, I've enjoyed all the time we've spent together.

"Off the record, be honest with me." Dakota pauses, and I look at her again. It's like she's inside my head or something. Her expression is changed, and she now looks at me with anticipation. "How do you feel about him?"

"What? Why would you ask that?" I stare into her eyes and see the same concern she always gives me when men are involved.

"I just know you, Nelly, better than you know yourself sometimes." She shrugs and looks down at our garbage, tearing at the bag a bit. "Which means that I know when you're into someone."

"Yeah, well," I glance over at the office and sigh briefly. "You don't have to say, 'I told you so' this time because nothing is going on there."

"Don't do that." Dakota crosses her arms, and I look back at her to see her eyebrows furrowed and a hint of pain in her eyes.

"What?"

"Don't make me out to be the bad guy here. I just care about you, Ellen." She uses my full name, which is rare. I know I've offended her.

"I'm not. But you were right about Jake, and I'm always afraid I'm going to mess up again."

We both remain silent for a few seconds, and I hate the tension between us. We don't have many disagreements, but when we do, it's bad.

"I don't hate all men, you know." Dakota breaks the silence and shakes her head. "I just hate when you choose assholes and get yourself mixed up in bad situations."

"I guess getting involved with my boss constitutes as a bad situation, right?" I sneer and glance down at my feet, tracing the outline of the small heart tattoo on my ankle.

"Actually, I think Brennan is amazing for you," Dakota says, and my gaze shoots back to her. She's smiling, and I feel myself blush at the turn this conversation has taken. "So, tell me what is going on in that pretty head of yours."

"Dakota..." I look away again and bite my bottom lip.

How am I supposed to respond to that?

"Nelly, you know you can talk to me about anything, right?" She says softly and grabs my hand. "I want to support you, but I can't do that if you don't open up to me."

I meet her eyes again and sigh, not sure how to even explain my feelings to her.

"I don't know, Kody." I rub my forehead and consider everything I've felt the last few months. "It's different."

I stop talking for a second, trying to find the right words, and Dakota just waits patiently for me to speak again.

"I really don't know how to explain it." I pull my legs up to my chest and hug them, resting my chin on my knees. "I'm happy when I'm around him. Like, we don't even have to be talking, but there is just something oddly satisfying about being in his company. It's like my body just craves his presence."

"And?" Dakota urges me to continue, but I'm still at a loss for words.

"What else do you want me to say, Kody?" I shake my head and stand up, pacing around in small circles. "You want me to tell you that he makes my heart skip a beat when he looks at me with those intoxicating eyes? Or that his laugh fills me with so much joy that I can't ever be upset around him? Or that his voice alone sends chills throughout my body and I love hearing it as often as I can?"

Dakota still sits on the ground, grinning from ear to ear as I ramble on.

"Or how about the way he interacts with his children? The way I can tell from his face that they fill him with so much pride, and he loves them more than anything on this planet? He's an amazing father, and that makes me so, so happy."

"Nelly," Dakota says, but I keep talking.

"Or maybe you want to hear that he's the last thing on my mind before falling asleep at night and the first thing when I wake up every morning."

I stop walking and stand still, gazing at the water rushing in the fountain.

"Or even the fact that I get terrified every time I think about the day when he won't need me anymore, and I'll have to walk out of his life forever."

"Ellen." Dakota snaps me out of my daze and pulls my arm for me to sit back down with her. "Relax."

I sit down and look at the ground, ashamed of myself for my little rant and unable to bring myself to look my best friend in the eyes. This is the first time I've truly acknowledged my feelings for Brennan out loud, and I realize that I've done the very thing I said I wouldn't do. I've gotten myself in too deep.

"I'm sorry, Nelly." Dakota rubs my leg and smiles at me in dismay. "I didn't realize it was that serious. But I want to help you, and I'm glad you told me."

"I didn't want this to happen," I say through a shaky voice. "I told myself I wouldn't get myself in over my head and now I'm just drowning."

"It doesn't have to be that way," Dakota says. "What if he feels the same? Things can be completely different."

"I can't do that." I sigh and finally look at my best friend. "I can't risk everything I have with the kids. I just have to continue like I've been doing and then when the time comes for me to leave, I'll just have to move on."

"I just want you to know that it's not the only option." Dakota sighs. "If you feel this strongly, you might want to do something about it."

"It's so different than how things were with Jake." I shake my head, trying to remember a time when I felt this way for my ex-husband. "I never felt anything like this when we were together."

"That's because you didn't truly love Jake. He was just a young fling that went too far."

"What are you saying?" I ask skeptically, though I already know the answer.

"You know what I'm saying." She smiles and brushes my hair behind my shoulder. "You have time to think about this and make a decision. Just don't shut yourself out immediately, okay?"

I look back toward the office and let all my thoughts dance around in my head. I don't even know what to think anymore. My heart aches when I think about my feelings for Brennan, so I try to shove them as far back in my mind as possible. It's just easier that way.

"I would hate to see you miss out on something amazing." Dakota stands up and offers her hand to help me up. "You're my best friend, and I just want you to be happy."

"Thanks, Kody." I hug her once I'm standing and hold onto her for a second.

I don't know what I would do without this girl. She has been my biggest supporter for most of my life and knows me better than anyone. It feels good to confide in her with something this big, especially when I have no idea what I want to do about it.

"Let's get in there before we get into trouble." Dakota winks and carries our garbage to the nearest trash can.

We head into the office, and when we enter the lobby, I see Brennan and some clients walking back to one of the more private conference rooms. He catches a glimpse of me and smiles with a nod as he disappears down the hall. He has been so busy with meetings and clients lately that I rarely see him before lunch.

I part ways with Dakota and head upstairs to file some more paperwork. A few hours later I'm almost done with the files for the day, and I decide to take a small break. I haven't seen Brennan since this morning, but I know how busy he is. Plus, I think the less we see each other now, the better.

I walk over to the window and stare out at the busy sidewalk. Seeing the fountain makes me think of my conversation with Dakota this morning, and I instantly frown. How am I supposed to carry on like this? Can I just ignore everything I've been feeling?

I shake my head and wrap back around the desk to finish up my work, but before I grab the next file from the stack of papers, something else catches my eye. A yellow sticky note is placed in plain sight on Brennan's desk calendar, and I see the word "interview" written first. I read the rest, and my heart stops.

Interview: Sept. 8 @ 1 pm, Jake Mallory.

Chapter Twenty: The Ex-Husband

I freeze in my spot, still staring at the name on the note in front of me. I close my eyes tight and then open them again, hoping this is all my imagination. It doesn't change a thing and sure enough, "Jake Mallory" is still written on the sheet. I check my watch and see that it's already 12:30.

"Hello, Elle," a deep voice pierces through me like ice. I haven't heard that nickname in a long time and it makes my heartrate accelerate.

I lift my head but don't turn around just yet. This can't be happening. Maybe it's someone else who sounds like him and knows that nickname, and I've got time to sort this all out. Get a grip, Ellie. Don't be so naive.

I finally build up the nerve to turn, and my eyes meet the face of the one person in the world I don't want to see. My ex-husband stands in the doorway of Brennan's office, gazing at me with the same hunger he had when we first met.

Although it's been months since I've seen him, he hasn't changed one bit. His brown eyes still burn into me, and his blonde hair is short and combed back neatly. He still stands with his stupid cocky stance, hip out, so he's balancing all his weight to one side, and he still has that foolish smirk. At one point in time, that smirk made me swoon, and I would fall for him over and over again, but now it just makes me sick.

I must be dreaming. This is just some crazy nightmare that I'm going to wake up from any moment now. I want nothing more than for this to not be happening.

"You look great." He says as if nothing ever happened.

How dare he? After everything we've been through he has the nerve to act so casually about our meeting. As a matter of fact, he doesn't seem at all surprised to see me, now that I think about it.

"What are you doing here?" I finally manage to form some words, though I already know the answer.

"I can ask you the same question." He smirks again, and it makes me angrier. "I'm here for a job interview."

He watches me carefully like this is a game for him. Before I can give any sort of response, Brennan walks in.

"Oh, you're here early!" Brennan says to Jake, grabbing him in for a quick hug and patting him on the back. "How was your trip?"

I stare in disbelief as the two men in front of me embrace each other as if they were brothers. What the hell is going on?

"It was good. Traffic wasn't too bad," Jake replies. "Man, it has been way too long!"

His gaze shifts over to me quickly.

"Oh, my goodness, where are my manners?" Brennan shakes his head at his slip up. "Ellie, this is my old roommate from college, Jake Mallory. He's here to interview for Lorelei's position."

I just stare at Jake while Brennan speaks. Jake was his roommate? The guy I've heard a few stories about is my ex-husband before I met him? Brennan couldn't possibly know about us. He wouldn't do that, would he?

"Ellie?" Brennan says my name, pulling me out of my trance. "Are you okay? I was just introducing you to Jake, here, but you seem a bit lost."

I'm unsure where to go from here. How do I tell Brennan that his old friend is the man who abused me for years? That after their fun times in college, his old friend became an alcoholic who took his aggression out on his wife. I can't do that to him.

"I'm sorry, yes." I extend my hand in greeting without even thinking. "It's nice to meet you, Jake. I'm Ellen Mannis."

Jake takes my hand and shakes it. His head is tilted, and he is eyeing me with a hint of confusion on his face. Yes, two can play this game. As far as Brennan is concerned, I've never met this man. At least until I can figure out where to go from here.

"Ellie is my nanny slash personal assistant here" Brennan continues his introductions. "So, you'll be seeing her around if you get the job."

"Sounds great." Jake's lips form a mischievous smile, and I clench my teeth to hold my poker face.

"Well, I'll let you two get on with your interview." I break in, peeking over at the clock. "It's time for my lunch anyway."

"Of course." Brennan smiles innocently and steps aside so I can get to the door. "I'll see you later."

I nod and exit the office, breaking into a jog down the stairs straight to the door. I need to find Dakota.

"Nelly!" I stop in my tracks and turn to see Dakota running toward me from the break room.

She wraps me in a hug the moment she reaches me, and it takes everything I have not to cry. We turn and walk through the door before saying another word.

Out on the sidewalk, I look Dakota in the eyes and see her concern.

"I was trying to find you." She huffs, out of breath. "I was just about to leave for lunch when he came in and he led himself up to Brennan's office and I was hoping you had already slipped away for lunch."

I look down at my feet, and then out at the square. I'm not sure I'm even in my own body at the moment. Everything feels wrong. I still wish this were just a bad dream and I would wake up.

"Nelly, I promise you I did not know he was coming," Dakota assures me. "Brennan must have done this himself because I would have told you as soon as I knew."

"They were roommates in college," I whisper, still staring out at the square.

"What?" Dakota is exasperated. "So, they already know each other?"

I nod. "That's why Brennan did this himself. Because he knew him personally."

"Oh man. I can't believe this." Dakota sighs. "He's going to get Lorelei's position."

I finally look back at my best friend.

"What do I do now? I can't be around him. I just can't. And now Brennan thinks we don't know each other and are just meeting for the first time."

I glance up at the window to Brennan's office and see both men standing and chatting. I walk away before they notice me, and Dakota follows.

"You're going to have to tell Brennan." She links arms with me. "He needs to know the truth."

"He has already lost so much since I came into the picture." I shake my head. "I'm not destroying any more relationships."

Dakota stops me and turns me to face her.

"That man." She points back toward the office. "Is a terrible person, and you get to look at the proof of that every day."

I grab my shoulder at the mention of my proof and finally a tear rolls down my cheek.

"Do not give him this satisfaction." She continues. "Brennan does not need a man like that working for him. Or in his life at all, for that matter."

I nod in agreement.

"I know," I whisper again. "I'll figure it all out. I just need...time."

We begin walking toward Market Square again, and I dread going back to the office. My heart hurts, and I have no idea what I'm going to do. My stomach cannot handle food right now, so we sit on a bench in the square talking.

"How could this happen?" I stare at the pigeons wobbling around, looking for food anywhere they can peck.

I wish I were a pigeon right now. No abusive ex-husbands or disappointing life revelations.

"I was married to Jake the entire time you worked for Brennan. How could it not have gotten brought up that they know each other?"

"I have no idea." Dakota shrugs and shakes her head. "I've never heard Brennan mention his name once in the time I've worked for him."

I don't say it out loud, but that doesn't really surprise me. Brennan is a very private person and doesn't usually bring his personal life to work with him.

"You know what's even worse?" I look up at Dakota. "He didn't seem at all surprised to see me. He just acted like we were old friends who were catching up."

"Now that you mention it, he didn't seem surprised to see me either." Dakota points out. "He recognized me immediately, and just acted like we were best buddies." She shakes her head and snarls a bit. "That asshole."

If there is anyone who hates Jake more than my family, it's Dakota. She hated watching me go through everything so much you could swear it happened to her instead.

After talking it out, and realizing that I can't avoid the office all day, I decide Dakota is right and that I need to tell Brennan everything as soon as possible.

When we arrive back at the building, I walk up to his office and find the door slightly ajar. I knock gently and peek in, but no one is there. I hear people chatting in the hall and poke my head back out the door.

Keith and Joe are walking toward the stairs, so I stop them.

"Have you guys seen Brennan?" I ask quickly as they pass.

"He took a long lunch today with that guy he's interviewing," Keith replies. "Everything okay?"

"Oh yeah, I'm fine." I wave my hand and smile. "I was just wondering, thanks."

Once they leave, I enter the office once more and take a seat on the couch across the room from his desk. I look at the pile of papers near the filing cabinet that I need to finish sorting through and organizing. It's probably a good thing to distract myself until Brennan returns, so I drag myself off the couch and continue my work.

I'm finishing up with the last of the pile when I hear laughter in the lobby. It's Brennan and Jake; there's no mistaking that. I know both of their laughs all too well.

Not even a minute later, they both walk through the door.

"Ah, Ellie," Brennan says with a big smile. "We were just talking about you."

What? Talking about me? What did Jake tell him? It couldn't be anything about our past considering Brennan is smiling. No, that's not it. So, why were they talking about me?

"I was telling Jake that you cook a mean pot roast." Brennan continues, and I sigh a breath of relief. "If it's not too much to ask, would you mind cooking some tonight for us?"

"Us?" I ask, not liking where this is going.

"Yeah, I thought it would be nice to have Jake over for dinner to catch up. Plus, it's Friday, and we won't need to be at work early tomorrow."

Great. Now he's going to be at the house, and he's most likely going to be drinking.

"If that's what you want, sure." I fake a small smile.

After all, I still have a job to uphold here.

I finish my work for the day by organizing things going into the weekend, so it's set for Monday morning while Brennan and Jake chat at the desk. Somehow Brennan is oblivious to the fact that Jake keeps peeking over at me and smiling. It's that damn mischievous smile of his that lets me know he's up to something. When I'm finished, it's time for me to pick up the kids from school.

"Ellie, wait," Brennan calls before I walk out the door. "Do you mind bringing a few things back to the house for me? I've already got a lot in my car, and there's more that needs to go in my home office."

"Not a problem." I nod, though I want nothing more than to just leave.

"Great, let me go grab it quick. I'll meet you in the lobby." He replies quickly before jogging out the door and down the stairs.

I'm left alone in the room with Jake, and I immediately regret my decision. To avoid any more conversation with him, I nod and turn to leave the room. I am unsuccessful as Jake's hand grabs my arm to stop me. The feeling of his hand on my skin makes me sick and I close my eyes and take a deep breath to center myself.

"Elle." He says, but I don't turn to look at him. I am staying strong this time.

"I look forward to seeing you later" He whispers in my ear.

I yank my arm away and head downstairs to wait for Brennan.

Once I say goodbye to Dakota, Brennan brings me a box and heads back upstairs. I watch him go, and when my eyes reach the top of the stairs, Jake is standing there smiling at me. I stare at him, taking a stand to prove that I am stronger than I was before, and don't move until he finally turns to follow Brennan into his office.

I climb into my car and look at myself in my mirror. How did today turn into the day from hell? I finally let everything out that has been building up inside me for the past few hours. I sob for what feels like forever when I finally wipe my face and pull out of the parking garage.

Chapter Twenty-One: The Dinner

I run to the store for everything I'll need for dinner and arrive home with the kids about an hour and a half later. We go about our usual routine of homework and chores and then it's time for me to get started on the food.

Before I begin cooking, I decide to bring Brennan's box into his office. It's only the second time I've been in that room of the house, so I take a moment to appreciate it.

It truly is a mess, with boxes and paperwork scattered everywhere. The hutch above the desk holds a few pictures I did not notice last time and I step closer to look.

One is the same picture at his parents' house of the family last Christmas. Another is the kids when Noah was born. Sophia is holding him, and Asher is laughing. Another picture is of the kids with Anna and William in the backyard near the pool. And the final picture makes me gasp out loud.

The last picture is from Brennan's wedding. He and Kayla stand in the center of the bridal party and standing by Brennan's side is Jake. He was the best man at Brennan's wedding, and yet I didn't even know they were acquainted until today. How did this happen? The answer was here the whole time.

Asher and Noah start talking loudly, and I assume that means Brennan is home. I leave the office and meet them all in the kitchen, where I make a quick cup of coffee before cooking dinner. I hope the caffeine will give me the boost of energy I need to get through this night.

"Hey, Ellie." Brennan greets me as I sit down at the island. "Are you sure you're still good with tonight? I'm sorry to throw it at you so last minute, but I figured it's best to get it out of the way tonight and then have the weekend for other things."

"Actually, I wanted to talk to you about something," I say as my heart rate quickens. How do I even begin?

"Can it wait?" Brennan smiles, not picking up on my tone of voice. "I'm dying to get out of these clothes, and I promised the boys a quick game of Go Fish before Jake arrives."

"No problem, I understand." I nod with a weak smile. "I was just about to throw the roast together anyway."

"Alright, great." Brennan smiles, retreating to his bedroom to change out of his work clothes. "Jake will be here around six."

Fantastic. I lift my mug in acknowledgment before chugging the last of it. Here's to the horrible, awful night ahead of me.

I prep and throw the pot roast in the oven and head upstairs to change into something more comfortable. I look at myself in the mirror and cry a little, angry with myself for not being more adamant with Brennan. He needs to know the truth. This has been the worst day in a very long time, and it's not even over yet. Everything just feels like it's falling apart.

Jake arrives a little bit before six o'clock, just as I am finishing up with dinner. The table is already set, thanks to the kids, and we all gather around to eat. As if I weren't already dreading this dinner, Jake sits across from me and smiles. I look down at my plate and try my best to ignore him without giving myself away.

"So, Jake," Brennan says, scooping vegetables onto his plate. "How has life been? It's been, what, eleven years now?"

Well, that would explain why I didn't know they were friends. They haven't even seen each other in over a decade.

"Yeah, I'm sorry man." Jake slices his pot roast while he speaks. "I've been traveling around, you know? Wanted to do some stuff before I settled into my career for good."

"Sounds fun," Brennan replies, though his tone says otherwise.

I know how he is, and I'm sure the thought of goofing around is not appealing to him at all.

"I know that's not really your thing." Jake laughs, peering over to me for a split second. "I guess the whole career and family thing isn't mine."

His smile fades for a second, and I break eye contact.

"Yeah, yeah." Brennan chuckles. "You never were that type." He takes a quick bite of his food. "But you still should have come around more. It's hard to believe you haven't even met the boys."

"We didn't even know you existed," Sophia says blatantly, almost causing me to spit out my drink. "But Daddy has told us stories about you before."

"Well, I'm glad I wasn't completely forgotten." Jake smiles and then points to his plate with his knife. "Ellie, this is seriously the most delicious pot roast I've ever eaten."

He stares into my eyes as he speaks and I want nothing more than to make a snide remark. I've cooked this for him many times, so he's just messing with my head right now.

"Thank you." I nod and force a smile. "I don't make it very often."

"Well, thank you for taking the time to tonight." Jake smiles even wider, and I look over to Brennan, who is watching me curiously.

I'm not sure what's going through his mind, but I don't want to blow this, so I look back down at my plate.

Jake makes small talk with the children, periodically looking over at me and smiling, but I stay silent for the rest of the meal. Brennan offers to clean up while I put the kids to sleep, and I'm grateful to not have to be alone with Jake.

Sophia goes into her room to wait for me and I head over to the boys' room to read them their bedtime story.

"You don't like Jake," Asher states as he's climbing onto the top bunk once I've finished.

"What?" I gape at him, astounded by his intelligence. "Why would you say that?"

"Because you were quiet and I saw the way you looked at him." He plops down on his pillow and reads my face. "I won't tell Daddy if you don't want me to."

"There's nothing to tell, Asher." I smile and kiss his forehead. "Now get some sleep, silly."

I kiss Noah and slowly stalk out of the room, entering Sophia's room a few seconds later.

"He's right, you know." Sophia says as I approach her bed where she's sitting up waiting for me.

"Eavesdropping now, are we?" I raise my eyebrow as I sit on the bed beside her and she smiles faintly.

"I'm sorry, but I was curious about the same thing, and I knew Asher would say something about it before you left them alone." She plays with her comforter as she speaks and finally meets my eyes again. "I don't like him either."

I am astounded by her words and can't decide how I want to respond. She's so young, and she shouldn't understand any of this, and yet she does. She is very intuitive, and I know that is a great quality for her to have. However, she doesn't need to know the truth about Jake yet, so I think up a response quickly.

"He's a bit strange and silly, but he's your dad's friend and that's what matters," I smile weakly and brush her hair behind her ear. "I'm sure he'll get better once you get to know him."

Sophia nods and I do my best to ignore the pit in my stomach. I hate lying to her, but she's too young to understand right now, and I've got to keep this a secret until I speak with Brennan.

"Goodnight, sweetie," I kiss her forehead and she climbs under the covers. "See you in the morning."

"Goodnight, Ellie." Sophia whispers while I walk into the hall and slowly shut the door behind me.

I stand in the hallway for a few seconds, listening to the faint echo of Brennan and Jake laughing on the deck. I don't want to join them, but it would look so suspicious if I don't, so I take a deep breath and head down.

I slowly walk toward the back door, and I can feel my heart rate increase as Jake's face comes into view on the deck. He's laughing about something with Brennan, and for just one second, I remember when things were good. His smile would always give me butterflies, and his laugh was once one of my favorite sounds. Now everything about him scares me.

Both men look my way as I walk through the door.

"Ellie! We were just talking about you!" Brennan laughs with a hand up, inviting me into their conversation.

I wish he'd stop starting out his sentences with that.

"Oh yeah?" I play along. "Only good things, I hope."

"Of course!" Brennan chuckles. "I was telling Jake about the boating incident up at my folks' house."

"That doesn't sound good to me." I laugh at the memory. "And if I recall, that was your fault anyway."

"Yeah." Brennan sighs at the memory of him falling out of the boat while I was driving. "I suppose it was. You did give me a fair warning that you've never driven a boat before."

"I'm just glad the kids weren't with us." I shake my head in amusement. "That could have been bad."

I find myself smiling at the memory, and for a split second, I forget why I've been upset all day. That is until I look up at Jake, who is watching mine and Brennan's exchange with curious eyes.

"Sounds hilarious." He chimes in after a second of studying me. "I would have paid to see that."

He laughs and takes a swig of his beer.

"I'm sure you would have," Brennan responds, taking a sip of his own beer.

"So, Ellie got to meet ole Ann and Will, huh?" Jake asks, his beer still close to his lips, covering the smirk that only I can see. "That must have been fun."

"Of course," Brennan explains. "I thought it made sense that my parents meet the woman who has been helping me with their grandchildren. It was a nice trip."

Brennan doesn't mention the confrontation between Anna and William, and I wonder if his trust in Jake has faded over the years. Your parents' divorce seems like something you'd want to tell your best man, but I guess it's been so long since they last spoke that Brennan wants to ease back into things.

"I'm sure." Jake sneers a bit, but Brennan doesn't pick up on his tone.

Jake continues to stare at me, and I can't tell what he is up to, but I don't let it get to me. Not yet.

"So, Ellie." Jake begins, placing his empty beer bottle on the table in front of him. "What's the deal? I mean, how did Brennan get so lucky?"

I feel blood rush from my face as I realize where Jake is going with this. What is he playing at? He can't reveal our secret without making himself look bad.

"What do you mean?" I play dumb, refusing to take my eyes off him. He needs to realize that I'm not the weak, vulnerable woman he once took advantage of.

"How is it you were available for this job?" He smiles flirtatiously. "No significant other tying you down?"

"Nope, not at all." I respond bluntly without a second thought.

Jake stops smiling, and I realize that my answer is a slap in the face to him. Brennan doesn't even understand the meaning of my statement. He knows my past, but he doesn't realize it's sitting in the chair beside him. He must have noticed my change in mood, though, because he looks at his watch and sighs.

"Well, it is getting late." He sits forward in his chair. "Jake, where are you staying?"

"Some hotel in downtown." Jake sighs in defeat, all signs of happiness wiped from his face.

"Woof. That's a drive." Brennan shakes his head. "You've been drinking a lot, and I'm not sure you should drive."

"I'll get a cab or something, man. No worries." Jake shrugs and then looks at me. "Or maybe Ellie can –"

"No, no." Brennan immediately objects. "I don't want to make Ellie go out of the way."

I sigh in relief at the save, but can't help but notice Brennan's demeanor. His objection almost seemed like jealousy. Like he didn't want Jake to be alone with me and was trying to think of a way to prevent it from happening.

I think this entire situation has gotten very confusing. I've been trying to distance myself from Jake because of our past, but I realize now that Brennen must think that Jake is just hitting on me.

"I've got the pull out in the office." Brennan quickly recovers himself, aware of how abrupt his response was. "You can just crash here for the night."

My heart drops once more as I shift my gaze back to Jake, who still has his eyes glued to me. This is not good.

"Sounds perfect." Jake grins and stands up to head inside.

Brennan glances at me and nods before following Jake inside, leaving me alone on the deck. I let out a sharp sigh and curse to myself. This is getting out of hand. How am I supposed to do this?

I cautiously walk inside, hoping not to find myself alone with Jake. Instead, I find Brennan standing alone in the kitchen, and I approach him quietly. Maybe I just need to tell him now.

"Hey." He smiles as I walk up next to him. "I just wanted to say thank you. For everything today."

I listen silently and watch his eyes as he speaks. He seems genuinely happy, and I don't have it in my heart to take that away from him. My news can wait. At least until Jake leaves tomorrow.

"You've been very welcoming, and I appreciate it so much." Brennan continues. "I know I threw this at you last minute, and it's not your job to entertain my guests, but you've been great. So, really, thank you."

"You're welcome." I force a small smile. "I like seeing you happy."

Brennan's smile grows, and we just stare into each other's eyes for a few seconds.

"Sorry to interrupt." Jake's voice pulls us out of the moment, and we both look over to see him walking in from the living room. "I just wanted to say goodnight."

"You have everything you need?" Brennan asks.

"Yeah, man. I'm good." Jake replies without a hint of a smile. He looks between the two of us and nods. "Goodnight to you both."

"Goodnight," I say, looking down at my feet as he turns to walk away. I look back up at Brennan. "See you in the morning."

"Goodnight, Ellie." Brennan kisses my cheek before leaving, and my heart skips a beat.

He's never done that before, so I'm not sure what has gotten into him. Everything just feels so jumbled right now, and I need a moment to decompress.

Chapter Twenty-Two: The Memories

Now that I am alone, I've got time to reflect on everything, so I step outside onto the deck. I'm not quite ready for sleep yet, and I'm still racking my brain about the whole night. The weather is cool, and I can tell fall is upon us. Instead of staying on the deck, I walk out towards the pond. All I need is some time with my thoughts, and I should feel better.

I glance back at the house briefly, covered in darkness and filled with the slumber of its residents. I've only been here for a few months, but this place just feels like home to me. I'm not sure I'm ready to give that up just yet.

I love those kids with all my being, but I don't think I'll be much help to them if I can't help myself. And as long as Jake is around, I can't be myself. I can't be happy. It's the whole reason I moved back to Pittsburgh when everything happened. I didn't want to be anywhere near him.

"So, you and Brennan, huh?" I turn around again to see Jake standing a few feet away from me.

For a moment, my heart does somersaults, and I'm not sure if it's because he's always had that effect on me, or if it's because I truly do not feel safe being alone with him anymore.

"What are you doing here, Jake?" I ask, ignoring his comment and cutting right to the point.

"Same as you." He shrugs. "Just enjoying a nice walk because I'm not tired yet."

"No." I stop him before he continues his little charade. "I mean in Pittsburgh. Why did you come here?"

"You think I have ulterior motives?" He smirks and inches closer toward me. "A job opportunity presented itself to me, and I took it."

"You're lying." I take a step back away from him, trying my best to distance myself. "You forget I know when you're lying."

He continues to move closer to me, and I'm running out of places to go. I can't exactly go back inside because everyone is asleep and I don't want to wake them up. And I very well can't just jump into the pond, though it sounds tempting at this point.

"You know me so well, don't you?" Jake is only inches away now. "I guess six years of marriage does that to you."

He reaches his hand out to brush his fingers along my face, and I lower his hand.

"Jake" I turn my face to look away. "I'm not doing this with you."

"Elle." He tries to grab my waist, but I pull away. "I miss you. You don't even know."

"No." I look him in the eyes and feel the anger rush through me. "Stop calling me that. You don't get to do this. You had your chance, and that's over now."

"No, it's not. It's not over, Elle, and that's why I'm here." His demeanor shifts and I become slightly more uncomfortable, if that's even possible. "You're right. I'm not here for the job. Not entirely."

Goosebumps roll up my arms as the recognition hits me. He is angry now, and I'm afraid of where this conversation is going. Flashbacks flood my mind as I realize that he's getting to the point where he is dangerous and capable of harming me, and I regret coming outside at all. I try to take another step back, but he grabs my wrist to hold me in my spot.

"Do you think I just randomly decided to call up my old friend who I haven't talked to in over a decade? No. I called him because I knew it would get me to you." He explains, still gripping my wrist. "I've had my eye on you, Elle, because I was waiting for the right time to make you understand that you did me wrong."

He has been watching me? For how long? My nerves turn to fear, and I realize the terrible situation I've gotten myself into. I knew it was strange that he didn't seem surprised to see me. It was his plan all along.

"You shouldn't have left me, Elle." His voice is fiercer now, and his hold on my wrist is tighter. "We could have worked it out. I could have been better, but you didn't give me a chance."

"Jake, I tried to make this work," I respond, trying to yank my hand from his grip. "I almost died because of you. Do you think I like living with that? Huh? If I had stayed with you, I'd probably be dead at this point."

SLAP! My cheek burns as Jake backhands me and the taste of blood leaks into the corner of my mouth. There's the man I know.

"Elle, baby, I'm sorry. I didn't mean it." He tries to hug me, but I shove him away.

"Don't touch me!" I shout louder than I intended to and try to make a run for the house but I'm not quick enough.

This time, Jake has both of my wrists in his grasp, giving him complete control over me. He's too strong, and I can't get away from him now.

"You can't escape from me. I will find you. I always will." He squeezes my wrists tighter with each word. "I came to Pittsburgh right after you left, and I knew I'd find a way to contact you. It was so easy when I found out that you were working for Brennan. It was like taking candy from a baby."

"So, you've been stalking me?" I try to yank my hands away, but he squeezes his grip even tighter.

"It was even easier when I got a hold of that old paralegal of his."

I stop struggling for a split second and stare at Jake in disbelief.

"You talked to Lorelei?"

Jake laughs to himself "Boy, does she hate you. Told me all about your arrangement here and delivered all the information I needed on a silver platter."

I shut my eyes tightly and shake my head as all of this information whirlwinds in my brain. Jake's been stalking me, and Lorelei has practically been helping him as a way of getting revenge on me.

"You're insane, Jake. This doesn't change anything." Once again, I struggle against his grip.

"You still love me; I know you do." His face is inches away from mine, and I smell the whiskey and beer on his breath. "Don't resist me, Elle."

"Jake, you're hurting me." I plea, still trying to free my arms from his grip.

My forearms burn from the tension, and a numbing feeling is taking over my hands. Tears saturate my cheeks, and I'm overwhelmed with hopelessness.

"Let her go." Brennan's voice rings through the darkness and Jake and I both glance over to where he emerges from the back door.

It's not until now that I realize I'm almost completely kneeling in the grass while Jake hovers over me.

Jake releases me, and my knees give out, dropping me onto the ground. I don't even try to get up. I just sit in the grass and glance up at Brennan who is now by my side, holding my arms in his, examining them. He cups my face to get a look at my lip, and I see the anger in his eyes.

"Get the hell out." He stands back up and puts himself between Jake and me. "Now. And don't come back."

"Ren, come on man. I didn't mean it." Jake says. "It's not what you think. It's me."

"I don't even know who you are." Brennan snaps, his hands in fists at his sides. "I know what you've done, and I am not going to let you do it again."

I shake my head as I cry, realizing that it's happening again. Brennan is losing another person because of me. Why do I keep doing this to him? I just keep causing these problems that destroy every relationship he has.

"Oh, you think you're so smart?" Jake gushes, switching his gaze to me. "You ran off and told your little boyfriend your whole sob story? Yeah, I bet you did. Well, what about me? I lost something too!"

He is now yelling, and Brennan blocks me a little more, knowing just as well as I do that Jake could pounce at any moment.

"That was my baby too, Elle!" Jake shouts, almost crying. His words hit me so hard I could almost swear he slapped me in the face again. "I lost just as much as you did."

Brennan glances down at me, and this time his expression is pained. I never mentioned the miscarriage when I told him about my past. I didn't think he needed to know about that. Tears continue to roll down my cheeks as my heartache grows more and more.

"It's your fault, Jake." I stare into his fierce brown eyes. "You're the reason I lost the baby in the first place. All because you couldn't just keep your hands off me."

In less than a second, Jake is lunging toward me, but Brennan shoves him away, clearly not trying to fight if he doesn't have to.

"This doesn't even concern you, Brennan!" Jake is fuming. "This is between me and my wife!"

"EX-wife" I angrily correct him. He's delusional. "It's over, Jake. Just let it go."

"So, you can live happily ever after here?" He looks around at the property. "I can give you nice things, Elle. You don't need him."

"Oh yeah, nice things," Brennan says. "Does that include more scars to match the ones she already has?"

Jake swings a punch but Brennan ducks out of the way. Angrier than before, Jake swings again, missing once more. He swings one last time and is instead punched by Brennan, causing him to fall to the ground.

"Shit, Ren. I didn't know you had it in you." He rubs his face in defeat. "What the hell, man?"

"I said get out," Brennan growls, fists still clenched. "Get out of my house. Get out of this city. Get out of our lives."

It's quiet for a minute. I'm still on the ground, watching Jake and waiting for his next move. Brennan is still guarding me, highly alert and waiting for Jake to stand up.

Jake gazes at me with bewilderment. He still cares about me, that much is true. It just can't work. Any consideration I had for that man went through the door the same day I did. I can't be with someone who deliberately wants to hurt me all the time. I shake my head, and that's when Jake finally stands up.

"Fine." He straightens his shirt and begins to walk toward the house. He turns back to look at me briefly. "I'll always love you, Elle. And I'll always find you. Remember that."

Brennan finally leaves my side to escort Jake out of the house. A few minutes go by, and I just sit on the ground, no energy to move my body. I hang my head in shame and regret.

This could have been avoided if I had done something differently. If I had gone to a local college, maybe I wouldn't have met Jake, and none of this pain would reside in me. After all, that's when it all started. Life could have been better for me. But that's not how life works. You learn from your mistakes.

I don't realize I drifted to sleep until I feel hands on my arm, waking me.

"Ellie? Ellie." Brennan is gently rocking me. "Let's get you into the house before you get sick."

He helps lift me, and it takes all my energy to stand up. We slowly walk into the house, and he directs me toward his room. He lays me on his bed and covers me with the quilt before leaving the room. He returns with a damp wash cloth and dabs the corner of my mouth, making me flinch. I forgot about the bloody lip.

Once he's done wiping my lip, he lays down on top of the quilt beside me. He takes my arms and begins softly caressing my wrists where Jake was holding me. I know they're going to be bruised in the morning.

"Ren –" I whisper because that's all my voice will allow.

"Shh." Brennan brushes hair out of my face and tucks it behind my ear. "Get some rest. We can talk later."

Brennan begins to rub my upper arms, and my body begins to warm as a sense of security washes over me. I remember what Brennan told me a few months ago when I told him about my past. He had said 'you're safe now', and I believe that in this moment. He watches me with sad eyes, but quickly my own close and my exhaustion takes over.

Light shines in my face and wakes me from my slumber. I open my heavy eyes and look at my surroundings, realizing I'm still in Brennan's room. The bed next to me is empty and I slowly sit up, rubbing my face and wincing when I touch my swollen lip.

I lift my arms and examine my wrists, which are already faded red with bruising. I look over at the window and see the sun shining in a clear, blue sky. I hear the kids outside laughing, so that means they're already up and dressed for the day.

What time is it? The clock on the end table tells me it is already almost ten o'clock, which is much later than I normally sleep. I climb out of bed and walk out into the kitchen, where Brennan is cooking breakfast.

"I should be doing that," I speak through a cracked voice.

Brennan's head shoots around, and he is obviously surprised to hear me in the room with him.

"How are you feeling?" He walks over to me. "I was trying to let you sleep as long as you needed." He touches my cheek and checks out my arms. "Damn."

"I'm okay." I sigh. "I'm just...tired." I sit down at the island and look down at my wrists again.

All I want to do is cry, but I can't do that. I have to stay strong. Brennan skeptically returns to the stove to finish breakfast and I just sit in silence, unsure of where to go from here. Brennan periodically glances at me, and I'm sure he's wondering the same thing.

"Ellie?" Brennan begins to ask something, but the kids run in yelling and laughing before he can get his words out.

"Ellie!" Noah shouts as he climbs onto a stool beside me. "You're awake!"

"What happened to your mouth?" Asher asks, leaning in and gazing amazingly at my swollen lip.

I glance at Brennan to see if he has an answer because I hadn't thought about what to tell the kids.

"Ellie slipped by the pool last night and hit her face on the way down," Brennan responds as if he's had the answer in his head all morning. "Let's leave her be, okay?"

I pull my arms down onto my lap before Asher notices them as well. He is quite the perceptive boy.

"Nothing to worry about." I smile at Asher and watch him skip into the living room where Sophia is now sitting with her book.

I manage to avoid any talk of Jake all day because Brennan is surrounded by the kids and we don't get a moment alone. I'm thankful for that because I get to really think about everything.

Once the children are asleep, I brace myself for the conversation I'm about to have with Brennan. I've thought about it all day, and I'm not looking forward to it at all. I need to leave, and Brennan needs to understand why.

I sit at the patio table on the deck, staring at the spot near the pond where everything happened the night before. Jake's words repeat in my head like a broken record. Yes, he lost a baby too, but it was his fault. At least, that's what I need to remind myself when I think about it.

The back door opens, and Brennan steps out onto the deck. He just looks at me before coming to join me at the table, and I feel an even worse sense of dread. I can tell he's not looking forward to this talk either.

"How are you feeling?" He asks as he sits down at the table with me.

"Um, better," I respond, not meeting his eyes. "Given the circumstances."

"About last night." Brennan immediately touches on the topic, not wasting any time.

"Small world, huh?" I sigh and shake my head in disbelief.

Who would have known this would happen?

Brennan just sighs and I finally look at him. He seems distraught and confused and I know I owe him a huge explanation. He didn't deserve any of this.

"I'm sorry, Brennan," I say with a heavy heart. "I'm so sorry about everything."

"Ellie, please." He takes my hand in his. "Don't apologize. You didn't ask for this to happen."

I nod in response, trying so hard to prevent the tears that want to fall.

"Why didn't you tell me?" Brennan asks with disappointment on his face. "I made you sit through dinner with him. Hell, I almost made you work with him. And you just pretended you didn't know him. Why?"

"You've already lost so much because of me," I explain. "How was I supposed to tell you that your good friend from college was my abusive ex-husband? I just couldn't do that to you."

"But look what it did to you, Ellie." He says, holding up my hand to remind me of my bruises. "He could have seriously hurt you last night."

He rubs over my bruises with his free hand. Goosebumps run up my arms and it takes everything I have to ignore my feelings and put them to the back of my mind.

"I know."

I think about how much worse it would have been had he not come out when he did.

"I heard you yell for him not to touch you and that was when I knew something was wrong." He stares at my wrists. "I should have been here sooner."

I pull my arms away abruptly.

"Don't do that. That wasn't your fault. I don't know if you heard the part where he said he's been watching me. He would have found me no matter what, with or without Lorelei's help. He said he'll always find me, so none of that is on you."

"I didn't realize Lorelei would be so dangerous, and I certainly wouldn't have invited Jake into my home had I known who he was to you." Brennan shakes his head. "I hate that he did this to you. That he hurt you again."

We sit in silence, both looking at the ground, disappointed in ourselves.

"You had a miscarriage," Brennan says as a statement rather than a question, like he's still processing the information. "You never mentioned that."

"It's one of the more difficult things to talk about," I explain. "I didn't think it was worth mentioning when I told you the story, but the night he pushed me, we were arguing about that."

I look down at my belly where a baby once developed and let the tears soak my cheeks again. I hate thinking about my past, but I can't seem to escape it.

"A few weeks after we found out about the baby, Jake had a bad night where he was just arguing about anything. We had some friends over for Valentine's Day, and after they had left for the night, he got aggressive again.

"Valentine's Day," Brennan remarks with realization.

He remembers when I mentioned my ex not making Valentine's Day a good time for me. It's one of the worst memories I have of Jake, and now Brennan can understand why.

"Yes, Valentine's Day." I nod with a sigh. "His gift to me was a slap in the face that caused me to fall down the stairs."

Brennan looks away furiously, clenching his teeth and shaking his head. He stays silent though, so that he can hear the rest.

"We played it off like I tripped and fell, but then I lost the baby in the hospital. There was a lot of bleeding and –" I close my eyes. "I needed a hysterectomy to survive. So, Jake and I were both angry, and that's what led to the argument the night with the glass door."

"I'm so sorry, Ellie." Brennan holds my hand again, and I look into his eyes. "He ruined everything for you. He took away so many opportunities."

"He did." I nod. "But maybe it was for the best. He shouldn't have been a father, and I think that is what got me through everything. I used to feel like it was my fault. That if I had caught myself, I wouldn't have gone down the stairs. But knowing that I didn't bring a child into that kind of life made it easier to move on."

"I guess I can understand that." Brennan agrees, still holding my hands in his. "But I can tell you honestly; you would have made a great mother."

"Thank you."

I smile for the first time all day. It's not a huge smile, but it's something. Then I remember what I had to tell him tonight and my smile falters.

Brennan notices my expression and tilts his head. "You okay?"

I look into his blue eyes. Those beautiful eyes that I love so much. For some reason, I thought this would be easier, but it is proving to be one of the hardest things I've ever done. He looks so innocent right now, and I don't have it in my heart to hurt him.

"I'm fine." I lie, forcing a small smile. "I think I'm just tired."

"I'm sure you are. It's been a long weekend, and you've been through a lot." Brennan nods and stands up. "You should get to sleep."

We enter the house and go our separate ways for the night. The moment I enter my room I grab my cell phone to call my mother and Anna. I need a plan.

Chapter Twenty-Three: The Resignation

Sunday morning arrives, and I wake up hating myself more than yesterday. I remember my phone call with Anna and realize what I must do today. I hop out of bed and organize my belongings the best I can. I am dedicating today to spending as much time with the kids as I can and enjoying this day with them. They'll never forgive me for what I'm about to do, so I need to go out with a bang.

After our typical morning routine of breakfast and cartoons, the kids and I play outside for a while before lunch. Instead of staying in, I treat them to lunch at their favorite restaurant while Brennan stays home to sort through his office.

Games, movies and lots of giggles take up the rest of the day, and as we are getting ready for bed, I help the kids with everything and then read them a story. It brings me back to the night Noah asked me if I could stay forever. I'm thankful now I didn't make that promise.

"Ellie?" Asher quietly calls as I am about to close their bedroom door.

I peak my head back in and tiptoe my way over to where he lays on the top bunk.

"Yes, Asher?" I ask him and I rest my chin on his mattress, looking into his eyes.

"I had a lot of fun today. Can we do that again tomorrow?" He whispers sleepily.

I think for a second before responding because I'm not quite sure how to answer his question without lying to him. His innocence is making this even harder on me.

"I had a lot of fun, too. But you have school tomorrow, and you can't miss that. Get some sleep, sweetie." I smile and run my hand through his hair as he closes his eyes to drift off.

Before I can walk away, he whispers something else with his eyes still closed.

"I love you."

His whisper reaches my ears and a small gasp escapes from my lips as I stare at the little boy laying before me. I kiss his forehead once more and leave the room as quietly as I can.

In the hallway, I lean against the door and let the tears stream down my face as Asher's words echo in my head. I never knew I could feel like this about someone else's children, but they have stolen my heart and I hate that I need to leave them.

"I love you too, Asher." I whisper to myself as I wipe the tears away, "I love you all."

I regain my composure before meeting Brennan in the kitchen. Misery consumes me as I make my way downstairs, but I shake it off the moment I see Brennan so he doesn't suspect anything.

"It seems like you had a great day with the kids today." He says as I approach the island where he's sitting. "I know they enjoyed themselves."

I nod with a smile. "It was just what I needed."

"Good, I'm glad." Brennan smiles and looks around in the kitchen. "Are you feeling a bit better?"

My smile fades a little, guilt rising again.

"For the most part, I guess." I look away because looking at Brennan is making this hard. "I just need time."

"Sometimes that's all we need to be able to move forward." Brennan sighs.

I watch him from across the island, unable to fathom the idea of what I'm about to do to him. But he deserves better than everything that has happened to him since I've been here, and this is best. For him and his children.

"Thank you, Brennan." My statement has so much more meaning than he knows. "Goodnight."

"Goodnight, Ellie." Brennan stands and leaves the kitchen as I do and disappears toward his bedroom.

In my room, I check to make sure everything is ready, and then I sit down at the window and begin to write my letter:

Brennan,

I apologize immensely for doing this to you and the children. I care about you all very much, but I need to let you move on now. The past few months have been nothing short of amazing, but I've also caused too much chaos to continue on like this. I refuse to stick around while you lose people from your life. I am grateful for the opportunity I have had to meet you and those beautiful children of yours, and I will cherish the memories we have made. Please understand that you have done nothing wrong, but I need to be on my own right now, especially given the recent circumstances. I do not want to put you and your family at risk with everything I've got going on right now. If we never cross paths again, I wish you nothing but love and happiness, and I will miss you all very, very much. This is the hardest thing I have ever done, so please try to understand. I have spoken with your mother, and she will be staying with you until you can find a new nanny to help care for the kids. She will be arriving in the morning. Take care of yourself and Sophia, Asher, and Noah.

With love,

Ellen

I wipe tears from my face and close the letter in an envelope, addressing the outside to Brennan. I sneak downstairs to investigate and, thankfully, Brennan is already sound asleep. I prepare everything for the kids' lunches tomorrow morning, so Brennan won't have to do it when he finds my letter, which I place in plain sight on the island. Then, I bring my things out to my car, returning to the kitchen afterward.

I stand there for a moment, looking around at the house and remembering the first time I stepped foot inside. I remember the first time I saw the kids, and realize how much they've all changed since then. Sophia wouldn't even speak to me, and now she shares everything with me. The boys had no idea who I was that day, but they were so quick to welcome me into their lives and I am so grateful for that. I will truly miss everything about this place, and I begin to tear up again just thinking about it. This was not how I wanted things to be when I left.

Beside the envelope, I place my copy of the house key and garage door opener.

I don't want to risk Brennan waking up, so I leave immediately and never look back. Just minutes later, I'm on the highway on my way to my parents' house with the music blasting to drown out my sobs.

I arrive at the house, shrouded in darkness, and quietly let myself in, going straight to my room to plop down on the bed. My heart is broken, and all I want to do is sleep.

***

My phone rings and I'm pulled from my dreams, which weren't pleasant at all. I look at the screen and see Brennan's number. I figured this would happen.

I ignore the call and sit up in bed. It's already seven o'clock and that means Brennan has found my letter and everything with it.

My phone rings again, and I see that it's Brennan again. I ignore the call once more, and drag myself up to go to the kitchen.

In the hall, I'm greeted by silence, which means my parents are already at work and I have the house to myself. In the kitchen, a note hangs on the refrigerator door, written in my mother's handwriting:

Ellen,

We are glad to see you made it safely. Help yourself to anything you need. We will see you when we get home. Love you, sweetie.

Mom

Just before I can open the fridge for some juice, my phone dings with a text from Brennan:

Ellie, please don't do this. I can help you work through whatever you need, but the kids need you here. Please, Ellie. Let me help you. Come back.

I don't respond, placing my phone on the counter while I make myself some breakfast. Anna planned to arrive at the house around 7:30, so she will be there to help him. He will be fine once he has the help.

I grab Dad's newspaper from the foyer table and sit at the dining room table with my bagel. I need something to keep my mind off everything. Maybe I can take up a hobby, or volunteer somewhere. For now, I settle on the crossword puzzle.

Around nine o'clock, my phone rings again, and this time it's Dakota. Again, I don't answer. She's at work and wondering where I am and I'm just not ready for that talk yet. After I don't answer, she texts me immediately:

Ellen, where the hell are you?? What is going on?? Brennan isn't talking to anyone and I'm worried. Please call me!!

I decide to unpack my van and get everything settled in my room. I leave most of the boxes packed, hopeful that I'll find my own apartment soon and not have to put my parents out for too long. I didn't even consider moving back in with Dakota because it wouldn't be safe for her either.

In my box of clothing, I come across a beaded necklace that I made with Sophia which says her name with a bunch of hearts. I hold it in my hand and start to cry again. I was hoping the heartache wouldn't be this bad. I shouldn't feel this way because I was bound to leave eventually. I knew this was coming, so I should have no problem moving on with my life. That was always the plan.

Further in the box, I find the three roses from Valentine's Day. I pull one out and rub my fingers along its petals. I hold the rose to my heart, lay down and close my eyes, trying anything in my power to force the pain away.

***

The sound of the doorbell ringing nonstop wakes me up, and I jump out of bed. I sneak to the door, hiding from the view of the windows. I see Dakota's face through the peephole, distraught and worried.

"Nelly?" She calls, knocking as well as ringing the bell some more. "Nelly, are you here?"

I sigh to myself. I can't hide from her forever. I slowly open the door.

"Nelly!" Dakota is hugging me before the door is even fully open. "What are you doing? Why did you leave Brennan's house? He's freaking out. What happened? Oh my god, your face!"

She grabs my cheeks and examines my lip.

"Jake did this?" Her tone changes from worry to anger. "How did this happen? I swear, I'll kill him if I see him again!"

"Kody" I grab her arms and try to calm her. "Relax. I'm okay. Come in, and I'll explain it all."

We sit in the living room, and I explain the events of Friday night. Dakota listens intently, anger and disgust on her face. When I'm finished, she hugs me again and wipes a tear away from her cheek.

"Nelly, I'm so sorry this happened again." She shakes her head. "Why did you leave though? I know Brennan would help you through this. He cares for you more than you realize."

"How is he today?" I ask, curious about how he is handling everything.

I know I've hurt him by just leaving in the middle of the night, but it was the only way. If I had tried talking to him about leaving, he wouldn't have let me. He would have been adamant that I stay, and I just couldn't do that. It's not safe.

"Pretty bad. The moment he got to work, he locked himself in his office and didn't talk to any of us. He canceled his meetings for the day and the only time I heard from him was when he asked me if I knew where you were. That's when I knew something was wrong, especially since you didn't come in."

"It wasn't my plan to hurt him or screw him over, but I just couldn't be there anymore," I explain. "I'm not doing them any good when I'm this messed up. He needs someone else caring for the kids. Someone who isn't having an emotional breakdown or fending off a stalker ex-husband."

"I understand." She sighs. "But just think about it, okay? I know they miss you already. Once those kids realize you're not coming back, they'll be heartbroken."

I nod and look at my feet.

"Does your family know what happened?" Dakota asks.

"Of course not," I respond. "My sister's wedding is less than a month away. I am not going to bother them with this."

"So how do you plan on explaining everything to them?" She just keeps coming with questions I don't have answers to yet. "Especially your bruises?"

"Long sleeves and makeup, I guess." I shrug, unable to think of anything else. "That's the easiest solution, and it worked for me last time."

"Oh, Nelly." Dakota sighs and stands up. "I wouldn't keep it from them for too long. Especially since Jake is still in town."

I know she's right. It's even dangerous for me to stay with my parents for the time being, but I didn't have anywhere else to go. I realize Dakota's lunch break is almost over and she needs to get back to work.

"I know, Kody." I stand up and walk with her into the foyer. "It'll be okay. Just do me a favor? And promise me you'll do it."

"What's up?" She asks skeptically.

"Do not tell Brennan you saw me, and do not talk to him about where I am," I say, hoping she will do this for me. "He needs to move on."

"Whatever you want." She responds. I know she doesn't like it, but I know she wants to help me. "Just, be careful okay? I don't need you getting yourself into any more trouble."

I shake my head and smile. "Don't worry. I'll see you soon."

I hug my best friend and see her off. I watch her car leave from the window in the family room and a sense of emptiness hits me. I thought having time to myself would be better for me, but now I feel like I need to be doing something.

I step onto the back patio and sit in the swing, watching a squirrel scurry around a tree across the yard. The simple things always seem to be the most calming, and I just enjoy nature for a while.

I'm not sure how long I'm sitting outside, but it must have been a while because I hear my mother's voice carry through the house.

"Ellen?" She calls from the kitchen, and I step inside to greet her. "Ah, there you are honey."

She wraps me in a long hug and then smiles at me.

"Hey, mom." I smile genuinely for the first time since I arrived back home.

"How are you feeling?" She plays with my hair and then her smile vanishes. "What happened here?"

She rubs her thumb over my lip, and I curse to myself. I forgot to cover it up before they got home.

"Oh, I uh, tripped on the trampoline with the kids the other day and bit my lip." I lie horribly and mentally smack myself on the forehead.

She surveys my face and I know I'm doomed. She has always read me like a book, and I know she doesn't believe me.

"Sweetie, please don't lie." She sits me down at the kitchen nook and grabs two glasses, fills them with iced tea, and sets one in front of me. "Talk to me."

Chapter Twenty-Four: The Letter

I don't want to tell my mother anything. She doesn't need to worry about this on top of everything with Clarissa's big day. And yet, I want to gush all my feelings to her and have her support. I stare at my glass for a minute before saying anything else.

"I, um."

I look her in the eyes and see the same concern I saw in Brennan's eyes on Friday night. It's the same look my mother always gives me when she's helping me through hard times. It's a safe look. A look that tells me everything will be okay.

"It's Jake." I whisper.

I watch her countenance change the moment his name comes out of my mouth. Instead of calm and soothing, it almost appears to be horror in her eyes.

"You...um....what?" She almost doesn't get the words out, and they make no sense when she finally does. She's completely baffled, and it's as if she's forgotten how to speak for the moment.

"It's a long story." I sigh, feeling guilty now that I brought it up. "And one I wasn't planning on telling you guys until after the wedding."

"Ellen, honey." She lays a hand on mine with concern, finding her voice again. "Your safety is more important to us than a wedding. Tell me what happened."

"Well." I decide not to go into too much detail, so I give her a quick rundown. "It turns out Jake was Brennan's roommate in college. Jake came to Brennan for a job opportunity on Friday and Brennan had him over for dinner. Jake drank too much and had to spend the night, but when everyone else went to sleep, we argued outside. He got aggressive again and, well –"

I pull my sleeves back, exposing the bruises on my arms. My mother gasps with her hand over her mouth and then touches my arms. She's absolutely horrified.

"Oh, my goodness, Ellen." She looks me in the eyes again and I see tears forming. "Why does this keep happening to my sweet girl?"

"I'm okay, Mom." I nod and smile to reassure her. "It's alright."

"Why did Brennan have him over after everything he's done to you?" She asks angrily, as if it's Brennan's fault this happened.

"He didn't know." I defend him, knowing I'll have to explain my lie to her. "I pretended that I didn't know Jake because I didn't want Brennan to lose his friend."

I don't bother mentioning the fact that Jake has been watching me for months. She doesn't need to know that part.

"Why would you lie?" She seems confused, and I'm not sure I can make her understand.

"I don't know. I just feel like Brennan has already lost so much because of me. I didn't want to do that to him again." I look down. "I guess it doesn't matter now."

"So, how did you make it out of this argument with Jake?" Mom asks.

"Brennan came out before Jake could do anything worse." I shake my head. "I'm not sure what Jake would have done if Brennan hadn't saved me when he did."

"Well, I'm just glad we don't have to think about that." Mom hugs me again and rubs my back. "I'm sorry, sweetheart."

"Thanks." I lean into my mom and enjoy the hug. It's just what I need at this moment, and I revel in the security. "Can we not tell Dad about this?"

"You don't think he should know too?" She pulls out of the hug and looks at me.

"Are you kidding?" I huff. "He'll want to find Jake and put an end to him. No, I don't think he should be worried about that. Let's let him worry about one thing at a time. First, Clarissa's big day."

Mom nods and we move on, catching up while we finish our teas. Mom is just telling me about the kids in her English class when my phone rings. It doesn't surprise me that it's Brennan. I ignore it and help Mom start on dinner to keep busy.

Dad walks in the door right on time around six, and we eat our meal together. It's been so long since I lived under their roof, and it's nice to just spend time with them again.

I spend most of the week running errands for my mother while she is at work, so she doesn't have to do them over the weekend. We've got a few last-minute preparations for the wedding, and I know it's a big help if she's got everything else taken care of beforehand.

On Friday night, I'm helping Mom with wedding favors in the living room while Dad watches a movie. Small mason jars, mini pine cones, note tags, and red and purple glitter are scattered on the floor as we work to assemble each 'thank you' gift.

The doorbell rings, and we all look at each other and shrug, unaware of who would be visiting. I peek out the window, and my heart drops. Brennan's car sits in the driveway, and I drop to the floor, looking at my mother for assistance. My car is in the garage, so there is no way he knows I'm here for sure.

Mom strolls to the door, and I shake my head vigorously, not wanting to see him. It has taken me all week to move past everything, and I'm still not even over it. Mom just pauses for a second but then nods with despair.

"Hello, Brennan." I hear the door creak open, and I sit against the wall around the corner, listening. "This is a surprise. Everything okay?"

"Good evening, Mrs. Mannis."

Butterflies fill my stomach when I hear Brennan's smooth voice. I close my eyes and enjoy the sound while I can.

"I was hoping to find Ellen here? I just wanted to speak with her." He whispers glumly, causing me to pull my legs to my chest to hug them, feeling complete remorse for what I've done to him.

"I'm sorry, Hun." Mom gently responds. "She's with her sister for the weekend."

I can hear the regret in her voice.

"I see." Brennan sighs. "Thank you anyway. I'd best be going. I have to get home to the kids."

"I'll be sure to tell her you came by." Mom kindly offers.

"Actually," Brennan says. "Can you just give this to her? I'd appreciate it."

"I sure will, sweetie."

I hear them exchange something and try to peek around without being noticed. Mom is holding something by her side, and I grab a quick look at Brennan. He clearly came straight from work as he's wearing a business suit, but the tie is undone, and his hair is a mess.

"Have a good night." Brennan's voice fades as he walks away and I sneak back to the window.

I watch him drag himself to his car and climb in, pulling out of the driveway a few seconds later.

"Well." I hear Mom's voice right behind me, and I turn around. "Here you are."

I look at her extended hand and see an envelope with my name written on it. I slowly take it from my mother and then meet her eyes.

"I'm not going to ask what you're doing," She sighs. "But I just hope it's the right thing." She pats me on the back and proceeds back to the wedding favors.

We finish the favors in silence, and then I retreat to my room where I sit on the rocking chair by the window, staring at the envelope in my hands. Do I want to read this right now? Maybe I should wait until the morning.

I stare at the envelope for a good minute.

No.

I rip open the back and pull out the papers inside.

Ellen,

I'm sorry you left the way you did, and that I couldn't persuade you to stay. I've had a lot of time to think this week and, while I would have liked to say this in person, I need you to know a few things.

A few months ago, I felt completely lost. It was the anniversary of my wife's death, and an emptiness filled my soul. There was no one I could talk to and, although my children were mourning as well, I felt alone.

I saw your face in the lobby of my office the day we met and I felt something I hadn't felt in a long time. It was hope. Hope for a better life for my children, and hope for a positive energy at home to fill the void. My children warmed to you immediately, and I knew at that moment that you were perfect for the job. You were something special, and brought light into our lives again. It was gratifying to see Sophia and the boys so happy again.

As time went on, I got to know you better. Who you are and where you come from. You confided in me about your past, and I realized how much I was starting to care for you. I found myself wanting more so I invited you along on our trip to my parents' house, which was one of the best decisions

I could have made. You became closer with the kids, and I even developed a relationship with you that I can't explain. That emptiness I felt just weeks earlier was completely gone, and I wanted nothing more than to be in your presence.

Everything I was beginning to feel scared me, to be honest. I hadn't felt anything like it in over ten years since I met Kayla. That night at the lake, you said you want someone who would talk about you the way I did about her. What you didn't realize was that you already had someone like that. I had already fallen hard at that point, but I kept that to myself. I was afraid to make any kind of move because I was unsure if you'd reciprocate and I didn't want to ruin a good thing. I couldn't stand to lose you, so I decided to keep you in my life the best way I knew how, and that was to keep things the way they were.

Then Jake showed up. Words can't express how much I despise him for hurting you the way he did. I hate myself for not knowing who he was to you, and I wish I could have protected you better. Seeing the blood on your lip and the bruises on your arms filled me with complete grief, and I feel partially responsible. I welcomed that man into my home thinking he was a different person, but you made me aware of his true identity.

I know you need some time to recover from everything, but I hope that you'll come back to us when all is said and done. It's not just the children who need you. I'd be lying if I said that were the reason you need to come back. I need you in my life, Ellen, and I'll do anything to bring you back home.

When you left, a part of me went with you, and I don't think I can live the rest of my life knowing that I didn't at least try to get it back.

With love,

Brennan

I stare at the pages, written neatly in Brennan's handwriting, for what feels like an eternity. I didn't think Brennan or the kids would be losing anything if I left. After all, this was a job, and it was bound to end at some point. All I am is the nanny, and I'm replaceable.

I can't wrap my head around the idea that Brennan does have feelings for me because it just doesn't seem possible. Dakota said it, and I didn't believe her. He can have any woman he wants. So, why me? I'm broken and claiming more baggage than I'd like to admit. He can do so much better for himself and his kids. He can have someone like Emily, but he wants me.

I refold the letter and slip it back into the envelope, which I place on the end table next to my bed. Reading it only made things worse because it has brought to light the one thing I have been trying to avoid for a long time now; the fact that I have feelings for Brennan, too. And not just any feelings. I love him.

This whole transition after leaving him and the children has been difficult because I love all of them and it is hard to say goodbye to the ones you love.

I am lost and not sure where to go from here. I still need time to work on me. As long as Jake is still around, even I'm not safe. I'm not going to risk Sophia and the boys because I am selfish and want to be with them. No. I just need to be on my own for a while and figure everything out.

I walk into the bathroom and look at myself in the mirror, hating the person looking back at me. Not only did I screw myself up, but now I've hurt Brennan and his kids. They didn't deserve any of this. Things would have been fine for them if I hadn't dragged my baggage into their lives.

I turn the shower on, strip out of my clothes, and step into the cold water stream. I wait as the water gets warmer, and then I clean off. Nothing seems to be making me feel better, though.

No soap or shampoo can cleanse the damage I've done. I turn the hot water up until I can see steam rising from my skin. I stand and soak up the burning water, letting it drown away my sorrow. The heat makes me tired, so I towel off and crawl into bed, not even allowing my hair to dry before I fall asleep.

***

The next few weeks are hard for me, but I push through and focus on getting the final preparations taken care of for Clarissa's wedding.

The day before the wedding I wake up feeling a bit better than usual, so I decide to eat my breakfast out on the patio. As I walk through the door, I find my dad on the phone, so I quietly take a seat, trying not to bother him.

"I think it's a perfect idea." Dad smiles and then notices me, giving me a slight nod. "Yes, perfect. See ya tomorrow, then."

He hangs the phone up and joins me at the glass table.

"Who was that?" I ask as I take a bite of my bagel.

"Just more preparations for tomorrow." He shrugs it off and grabs a piece of fruit from my plate, popping it in his mouth with a mischievous grin.

"Hey!" I slap his arm gently, and he laughs. "Go get your own, greedy."

I scoot my plate closer to me and cover it with my arm.

"I can't help it." Dad chuckles. "I love food!"

"Oh, I know you do." I pat his practically flat belly and laugh.

"You seem to be in better spirits today, baby girl." He leans on the table, and I see his eyes become concerned again. "Still don't wanna talk to me about it?"

"It's not that, Dad." I sigh, placing my bagel down on my plate and wiping my mouth with a napkin. "I just think we have better things to focus on right now."

"Ya know that's not true." He shakes his head. "Your happiness means everything to your mother and me. You can come to us with anything, anytime."

"I know, trust me." I smile in appreciation. "But it's okay right now."

"I know you miss him," Dad says, and I just stare at him, astonished that he brought it up.

I look down at my plate and then meet his eyes again. I nod once, and he grabs my hand, rubbing his thumb over my knuckles.

"I'm not sure what happened, but I can tell you he misses you just as much." He smiles with a nod. "I know how things were in the beginning, but I think we all know this was more than a job in the end."

I stare into my dad's eyes and think about how to talk to him about what's on my mind.

"How did you know you wanted to be with Mom?" I ask quietly. "I mean, how did you know you were ready to step in as a father to her children and take on all of that responsibility?"

"Your mother is the greatest thing to ever happen to me." Dad begins. "I knew the moment I met her that she was something special and then when I met you and Clary, it was like the final piece to a puzzle set into place."

Dad smiles and I listen intently, thinking about how I felt about Brennan and the kids when I first met them. Things had changed so drastically in just a few weeks, and I found myself immensely happy all the time.

"I found myself wanting nothing more than to be with you all and it got to the point where I dreaded going home at the end of the day. I just wanted to be with your mother. She consumed my life, and I even started to miss her when we were together. Things didn't feel right until I made her mine forever, and that's when I decided I had to marry her. I didn't want to be without her, or you and your sister, for another second."

I can't help but think about Brennan and how much I truly miss him after all this time away from him and the kids. My heart aches and I feel a small tear escape from my eye. How have things gotten this messed up?

"That's what I thought." Dad's voice drags me back from my thoughts, and I look over to see a huge grin on his face.

"W-what?" I stutter and wipe my cheek.

"I think that you have some business to take care of once this wedding is over, eh?" He gently kisses my hand and stands up to go inside. "Listen to your heart, baby girl. It knows what it wants."

I sit in silence after my father steps back in the house. How does he do that? He knew just what to say to make me realize what I need right now. But it's going to have to wait. I need to get through Clary's big day tomorrow, and then I can worry about myself.

Chapter Twenty-Five: The Wedding

"Nelly!" Dakota skips into the living room holding two bottles of wine. "You ready to go crazy tonight?"

"Not too crazy." I laugh and grab the bottles from her, placing them in the box of stuff I've gathered to bring to our hotel suite tonight. Clarissa doesn't want a drunk fest of a bachelorette party, so we are all staying in a suite, drinking wine, and playing games.

"Girl, I think you need to live a little tonight." She laughs and grabs my face in her hands. "Stop thinking for once and just have fun."

"I'm going to have a great time! Just not gonna get wasted to do it." I slap her butt playfully and walk into the kitchen where my mom and Clarissa are eating lunch.

"You guys almost ready?" I pull my phone out to check the time. "I told the girls we'd meet at the hotel around two, so we should get going soon."

"Yay!" Clarissa giggles and jumps up and down excitedly.

She is so giddy, and I couldn't be happier for her. This is going to be a great weekend.

Within a few hours, Mom, Clarissa, and the rest of the bridesmaids are in their pajamas, tipsy and acting loud and rowdy in our suite. Karaoke, pillow fights, movies, and gossip take up most of our night like a slumber party from our childhood.

It is just after two in the morning when everyone has fallen asleep, and I make my way to one of the bedrooms. I grab my phone and sit by the window, looking out at the city, peaceful and illuminated by streetlights.

All I can think of at the moment is Brennan and what he's doing. If things hadn't gotten messed up, he'd be out with my dad and the guys enjoying Gareth's bachelor party. When I had asked him for the time off for the wedding, he offered to come to the wedding with me. That isn't happening now.

Brennan's number sits on the screen of my cell, and my thumb hovers over the dial button. I want to hear his voice so badly. I want to tell him I'm sorry and that I want to be with him but that will have to wait. I need to focus on the wedding tomorrow.

I lock my phone and place it on the end table before I climb into the bed and wrap my arms around a pillow. I close my eyes and let my mind wander. A memory of the kids at a fair in the Poconos pops into my head, and I fall asleep with a smile.

When I wake the next day, I walk out of the bedroom and make my way to the kitchenette, passing the crowded living room along the way. All the girls, except my mother, are scattered out around the room, sleeping wherever there was space last night. A smile creeps across my face, and I shake my head as I reach the refrigerator.

I know things will be hectic once everyone wakes up, so I quickly eat a croissant and enjoy some me time. As I'm popping the last bite in my mouth, Clarissa walks over from the couch, yawning and rubbing her eyes.

"There she is." I smile. "Big day is finally here."

She smiles and sits down at the table with me.

"I know, I can't believe it." She takes a sip of my orange juice and gently wipes her lips after.

I can sense her nerves and lean forward, laying my hand on hers.

"Do not be nervous." I watch her eyes as they shift from anxiety to comfort. "Gareth is amazing and you two are going to be so happy together. I know it."

"Thanks, Nelly." She hugs me. "For everything. I couldn't ask for a better sister."

As we share this moment, I feel closer to my sister more than ever. She's got a great life ahead of her, and I couldn't ask for a better man to lead that life by her side.

"Oh good, you're both awake!" Mom strolls in, already in her dress and ready to get the day started. "It's finally here! So much to do!"

She's smiling and humming to herself as she opens the fridge and I share a look with Clarissa that makes us both giggle.

Not even an hour later, the entire suite is a monsoon of hairspray, glittery makeup, music, and laughter. The commotion is loud and exciting, and I'm amazed anything is actually getting done with how much talking is going on.

Dakota and I decide to move to the bedroom to get ready with some peace and quiet before we leave. She's doing my hair in a chignon while we chat, and we eventually run out of things to say.

"So, how have you been?" She finally asks the dreaded question I know has been on her mind since we met up yesterday. "Hanging in there?"

"Yeah, I'm fine." I lie with a small smile, and she makes a face at me in the mirror. She knows I'm lying. "Dakota, it's fine. I know how to move on when I have to."

"Okay, Nelly." She sighs audibly. "I believe you." She bobby pins the last couple strands of hair and then douses it all in hairspray. "Perfect!"

I check it out in the mirror and grin. "It looks great. Thanks, Kody." I turn to face her. "We should probably get out there and join everyone else."

The girls are all starting to get dressed when we walk out of the room, and I find Clarissa to help her into her dress. Once she's fully ready, I gaze at her in all her beauty. She is the most beautiful bride I've ever seen, and I begin to tear up.

"Clary." I begin to say as I hug her. "You look so gorgeous, and I am so happy for you."

"I love you, sis." She pulls out of the hug, and I see her eyes are watery too.

I walk back over to Dakota, who is avidly typing into her phone, which she tosses into her purse the moment I reach her.

"Hey, wanna come with me quick? I have to run to my car for something." She says, rushing toward the door.

"Oh, um, sure," I tell my mom I'll be right back and head out with Dakota.

As we exit the elevator on the first floor, Dakota is intently looking around, and I'm not sure what she's looking for. As we are about to reach the lobby, she smiles and nods.

"Hey, look. Your date is here. So, I'm gonna run to my car quick, so... yeah."

"My date? What are you – "

I look around and stop talking the moment I see Brennan standing near the door. My heart skips a thousand beats, and I forget how to breathe for a minute.

"Please don't be mad at me." Dakota grabs my arm and kisses my cheek. "I love you so much! Bye!"

And before I can stop her, she has left my side, leaving me alone in the crowded lobby.

Brennan hasn't noticed me standing there yet, so I watch him for a second. He looks more handsome than ever in a three-piece suit with a burgundy-colored tie that matches my dress perfectly. His hair is combed back neatly, clearly exposing his perfect, clean-shaven face. I can't see them from this distance, but I just know his blue eyes would make me weak at the knees.

Butterflies fill my stomach as his eyes finally find me in the crowd of people conversing in the lobby. The smile that appears on his face gives me more joy than I can explain and I can't stop the smile that breaks out on my face.

I slowly start walking toward him, quickening my pace with each step. A second later I find myself running to him as he walks toward me and I throw myself into his arms. He wraps me in a warm embrace, and I dig my face into his neck, savoring his touch, his smell, his everything.

Right now, nothing else seems to matter. The bustle of the lobby fades away and all I can focus on is this incredible man with me. God, I've missed him so much.

Brennan pulls back, grabbing my face and grazing my cheek with his thumb. He gazes into my eyes for a second in silence before pulling me closer to him. His lips land on mine and my body goes weak. I lean into his kiss and melt into his embrace, and in this moment, it is just him and me. Once the kiss ends, we just stare into each other's eyes.

"I'm sorry to just show up like this." He apologizes and looks down at my hands which he's now holding. "I wanted to give you time, but I just had to see you. I don't want to be away from you anymore."

He smirks and meets my eyes again. This whole situation seems surreal to me, and I feel overwhelmingly giddy.

"I'm glad you're here." I smile briefly. "Ren, I'm so sorry."

He puts a finger over my lips to stop me.

"Not now." He says in a smooth voice. "Tonight, I just want to enjoy your company while you celebrate your sister's wedding. Okay?"

"Okay" I smile, and he kisses my forehead quickly before linking his fingers with mine and leading me toward the elevator.

We meet Dakota there and head back upstairs, running into my dad and the rest of the groomsmen the moment we step out on our floor.

"Brennan, good to see you lad." Dad smiles and shakes Brennan's hand, giving him a slight wink. "I'm glad you could make it today."

"Me too, sir." Brennan nods with a smile.

The realization hits me. I remember dad's phone call yesterday morning, and I now know who he was talking to."

"Dad?" I study his face curiously. "Did you – "

I point to Brennan and they both laugh.

"Ahh." Dad lets out a loud sigh. "Busted."

"Your dad called me yesterday to check up on me, and then we may have planned for me to surprise you here today." Brennan winks at me and grins.

For some reason, I'm not even mad that my dad interfered. I'm thankful.

"Thank you, Dad." I hug my father before turning back to Brennan. "Hey, why don't you go back down with the guys so I can go help Clarissa?" I recommend, and Dad agrees, wrapping his arm around Brennan's shoulder.

"Yeah, you'll get her all night. Let's get a quick drink before the ceremony." Dad laughs, and I give him a stern look.

"Don't go crazy! We'd like you all to be coherent before the reception."

I join Dakota down the hall towards our suite. I look back and see Brennan's face just as the door to the elevator closes and wave before entering the room.

In the room, Mom is just finishing up the ties on the back of Clarissa's dress. I grab her veil from the countertop nearby and approach my sister as she turns to look at me. I slide the comb which holds the veil into her hair just above her bun, letting it flow perfectly down her back. Stepping back to take a look, I smile and she does a little twirl.

"Thank you so much!" She cheers. "It's perfect!"

"You're perfect." I smile at her and pull her into a hug. "Most stunning bride I've ever seen."

"Oh, sweetie, you're so beautiful." Mom wraps us both in a group hug and starts crying.

"Don't start that yet, Mom." I roll my eyes and laugh. "It's going to be a long day!"

After taking some pictures in the room with the photographer, we all head downstairs to the hall where the ceremony is located. I stand outside the doors with the rest of the bridal party while we wait for our cue to enter.

"I'll see you on the other side, Mrs. Montgomery." I smile at Clarissa just before I enter the hall with Gareth's best man, David.

I walk down the staged aisle to the rhythm of the music my sister chose for procession. I catch a glimpse of Brennan sitting behind my mom and smile at him as I take my place up with the other bridesmaids.

Everyone in the room rises as my dad and sister enter the room and begin their walk. I immediately glance over to Gareth who couldn't have a bigger smile on his face as he watches Clarissa walk toward him. I'm fairly certain I see his eyes watering a bit.

The remainder of the ceremony is gorgeous and next thing I know I am standing with Dakota in the reception hall, chatting about the day so far.

"So, you and my dad are in cohorts now, huh?" I shoot her a side glance and smirk.

"Hey, I couldn't just stand by and watch two people I care about ignore their feelings for each other." She chuckles and takes a sip of her wine.

Leave it to Dakota to already be drinking.

"Speaking of, I'll leave you two alone." She nods her head toward the other side of the room and then slips away.

Brennan waltzes up to me with his hands in his pockets and then slinks an arm around my waist once he reaches me. He pulls me close and kisses the top of my head before looking at me again.

"You look so beautiful tonight, Ellie." He smiles and rubs his knuckles along my cheek.

"And you look very handsome." I smile in return and hug him again. "I'm so glad you're here with me."

"I've missed you so much." Brennan sighs, leaning his chin on my head as he holds me in his arms. "I can't stand being away from you any longer."

"Brennan, I – " I begin to apologize again, but before I can finish, Brennan kisses me once more.

"Dance with me." He smiles and offers me his hand.

He leads me to the dance floor, and we slowly sway to the sound of the song that has just started.

"So, what happens now?" I ask, completely at a loss for the next step.

How do you move forward from everything we've been through? It's not like we can run away from the past and live happily ever after. There are so many things we still need to handle before we can get to that point in our relationship.

"Well, for starters, I'd love for you to come back home," Brennan whispers as he gazes into my eyes.

I smile to myself and look down at Brennan's tie, running my fingers along its silky material. I can't think of a better place to call home than with Brennan and his kids.

"Home. I like the sound of that."

"I don't think you fully understand." Brennan lifts my chin, so I'm looking into his gorgeous blue eyes again.

"I want you to move in with me. Not as the nanny." There's a fire burning in his eyes, and I feel myself blush. "I want you to live with me as my girlfriend, and I want to make this work as a real relationship."

"Really?" I stop moving, and we both stand there, in the middle of a bunch of dancing couples, staring at each other. "You really want that?"

"I really, really do." He nods and then kisses my forehead again. "I should have told you what I was feeling sooner. I almost lost you, and I don't plan to let that happen again."

"Okay." My voice is barely a whisper as Brennan cups my face and kisses my lips before the song comes to an end. I could just lose myself in his touch.

***

The night carries on, and I enjoy every moment of it. The look on my dad's face when he dances with Clarissa is enough joy for the rest of us. I know he is proud of her and is just as happy for her as I am, if not more. She didn't make the same mistake I did, and for that, I am thankful.

The toasts are all heartwarming, and the cake cutting and bouquet/garter toss are all hilarious, to say the least. This night couldn't have gone any better, and I'm so glad Clarissa got the special day she always wanted growing up.

The night is coming to an end, and most guests have already started to leave, but I enjoy my time with Brennan and the rest of my family and friends. Brennan and I dance to one more song, and I soak up every second of it.

I stare into his eyes as we dance and I can't stop the smile that comes to my face. This moment feels perfect, and I never want it to end.

"Ellie, there's something I've wanted to tell you for a long time now." Brennan grins as we stop moving.

"Yeah?" I keep my arms wrapped around his neck and smile. "What's that?"

He brushes his fingers along my cheek and cups my face with a glow in his eyes. He opens his mouth to speak but something else catches his eye behind me, and his smile is washed away instantly.

"Get down!" He yells, shoving me and the next thing I know, I'm lying on the ground as a loud bang fills the room.

Chaos ensues.

Chapter Twenty-Six: The Intrusion

Everything has happened so fast, and I feel lost when I open my eyes. I look over to find Brennan on the ground, a few feet away from me, unconscious and bleeding from his left shoulder.

"Ren!" I cry, crawling over to him amongst the rush of the other wedding guests running around. "No! No, no, no, no! Brennan!"

I put my hands gently over his wound as tears fill my eyes. I look up, trying to find the person who did this and I finally find him through the crowd of people, staring at me from the door.

Jake aims his gun at the ceiling and shoots again, causing even more mayhem. Guests flow toward the doors, and in just a few seconds, I am left alone with Jake and Brennan's unconscious body.

"I told you I would always find you, Elle." He sneers as he slowly walks toward me.

I instinctually shift myself to block Brennan so Jake can't do any more harm. I hold my hand over his wound still, trying to stop the blood. He needs a doctor.

"Why are you doing this?" I cry. "Why can't you just let it go and leave me alone?"

"Because you are mine, Ellen." He continues walking towards me, stopping only a few inches away. "I don't like other people taking things that belong to me."

"I'm not your property, Jake," I yell as the anger bubbles up inside me. "I'm a human being, in control of my own actions and decisions. My decision was to never see you again."

My face burns as Jake pistol-whips me and cuts a small gash into my cheekbone.

"But you *are*, Elle." He growls. "You are mine. You promised that until death do us part six years ago!"

I hold my face in my bloody hand, feeling nothing but the throbbing in my cheek from the impact. I have to be strong. He feeds on my vulnerability, and I can't let him have that advantage.

"Not anymore, Jake." I cry, working hard to hide the fear within me. "That's a promise I can't keep."

"Get up." Jake barks and I look down at Brennan, who I'm still hovering over. "Now, Elle! Get up!"

I comply and slowly stand with my hands up. In less than a second, Jake grabs my wrist and yanks me toward him, throwing me down on the ground a few feet away from Brennan. I turn around immediately and see Jake facing Brennan, staring at his motionless body.

"Jake, please, no." I plead.

My words are drowned out by the slap that meets my face again. Jake's breathing becomes heavy, and he glares at me.

"Shut up!" He cries, and I can see that he isn't thinking straight.

His eyes look around the room, and it's almost as if he just realizes what he has done. He looks confused as he stares at the floor and continues to breathe heavily.

"I love you, Elle." He says. "We could have everything. Why don't you see that?"

He is starting to calm down, and I realize that this is my chance to talk him over.

"Look at you." I lower my voice and keep a calm timbre. "This isn't you."

Jake listens, still holding the gun and glancing over at Brennan. I continue talking, hoping to keep his attention on me so nothing worse happens.

"We were happy once, Jake" I shake my head. "Don't think I forget that. I loved you so much. And it was amazing in the beginning."

I remember what Dakota told me a few weeks ago about how I felt about Jake. She had said that I didn't love him and it was a fling that had gone too far. I know she's right, but Jake needs to hear something else if I want Brennan to remain unharmed. He needs to hear something positive, and I'm willing to do that if it keeps us all safe.

Jake slowly lowers the gun to his side so it's pointed toward the ground and I continue.

"You got lost along the way, and you just need to find yourself again." Sirens are whaling outside, but he doesn't seem to notice while I carry on. "You can be happy again. I just can't be the person to help you get there. I'm sorry, Jake."

Jake kneels in front of me, so we are face to face. He wreaks of alcohol, and I turn my head away as he tries to kiss me.

"Yes, you can, Elle." Jake grabs my face and turns it back to his. "You're the only person who can make me happy."

Jake kisses my neck as his hand snakes up my dress. I calmly lower his hand and shake my head.

"Jake, no."

My face goes numb as Jake slaps my cheek once more and I fall backward to the ground. He climbs on top of me and presses his body against mine as he grabs my face again.

"Stop resisting me, Elle," Jake whispers in my ear as he slowly grinds against me.

I try my best to shove him off, but he's too strong. He has always been too strong. He now has both of my arms pinned to the ground as he runs rough kisses over my neck and onto my shoulder.

"Jake, please." I cry as the tears escape my eyes.

Jake ignores my pleas, though, and begins to unbutton his jeans. I brace myself for the inevitable and stare at the ceiling above me. I close my eyes and think about Brennan and the kids, hoping to find some more strength to fight back.

Before I can understand what's happening, Jake screams in surprise as he is knocked off me by something that hits his back. He instantly flips around and points his gun at Dakota, who is holding a fire extinguisher above her head.

"Dakota, how nice of you to join us." He growls as he stands back up. "Drop it and sit down"

He nods his head in my direction, and Dakota does as she's told, kneeling beside me and helping me up. I watch as Jake readjusts his pants, and realize that he didn't get his way. Had Dakota been a few seconds late, he probably would have completely violated me. Her timing was perfect.

"You're a piece of shit, Jake." She shouts as she grips my hand in comfort.

"Shut the hell up!" Jake yells, holding the gun in her face.

"Jake." I plead. "Please."

I stare into his eyes with concern, hoping he'll lower the gun again and calm down. He stands there for a long moment, just staring at me like he's studying me. I can tell he's considering everything I've said to him and I'm not sure if that is good or bad. I see tears fill his eyes and it worries me.

"I'm sorry, Elle." He finally whispers, pointing the gun at me. "But if I can't have you, no one can."

I take a quick breath and prepare for my fate. This is it.

Wham!

Jake is knocked to the floor by my father and a bullet goes into the wall in the distance. The two men wrestle on the floor while Jake still holds the gun, trying to gain control again. They struggle for what seems like forever when Jake finally lowers the gun and shoots again.

BANG!

"Dad!" I shout, unable to see where the bullet went.

"Ah, ya fucker!" Dad shouts in agony, punching Jake's arm and sending the gun flying across the room.

I see Dad's thigh bleeding, but he continues to fight Jake. It's a bit of a struggle for him, but Dad manages to get on his feet and drag Jake with him. He throws him into a wall and screams in pain again. In the meantime, I glance over at the gun, unattended and sitting just a few feet away from me.

"Nelly!" Dakota says, but I ignore her and stand up with my eyes still glued to the gun.

Without thinking, I run over and grab it, staring at it in my hand. This is too much power, and I'm not sure I can handle it. I've only ever shot a gun a few times when I first received my concealed carry a few years back, and I'm not sure how good a shot I have anymore.

I turn to see Dad and Jake over by the cake table, where Dad has fallen over and Jake hovers over him. They are still wrestling and I can't do a thing to stop them without risking Dad's safety. They're too close to each other and if I miss Jake, I'll surely hit my father.

I notice Jake peek at the top of the table, and realize what it is that he sees the moment his hand begins to reach up for it. He's going for the cake knife. My heart races even quicker in my chest and I raise the gun at Jake. I steady my breathing as I follow him in my sights, and wait for the opportune moment to take the shot.

Jake turns his body enough for me to get a clear shot of his back and, without hesitation, I pull the trigger as his hand grabs the knife.

BANG!

Jake falls over in agony, still gripping the knife in his hands.

"Damn it!" He rolls over and looks at me, reaching for the wound in his back where I hit him.

He falls back over and lays there, looking at the ceiling and mumbling to himself. The knife falls from his grip and I drop the gun, staring at my blood-covered hands, shaking from the adrenaline.

Dad stares at me in astonishment, panting as he grips his leg where the bullet went through. He finally manages to get to his feet and limps in my direction at the same time Dakota runs over and wraps me in a hug.

I shot him.

The door busts open and a swarm of armed cops enter the room shouting.

"Everyone, freeze!"

The moment the cops see Jake on the floor, they lower their weapons and walk over to our huddle. My breathing is heavy and I can't stop crying as I stare at the gun on the floor in front of me. My gaze shifts all around the room.

I shot him.

Dad limps over to the approaching cops. Jake lays motionless on the floor. Brennan is being lifted by two EMTS. Dakota still has her arms wrapped around me.

"Are you guys alright?" I hear a man ask Dad, and then everything begins to get fuzzy.

I can't think straight.

I shot him.

I shake my head and look down at the blood on my hands again. Nothing feels real right at the moment. There's no way I just shot my ex-husband. During my sister's wedding, nonetheless.

"Oh my god, Nelly." Dakota finally looks me in the eyes and brushes hair out of my face. "I was so worried about you."

I just stand there, completely silent, as the world moves around me. Mom and Clarissa rush in and go straight to Dad, who is now sitting on a gurney near some EMTs. I then watch Brennan as he gets carried away on another gurney.

"Ellen!" Dakota has me by the shoulders, trying to get my attention. "It's okay. You just need to talk to Officer Willis quickly, okay? Then I'm going to take you to the hospital."

I nod, still silent, as I wait for the officer to come take my statement. As I tell him everything, I watch as Jake is taken away on another gurney, and I suddenly feel safe again.

"Thank you, Ms. Mannis." Officer Willis says as he tucks his notepad into his pocket. "I'm very sorry for all of this, and I'll keep in touch."

The moment he leaves, Dakota is back by my side, dragging me back to our room so I can change to go to the hospital. Once in our room, I realize I need to call Anna, so I find my purse and dig out my cell.

"Hello? Ellie, is that you?" Anna answers after a few rings and I don't know where to start.

"It's Brennan....you need to go to the hospital....he's been sh –" I start rambling, and before I can say more Dakota grabs my phone from me and throws clothes into the bathroom for me.

"Mrs. Grant? I am so sorry. This is Brennan's receptionist, Dakota." She begins to explain. "There was an accident, and Brennan was shot in the shoulder. He's on his way to —"

Dakota's voice trails off as I close the bathroom door. I strip out of my blood stained dress and thoroughly wash my hands. I rub until my skin feels raw while tears stream down my face. Once I decide my hands are clean enough, I dress quickly and meet Dakota back in the hall, where she is already out of her dress and waiting for me.

"Nelly, are you okay?" She looks me in the eyes, and I nod. "Anna is going to meet us there. It's okay. Let's go."

We leave the room and find my Mom and Clarissa walking toward us.

"Ellen, sweetie." Mom hugs me as she cries.

"I'm okay, Mom. Was Dad alright?" I ask immediately.

"He's just fine. The bullet only grazed him, but they took him to the hospital to make sure there was no major tissue damage." Mom releases me and I hug my sister.

"Clary, I am so sorry." I cry in her arms. "I ruined everything."

"Nelly, stop." She says. "I'm just glad you're alright. We are okay, now go. You need to go to Brennan."

She kisses me on the cheek and turns to enter our room with Mom. The short car ride to the hospital is quiet, and I just look out at the city lights as we pass.

"Why did you do that?" I ask Dakota while I stare out the window.

She's driving so fast that everything outside is a blur and I can't focus on anything.

"What?" I see her glance at me through my peripheral vision and I finally turn to face her.

"Why did you go after Jake?" My voice is pained, and I can't shake the feeling that I want to burst into tears again. "You almost got yourself killed."

"And you almost got yourself raped, Ellen." She exclaims, sneaking another glance at me. "I don't even want to think of what that maniac would have done to you if I hadn't hit him."

She returns her gaze to the road, and I look out the window again with my head against the glass. We drive in silence for a few minutes, and I feel exhaustion washing over me. I know what would have happened if she hadn't arrived. Jake would have gotten his way. He would have gotten me, and I don't think I could have lived with myself had that happened.

"Thank you," I whisper as a single tear lands on my lap.

"I love you," Dakota grabs my hand and squeezes it gently.

We ride the rest of the way in silence, and all I can think of is Brennan's unconscious body lying on the hotel floor.

Please let him be okay.

Chapter Twenty-Seven: The Hospital

I walk through the doors to the emergency room at the hospital and find myself running the rest of the way to the desk.

"Brennan Grant," I say to the nurse behind the desk. "Was brought in for a gunshot. How is he?"

"Are you a family member?" She asks, looking up from her computer with a bored expression.

She is a young nurse, with blonde hair tied in a messy bun and tired eyes. She's probably on the last leg of her shift and doesn't want to deal with my frantic self.

"I'm his live-in nanny," I tell her, losing my patience.

"I'm sorry, but unless you are next of kin, or have power of attorney, I can't release any information to you at this time."

"Are you kidding me?" Dakota blurts out, pushing past me and yelling at the nurse. "She's his goddamn nanny who lives with him and takes care of his kids, what more do you want?"

"I'm sorry, ma'am. Give me one second."

The nurse walks over to another hospital employee and asks her something while keeping her eyes on us. I think she's going to have security take us out until she returns.

"Mr. Grant is in the operating room right now. I'm sorry, I don't have any more information for you right now. If you take a seat, I will let you know as soon as anything changes."

Her eyes are sympathetic, and I feel my anger fade away. I nod and take Dakota by the arm to sit by the windows.

"Relax," I say as we sit down. "I'm the one who should be freaking out here."

"Sorry." Dakota sighs and leans on her arm. "These damn nurses just piss me off. Next of kin. Power of attorney. Seriously?"

"Anna will be here soon anyway, so we would have gotten what we needed." I look out the window and realize how exhausted I am.

I just stare out at the city and take a few breaths. I need to calm down. I'm not doing Brennan any good if I lose control. I think about the wedding and everything he said to me before Jake ruined it all.

"Brennan asked me to move back in with him," I say, not taking my eyes away from the window.

"What?" She asks excitedly, sitting forward in her seat. "That's amazing, Nelly."

"Not as the nanny." I sigh and close my eyes as a few fresh tears fall down my face. "He wanted to make things work. He asked me to move in as his girlfriend."

"Oh, Nell." Dakota moves to the seat next to me and wraps her arms around me. "He will be okay, and you two will have your chance to be together."

"He lost so much blood." I sob, turning my face into her shoulder and hugging her back. "Jake just let him bleed out. He didn't even care."

"You have to stay positive." She rubs my back. "Have some faith."

A half hour goes by, and we still hear nothing from the nurses. Dakota returns from the vending machine just as the doors open, and Anna walks in. I run over and hug her tightly.

"Anna, I am so sorry," I say, tears filling my eyes again. "I didn't mean for this to happen."

"Shhh, sweetie it's okay." She hugs me and rubs my back. "This is not your fault. He's going to be okay. My boy's a trooper."

Anna pulls back to examine my face, and I can tell she's distraught. She gently grazes her thumb over my bruises and shakes her head in disappointment.

"Your face." She sighs and hugs me again. "Your poor, sweet face."

She sits down with me, and I explain everything that happened, keeping a steady voice as I run through the events again. Anna comforts me, and we wait together impatiently, hoping to hear some news soon.

"I never did like that man." Anna shakes her head after looking at my face again.

"Me neither." Dakota quips and then leans over to Anna with an extended hand. "I don't think we've ever officially met. I'm Dakota Warren, Brennan's receptionist."

"It's so nice to meet you, Dakota." Anna shakes her hand and smiles weakly. "Though, I wish the circumstances were better."

"I'm sorry this happened to him," Dakota says. "He's such a wonderful man."

"Thank you." Anna nods and places a hand on Dakota's arm. "And thank you for helping them both. I greatly appreciate it."

They exchange a brief smile, and then we all fall into silence again. A few minutes later, the door to the ER opens and my father walks through on crutches. I jump up from my seat and run over to him, carefully hugging him the moment I reach him.

"I'm so glad you are okay!" I say, examining the cast around his thigh. "Everything looks alright?"

"I'm fine, baby girl." He smiles. "A little bit of damage to the tissue, but the bastard didn't hit anything else, thankfully."

I nod in response and meet Dad's eyes again. He's watching me quietly and I can tell he knows what I'm thinking. His expression changes immediately and he now looks dejected.

"I just asked the doctor if he knew anything about Jake," Dad sighs and I already know this isn't good news. "He, uh, he didn't make it."

"He's...dead?" I ask as the blood drains from my face.

Dad nods slowly and I look down to the ground as a thousand thoughts race through my mind. I killed my ex-husband. I shot him, and now he is dead. I thought that my shot would only harm him and prevent him from injuring Dad, but it killed him.

I'm a murderer.

"I guess your bullet went deep enough to penetrate some major blood vessels and he didn't last long after they got him into a room." Dad rubs my arm in comfort and I shake my head.

"I can't believe I killed him." I whisper.

"It was self-defense, Ellie." Dad reassures me, but it doesn't make it any less true. "You're gonna be okay."

I nod and lead Dad over to meet Anna while he waits for Mom to pick him up. We all sit in silence until Mom walks in the door and runs over to Dad.

"Eamon!" She hugs him and kisses him passionately as I smile to myself.

Their relationship has always been something I admired, and I had always hoped to have the same bond with someone special.

I immediately think about Brennan again and my smile is wiped away. Jake didn't survive his gunshot. What if the same happens to Brennan? I'll never be able to share with him what my mom and dad have, and that breaks my heart to consider.

"How are you holding up, Ellen?" Mom approaches me and takes a seat beside me.

"I'm as good as I can be, I suppose." I say. "I'm not sure how else I should handle the news that I killed my ex-husband and still know nothing about the man I just reconnected with."

"Jake's dead?" Dakota leans forward and rests a comforting hand on my knee. I nod in response and she sighs. "Shit."

"It's going to be okay, Ellie." Mom hugs me and rubs my back. "You did what you had to do. And I'm sure Brennan will be alright. I have hope."

"As do I." Anna chimes in and my mother turns to look at her. "Hi, I'm Brennan's mother, Anna."

"It's so nice to meet you, Anna. I'm Linda, Ellen's mother." The two shake hands and exchange a mutual smile.

It's actually strange to see them both together, but it's comforting all the same.

"Your son is such a wonderful man, and he has done so much for Ellen in the past year." Mom continues to rub my back as she speaks to Anna. "We really hope he will be alright."

"Thank you," Anna nods and meets my eyes again. "Your daughter has done wonders for him as well. I'm sure he will make it through this, and life can continue to move forward the way it's supposed to."

I understand the meaning in Anna's words and she winks at me before sitting back in her chair and sighing to herself. I look back to my Mom, who is staring at Dad with caring eyes.

"Why don't you get Dad home?" I rub her hand, which rests over mine in my lap. "I'll be alright here. I've got Anna and Dakota."

"Are you sure, sweetie?" Mom asks skeptically. "I hate to leave you like this."

"There's no point in all of us waiting here." I urge. "Honestly, I'd rather you get Dad home and comfortable."

My father scrambles to his feet and gets situated on his crutches before reaching a hand out to me. I stand up and hug him again, but for longer this time. He squeezes me tight and I enjoy the security that washes over me.

"Thank you, Dad." I meet his eyes and speak with the utmost sincerity. "For what you did back there. You're crazy. But, you saved my life and I can't tell you how much I appreciate you being there for me."

"I told you, Ellie," Dad smiles. "I'll always make sure you're safe."

"You could have gotten yourself killed, though." I sigh. "I hate that you even got shot."

"Grazed." Dad corrects me with a smirk. "Just grazed, and I'd do it again if it meant keeping you safe from that psychopath."

"Well, thank you again." I smile weakly.

"I should be thanking you, too." Dad says. "You did a good job. I know it's scary and unnerving, but I don't know what Jake would have done to me with that knife if you hadn't stopped him. Thankfully we don't have to worry about that."

I nod in silence and hug my dad again before he leaves.

"Please keep us updated, okay?" Dad kisses the top of my head and rubs my arm.

"I will." I pat his back, and turn to hug my mom. "Drive safe, and I'll talk to you both soon."

I watch my parents walk out the door together, and am once again hit with exhaustion as I stand there in silence. I slowly drag myself back to the seat near Anna, and stare out the window.

Anna places a hand on my lap and smiles at me without saying a word. It's funny. For a woman whom I've only spent a few weeks with, she seems to know how to calm me, and I couldn't be more thankful for that.

I know we are in this together, and I am glad to have this support right now. I would probably be a complete mess if I didn't have such wonderful people in my life.

I glance over at Dakota, who is stuffing her face with vending machine donuts, staring out the window. I smile to myself and watch her for a moment. I still cannot wrap my head around what she did for me earlier. She almost got herself killed just to protect me, and I will never forget that. She is truly the greatest friend I could have ever asked for.

"Kody," I whisper, and she looks at me and stops chewing. "Why don't you go home, too?"

"No way, girl." She finishes chewing her donut and dusts off the powder from her shirt. "I'm not going anywhere. I'm here for you and Brennan."

"I hate to keep you here." I say. "I'm not sure how long we will be waiting."

"Fine by me," Dakota smiles. "It's a good thing I don't have anything else going on."

I shake my head and smile in response. Dakota looks back out the window and I look over to the nurses behind the desk. Why haven't we heard anything yet? Ever since I found out about Jake, I've been even more nervous about Brennan.

My thoughts are interrupted as the ER doors open and Officer Willis steps into the waiting room. Just behind him is Byron, casually dressed in some slacks and a button down he must have thrown on before he came to support me. Willis scans the room, and nods in acknowledgement when he sees us by the window, making his way over. Byron follows.

"Hello, again." He takes a seat across from me and nods. "I'm sure you've heard the news by now?"

I nod in silence and he sighs.

"Dakota called me, I hope that's alright". Byron sits down next to me and places a reassuring hand on my upper back. I nod again and he turns to Officer Willis. "I'm Ellen's lawyer, Byron Hart."

Willis and Byron shake hands, and then the former glances at me with compassion.

"I know you've been through a lot today, Ellen, and this is a lot to process, but just know one thing," He says, looking at Byron briefly and then back at me. "You're going to be fine. I've got the entire story from multiple sources, and this won't hurt you in any way."

"Okay," I nod and glance at Byron, who gives me a gentle nod. My heartbeat quickens at the thought of what happened again. "I just can't believe how everything turned out. I didn't have any other choice."

"I understand that." Willis says. "Earlier you told me about what happened at the wedding. I hate to bother you with this now, but do you mind telling me about your history with the deceased?"

Byron leans over and whispers into my ear, "Just tell the truth. You've done nothing wrong, and I've worked with Willis before. He's gonna do everything he can to help you."

I look down at the floor before meeting Officer Willis's eyes again. "He was my ex-husband."

In my peripheral vision, I see Byron shake his head in dismay, and Anna shift in her seat uncomfortably, still holding my hand while I tell my story to Officer Willis. I can imagine how awkward this whole ordeal is for her. She hadn't even known that I was married before tonight, and now she finds out that the man was her son's good friend from college.

Once I'm done with my story, Willis nods and stands back up.

"Everything I said about you being okay?" He smiles slightly. "A hundred times more so, now. I'm really sorry you've endured so much, but you're going to be absolutely fine."

"Thank you, Officer Willis." I smile in appreciation.

As I walk the two men back over to the doors, Byron turns to me one last time, "If you need anything, you know where to find me. Don't hesitate to call."

I nod in response and Byron pats my shoulder before leaving the ER.

"Between you and me," Willis whispers as we both watch Byron walk through the exterior doors. "Things worked out for the better, and this world will be a better place without someone like Jake."

"It's just going to take some getting used to." I admit. "But you're right."

"Have a good night, Ms. Mannis." Willis shakes my hand one final time. "Like I said, I'll keep in touch."

I rejoin Anna and Dakota and we continue to wait for news about Brennan. Anna asks about the wedding, and I tell her all about the night before Jake crashed the party.

The only thing we can do is wait, and it kills me every minute that we don't hear anything.

Chapter Twenty-Eight: The Admission

After another hour of waiting, a doctor comes out and searches the waiting room, stopping when he sees me. He walks over with an extended hand.

"Grant?" He asks, and I nod and shake his hand.

"I'm his nanny, Ellen Mannis," I say, hopeful for some good news.

"I'm Dr. Lee." He turns to shake Anna's hand. "And you must be?"

"Anna Grant." She returns the handshake. "I'm his mother."

"Great." He opens the folder in his hand and skims through the paperwork. "Well, it looks like Brennan took a deep shot to the shoulder. No nerve or joint damage, thankfully, and we were able to remove the bullet and tend to the wound. He's very lucky. However, he is still unconscious."

Blood rushes to my face as the nerves fill my body again. He's still unconscious?

"He's lost a decent amount of blood, but I don't think a transfusion will be necessary." Dr. Lee finishes as he closes the folder. "We are just monitoring him now."

"When can we see him?" Anna asks instantly.

"He's in stable condition, so you may see him now. But, as I said, he's not conscious." Dr. Lee shifts his glasses and scans his ID tag on the door. "If you'd follow me."

I look back to Dakota, and she waves me along. "I'll be right here."

Anna and I follow the doctor down the hall until we reach a dimly lit room. Brennan is laid out on the bed with a bandage covering most of his left shoulder. My heart aches as I look at the scene and I hold back the tears that want to fall. His breathing is slow, and the beeping on the monitor reflects his steady heart rate.

"Excuse me, Ms. Mannis?" Dr. Lee taps my arm, and I meet his eyes.

"Yes?" I say, waiting for his response.

"Would you like one of the nurses to tend to your wounds?" He points to my face, and I place my hand on my swollen lip, wincing at the pain.

With all the commotion, I almost forgot about the marks Jake left on me.

"I'd appreciate that, thank you."

A nurse comes in and cleans my cuts and treats them before covering them with small bandages. "Are you injured anywhere else, ma'am?"

"No, I'm fine. Thank you, very much"

I rub my leg as I respond, feeling the tender spot where Jake was grabbing my thigh. It will bruise, but there isn't anything I can do about that now.

The nurse nods with a small smile and leaves me alone with Anna and Brennan. I watch Anna and guilt consumes me once more. She must feel so much pain seeing her son in this condition. I sit down in the chair near the door so she can have her moment with him.

"Oh, Ellie. Don't be silly." Anna says once she notices where I am, and waves me over with a gentle smile. "Come over here."

I walk over and take the seat on the other side of Brennan. We sit in silence for a few minutes, and I watch his chest move in sync with each breath. This poor man has endured way too much since I came into his life, and I feel the worst I ever have through this whole ordeal. He doesn't deserve to be in this bed. Not for my sake.

"I know you feel like this is your fault, Ellie," Anna speaks up as if reading my mind. "But you can't beat yourself up over this."

"How can I not?" I meet her eyes with sorrow. "He wouldn't be here if I hadn't brought my problems with Jake into the picture."

Anna looks down briefly before looking back over at Brennan.

"I saw the letter you left for him. I don't know what other stuff you two have been through, but I can assure you that what happened between Will and me was not your fault."

I watch her as she speaks, surprised that she knew I was referring to them in my letter. Her tone is calm as she continues.

"That was a long time coming." She meets my eyes again. "I guess it just took a little extra nudge for us to do something about it."

"I'm sorry, Anna." I shake my head, still angry with myself for the events of our visit in July.

"You shouldn't be." A small grin appears on her face. "In fact, I should be thanking you."

"Um... what?" I ask, bewildered by her response.

"Not only did you guide me out of a bad lifestyle, but you also gave my family something amazing." She looks back at Brennan and rubs his hand. "You brought love back into their lives."

"I –" I trail off, unable to find the words to respond.

She is right, but to me, it's the other way around. Brennan and his kids have shown me a love that I have never experienced before. And it couldn't have come at a more perfect time. Life seemed so depressing before I met Brennan, and he and his kids have given me so much joy over the past year.

"It was very hard on Brennan when Kayla passed, and I had to sit back and watch him live through that pain. But one thing is certain." Her eyes meet mine again, and I see admiration. "You changed everything the moment you came into his life. I saw that change hands on when you came to visit over the summer, and it was a very refreshing sight."

I sit and listen to Anna as my eyes begin to water again.

"The way you two interacted was enough to convince me that this was more than a business arrangement, and then I saw the way he looked at you." Her smile grows larger as she rubs her hand over Brennan's face. "I don't think William ever looked at me with that much adoration and I knew then that you two shared something special. The fact that the kids love you so much made it even better."

I stare at Brennan's face as I think about our time together. I've cared about him immensely for most of the time I've known him, and it's crazy to think that he felt the same way.

"I tried to get something out of him, but this boy is almost as stubborn as his father." She smiles. "Kept saying it wasn't what I thought, but I know my son, and I knew what he was feeling for you."

I think back to our visit and all the times Brennan and his mother were whispering, or whenever he seemed nervous that I had heard their conversation. Anna was talking about his feelings for me, and he didn't want me to know. She had whispered in his ear the day we left, and he looked at me, and I had thought the whole exchange was strange. It all makes sense now.

Anna finally looks back at me, and I see the glimmer of a tear in her eye.

"Thank you, Ellie." She nods. "For giving him life again."

I smile for the first time in hours and wipe a tear from my cheek.

"He's done the same for me, I can assure you. The feeling was completely mutual."

She nods with a smile and then slowly stands up as she releases Brennan's hand.

"Well, it looks like he is in good hands right now, so I'm going to get home to my grand babies." She grabs her jacket and slips it on as she looks back at me. "Ruth is probably going crazy taking care of all of them on her own. Keep me updated."

She walks around the bed and pulls me in for a long hug. After she pulls away, she holds my face in her hands, gazing lovingly at me. She brushes hair behind my ear and then heads for the door.

"Anna?" I grab her attention, and she stops in the doorway, turning to look at me. "Thank you for everything."

"Anytime, sweetheart." She smiles and walks away.

I glance back at Brennan and my spirits drop again. I truly hate seeing him in this state.

I lean forward and grab Brennan's hand, rubbing my thumb along his rugged knuckles. I bring our hands to my face and gently kiss his a few times. I sob in silence and look back to his face, illuminated by the lights from the machines.

An hour goes by before I decide to tell Dakota to head back home. I want to stay with Brennan, and I'm not sure how long it will be before he wakes up, if he does.

I don't realize how hungry I am until my stomach makes a loud gurgling noise and I decide to grab some pretzels from the vending machine.

When I enter the room again, I stand in the doorway looking at Brennan, wondering if Dakota is right about everything. Can we really be together after all of this? After everything we've been through, I don't know if I could live my life happily without him in it. The thought brings a tear to my eye, and I take a seat beside the bed again.

I fall asleep in my chair, and the doctor wakes me as he is checking up on Brennan. I glance at my phone and see that it is already three o'clock in the morning.

"Are you holding up alright, Ms. Mannis?" Dr. Lee asks after he's finished with Brennan.

"Honestly, no." I shake my head and continue to stare at Brennan.

"The nanny, huh?" He says from the other side of the bed, and I glance up at him.

His expression is curious, and all I can do is nod in response. Dr. Lee nods with a weak smile.

"I understand." He says as he glances down at the clipboard in his hand. "Well, his vitals are very good right now, so it's just a matter of him waking up. Let me know if you need anything."

I nod again and glance back at Brennan as the doctor leaves. I grab Brennan's hand again and whisper just loud enough for him to hear.

"I don't know if you can hear me right now, but I have so much to say." I pause and listen to his monitor beep and gently lay my head on his hip, closing my eyes.

"I'm so sorry, Brennan. I'm sorry for leaving. I thought I was protecting you all, but all I did was hurt us even more. The truth is – "

I pause briefly. Why is it so difficult to say what we feel? He isn't even conscious, yet I'm still finding it so hard to open my heart to him.

"I was afraid." I reach up and gently run my fingers through his hair. "I knew what I was feeling for you, and it scared me to be in that situation again."

I run a thumb across his cheek before laying my head back down on his waist.

"It's only been a few months and yet I feel as if I've known you my whole life. My soul feels connected to you in so many ways that I'm sure I'm not complete without you."

I take a moment to listen to his breathing. The steady rhythm is slightly comforting, but I still feel dread coursing through my veins. Finally, I lift my head to look back up at his face again.

"Your letter said I brought light into your life, but really you did the same for me. I was in a dark place for a long time, and things finally felt normal with you. I never thought I'd feel so secure again and all I want is to be back in that place."

I continue to stare at his face, handsome and serene. As I look at him, I know that I never want to be without him. This man is my life now, and I can't lose him.

"Please come back to me. Please."

I squeeze his hand for a second and just cry.

"Come back to me so we can go home."

For a few minutes, I cry while listening to the monitor beep. I feel so alone, and I want nothing more than to hear his voice once again. I need to hear it.

"I love you, Brennan." I sob in between words. "More than words could ever explain. I need you."

I cry to myself for what feels like hours but is realistically only a few minutes. I continue to rest my head on his waist and watch his face.

After a moment, I feel a weird sensation in my hand. At first, I think I'm imagining it, but then I realize Brennan has wrapped his fingers around my hand. His heart rate quickens, and I lean forward to see him better.

"Ren?" I watch as his eyes slowly open and find me.

"Ellie." His voice is cracked, but he forces himself to speak. It is hushed and slow, but he manages to talk to me. "You took the words… out of my mouth."

He smiles and carefully reaches his hand to cup my face.

I lean over and put my face near his. He guides my chin in the rest of the way and my lips land on his. His kiss is warm and tender, and I savor the sensation that pulses through me. I pull away slowly, keeping my face close to his. He leans his forehead against mine, and we sit like that for a moment.

"Knock, knock." Dr. Lee says as he enters the room with his folder. "Good to see you awake, Mr. Grant. You gave us quite the scare."

I step away from the bed so he and the nurses can go about their business. Dr. Lee smiles at me before he speaks to Brennan.

"I was just telling Ellen here that your vitals are normal, which is excellent." Dr. Lee states. "However, we do need to keep you for a day or two just to monitor you after your excessive blood loss."

"I understand." Brennan sighs.

"And I'd like you on bed rest for at least two weeks once you're home." The doctor adds. "That means no going to work or leaving the house."

"That's a tough one, Doc," Brennan smirks. "But I guess I can work from home."

"Very good, sir." The doctor chuckles and turns to leave the room, stopping in the doorway. "One more thing, Mr. Grant. The police are here and would like to speak with you now that you're awake. I can send them in if you're feeling comfortable enough."

"Give us a few minutes, and then you can send them in." Brennan's expression becomes serious, and I hold his hand again as he looks back at me. "I just need a moment."

"Of course." Dr. Lee smiles again as his gaze shifts between the two of us.

He leaves the room, and I hover over Brennan again, running my fingers over his face as if it's the first time I'm seeing him. I lean my forehead against his again and sigh.

"I thought I lost you," I whisper. "I was so scared that things were over before they even started."

"Hey," Brennan whispers as he pulls me back to look at me. "I'm not going anywhere."

I nod and glance down at his patched-up shoulder. I don't know what I would have done if that bullet had been a few inches to the left where it would have hit his heart.

"You took a bullet for me," I say, staring into his sincere eyes.

"I would do it again in a heartbeat." He says. "You have no idea how glad I am that you are alright. I love you, Ellie, and I'll do whatever I can to keep you safe."

My heart does somersaults at the sound of those words coming out of Brennan's mouth, and I smile, still staring into his beautiful, blue eyes.

"I love you, too." I lean in and kiss him once more.

Brennan examines my face for a moment, and I can tell he is angry about my cuts and bruises again. He gently strokes my cheek where Jake hit me and shakes his head.

"I'll kill him if I ever see him again." He growls. "I can't believe that bastard got his hands on you again."

I stare at him for a second and bite my lip, unsure how to tell him. He senses my mood and eyes me curiously.

"What?" He asks.

How do I tell him the news about Jake? It feels so morbid to just come out and say it, but he needs to know, and that's the easiest way.

"Jake is gone." I say as I look down at Brennan's chest.

"Well, I hope so." Brennan sneers. "I hope he never comes back."

"No, Ren," I meet his eyes again and watch as the realization takes over his face. "He's gone."

"Jake's dead?" Brennan whispers, and I nod slowly. "How?"

Brennan watches me, and I can tell he already knows the answer to his own question. He pulls me into a hug and holds me there for a long time, rubbing my hair back and kissing my head.

We don't say anything else, and it's probably better that way.

Chapter Twenty-Nine: The Scars

Brennan gives the police his statement, the doctors move him to a regular room, and I call Dakota to pick me up so I can stay in the apartment with her for the rest of the night. As much as I hate to leave Brennan, I know he will be fine until later, and I've got to get some much-needed sleep.

Two days pass quickly, and I spend most of them gathering my things to move back to Brennan's house and visiting him in the hospital. After loading up my van with my belongings, I head back to the hospital, where Brennan is ready to be discharged.

"Well someone is eager to go home." I chuckle after seeing a fully dressed Brennan standing by the window of his hospital room.

Anna had brought him clothes when she brought the kids to see him while I was gone. I wasn't ready to see them yet, and I wanted Brennan to be home with me when I finally did.

He turns around and grins as I walk up to him and plant a kiss on his cheek.

"More than ready." He places his hands on my waist and pulls me close, so my body presses against his chest. "Are you ready to go home?"

I smile at his words again. Home. It just sounds so perfect right now, though I am a bit nervous to see Sophia and the boys. They probably hate me.

"Absolutely." I nod. "But, um, how do we explain everything to the kids?"

Brennan sighs and glances out the window briefly before looking back down at me with a shrug.

"I'm not sure yet, but I know they will be thrilled to see you."

"I hope you're right." I sigh as I lay my head against his chest and look out the window at the city.

His embrace calms me so much, and I don't ever want to let go.

"Alright, Mr. Grant, here are your discharge papers." Dr. Lee enters the room and hands a packet of papers over to Brennan. "You're free to go, but please follow up with us in two weeks. And remember what I said, you need to rest."

"Sure thing." Brennan shakes the doctor's hands and then takes my hand. "Thank you for everything, Dr. Lee. Take care."

"Make sure our guy stays out of trouble now, Ms. Mannis." Dr. Lee grins at me before walking out of the room.

"Come on, let's go home." Brennan kisses my cheek and leads me out of the room like a man on a mission. I can tell he wants to get out of this hospital as soon as he can.

We arrive back home about a half hour later, and the moment we walk through the front door, we are greeted by all of our family. My parents, Dakota, Anna, and Ruth are all smiles and saying random cheers while Sophia, Asher, and Noah are holding up a sign that says, "Welcome home, Daddy!"

Brennan rushes over to his kids and wraps them in a huge group hug and holds them there for a few seconds while I greet everyone else. It's not until they pull out of their father's embrace that the kids finally notice me.

"Ellie!" They all shout in unison and run over to flood me with hugs.

"You're back!" Sophia smiles at me and claps. "We've missed you so much!"

"I've missed you guys, too." I kneel and give them each a huge kiss on the cheek. "More than you know. I thought about you all the time."

"Don't leave us again!" Noah shouts as he throws his arms around my neck again for another hug.

"I'm not going anywhere." I return his hug and glance over at Brennan, who has been watching our exchange with a big smile.

"You're moving back in?" Asher beams with pride as he looks from his father back to me.

"I am." I nod with a grin and glance at Brennan to see where he wants to go from here.

"Kids, Ellie and I have something we need to talk to you about." Brennan looks around at everyone, and the adults take that as their cue to retreat to the living room, leaving us alone with the kids.

Brennan joins me by my side and kneels to their level with me.

"Ellie is moving back in with us, but she isn't going to be your nanny anymore," Brennan speaks as he relays the news to the kids.

Their faces light up the moment he finishes his sentence, and I know they understand what this means.

"Are you guys finally dating?" Sophia looks back and forth between Brennan and me, looking for answers on our faces.

Finally dating? I'm almost surprised to hear her reaction because I wasn't aware the kids wanted that for us.

"Yes, we are." Brennan chuckles, and the kids all break out into cheers.

"Yay! I knew this would happen!" Asher throws his hand in the air like he just earned the greatest victory ever.

"I love you guys!" Noah hugs us both at the same time, and I can't help but laugh.

I am so grateful that they are not mad at me for leaving, and their support for our relationship means the world to me. The moment Brennan said he wanted to make this relationship work, I immediately wondered what Sophia and the boys would think. I'm glad to know they are more than happy with it.

"I hope you guys aren't too mad at me for leaving without saying goodbye." I frown a bit as I look at each of their sweet faces.

I've missed these kids so much.

"We were hurt, but we aren't mad at you." Sophia smiles, resting a reassuring hand on my shoulder.

Such an old soul. I love it.

"Why did you go, though?" Asher asks curiously, and I glance at Brennan.

"That's a story for another time." Brennan stands up and begins leading us all toward the living room. "What matters is that we are all here together now and we can move on with our lives."

"I'll drink to that!" Dakota calls from the kitchen and my mother and I both laugh. That girl will drink to anything.

We enjoy the evening with our families and settle back into the house. It is a perfect homecoming, and I'm glad everyone could be there for us. The support system I have is incredible, and I know I wouldn't have made it this far without every single one of them.

Once the kids are sleeping and it's time to turn in for the night, I find it strange not going to the room upstairs. I take a quick shower in the master bath in Brennan's room and throw on some simple pajamas.

I run a hand over my thigh where the bruise from Jake is at its prime purple and blue, and I pull my short leg down as far as I can to cover it up before leaving the room.

Brennan is sitting by the window with his laptop when I enter the bedroom. He watches me walk toward him, and I see his eyes scan my body. A shiver runs down my spine as satisfaction washes over me. I love the way he looks at me.

As I'm about to sit down beside him, Brennan places his laptop aside and grabs my arm to bring me to sit on his lap. He runs a gentle hand over my thigh, lifting my shorts a few inches and exposing my bruise.

"Ellie." He whispers as he stares at my leg.

I can sense the pain in his voice. He runs a hand down my back and rubs his nose along my shoulder before he continues.

"What happened after Jake shot me?"

I close my eyes and turn my face away from him in embarrassment. I knew he would want to know, but I don't know if I have it in me to tell him the whole story.

"You don't need to worry about that," I say. "I'm okay now, and he's gone."

"Ellie, please tell me." I meet his eyes again, and I see the desperation in them.

He needs to know so that he can have closure. I nod and stand up with my back to him, trying to gather my thoughts.

"Once I realized you were shot, I tried to put pressure on your wound until help arrived." I begin to explain. "But before I knew it, I was alone with you and Jake, and he had the gun pointed at us."

I feel my body begin to shake a little bit as I recall the events of that night. Brennan takes my hand and gently rotates me, so I'm facing him. He looks up at me and runs a hand down my arm to comfort me, and I continue.

"He made me move away from you and was going to shoot you, so I had to distract him until the cops came." I shake my head in frustration. "I tried to talk to him and calm him down, but he didn't seem to understand what I was saying to him. And then he —"

I start to cry and turn to look away from Brennan, but he guides my face back to look at him again. He watches me compassionately, and I know this is one of the parts that worried him.

"Did he –" Brennan begins to ask the question I know has been on his mind but trails off.

He doesn't need to finish for me to understand and I shake my head in response.

"He almost did, but Dakota stopped him before he could do it." I sigh, knowing that one hard part of the story is over with.

"Remind me to give that girl a raise," Brennan smirks for a second, but his smile is washed away again as he examines my bruise again. "Can you tell me the rest?"

I stare at him for a second before continuing.

"Jake was about to shoot me. He had said 'If I can't have you, no one can', but before he could shoot, my dad came out of nowhere and tackled him to the ground."

"Your father is an amazing man." Brennan whispers and I nod once more.

"Jake shot at Dad's leg, but only grazed it." I continue. "Then he dropped the gun and I took it. I didn't think I would be able to do anything, and it felt so wrong holding a weapon at someone, but Jake started to move for the cake knife while he hovered over Dad and –"

Brennan pulls me into another hug to calm me down, and I sob for a second as I recall the events of that night. I wonder how long it will take for me to feel normal again after thinking about it. Will I ever be the same again? I killed someone, and I'm not sure how anyone can rectify that in their mind.

"I am so proud of you for defending yourself," Brennan whispers in my ear. "I should have been there for you. I should have been able to save you from all of that."

"Are you kidding?" I step back a bit and take Brennan's face in my hands. "Ren, you took a bullet for me. That is more than enough."

"I just hate that I couldn't do more." He shakes his head and closes his eyes. "If Dakota hadn't come to your aid, he would have ra—"

He doesn't finish the rest of his sentence as tears fill his eyes.

"You know what else could have happened?" I ask, lifting his chin, so he looks at me again. "If that bullet had been just a few inches to the left, it would have hit your heart."

Brennan gazes into my eyes, and I can tell he understands where I'm going with this. I place a hand on his heart and shake my head again. My hand trails over to the scar on his shoulder, which now resembles the one I have. Two identical scars, for two separate people, as a result of the same reckless individual.

"Your kids would have lost you," I whisper. "So, please, don't think that you didn't do enough for me. You risked your life to protect me, and I couldn't be more grateful for that."

Brennan places his hands on my hips and guides me closer, resting his forehead on my stomach. I run my hands through his hair, and we remain silent for a moment.

"I need you to understand something, Ellie." Brennan finally looks back up at me with complete misery. "I have to protect you. I failed to protect Kayla, and I can't let the same thing happen to you."

"Brennan," I take his face in my hands. "You can't say that. Kayla's accident wasn't your fault."

"But, it was," Brennan shakes his head as tears trickle down his cheeks. "It's my fault she got into that accident, and I hate myself for that to this day."

"What are you talking about?" I ask, searching his eyes for some answer.

"Kayla shouldn't have been out when she was. It was my fault." Brennan takes my hands and pulls them away from his face. He looks down at the ground as he remembers that night.

"I was too invested in my work around that time. I was turning into my father and I cared about my career too much, and it was to the point where I would forget to do the simplest things. Kayla hated that and we fought a lot because of it."

I listen to Brennan's story and remember what he told me at his parents' house. He had said there was a point where he was turning into his dad and he had been trying to change that recently. His wife's accident was the reason he needed to change, and I feel awful knowing that.

"The day of the accident, Kayla had asked me to grab some milk on my way home from work, but I forgot, as usual. We argued when I got home and that's when she left to go to the store for it herself."

Brennan closes his eyes and hangs his head in shame. Kayla's death wasn't his fault, but he has always forced himself to believe it was. He couldn't have known what was going to happen that night.

I silently kneel in front of Brennan and lift his face to look at me. His gloom depresses me and I wipe his tears away as he watches me for a reaction.

"She was so angry when she left, and that's the final memory I have of her." Brennan whispers through a cracked voice. "Everything would have been different if I had just remembered to pick up the milk after work."

"You can't do that to yourself, Brennan." I sigh. "I know you blame yourself, but what happened was out of your control. You didn't know what was going to happen when she left, and you can't keep telling yourself it was your fault."

"I just hate the person I was back then. I hate that it got to that point, and I wish I could take it all back." He says.

"I know you do," I nod. "I know you hate that final memory of her, but you have to remember the good instead of the bad. Couples fight, and that's just the way of life. But you two made a beautiful life together and you have three amazing children to show for that."

Brennan nods as he listens, and I can tell he's coming around a little.

"You are not a bad person, and you weren't back then either." I assure him. "People like Jake are bad people. You have always loved and cared for your family, and it's one of the many things I love about you. So, please, do not feel like you don't do enough. You are an incredible father to those kids, and you give so much more than you take."

"Thank you." Brennan says. "I work hard every day to be the best father I can for Sophia and the boys, and I just needed you to know the truth before we went any further."

"The truth doesn't change a thing." I smile and run a hand through his hair again. "You're still the same man you were this morning. You're a magnificent person with a big heart and a lot of love to give, and I'm happy to be by your side."

"I love you, Ellen." He looks at me tenderly, and my heart skips a thousand beats. I love when he looks at me that way, and I couldn't love him any more than I do at this moment.

"I love you, Brennan." I smile and kiss his forehead. "More than I think I'll ever understand."

He kisses me on the lips and then lifts me up with his good arm, carrying me to the bed. He lays down beside me, and we stare at each other in silence. Brennan caresses my arm the same way he had the night Jake was here and my eyes slowly close as slumber consumes me.

Chapter Thirty: The End

The night is cold, and I walk along the pond, shivering with each step. I can't seem to find my way back home, and I feel the loneliness wash over me as I search for someone, anyone.

I feel like I've been walking for miles until, finally, I see something ahead in the distance. As I get closer, I realize it is Brennan's body on the ground.

I shout his name, but no sound comes out. I try to run to him, but I don't move from my spot.

I'm stuck.

Laughter rings through the air, and I turn around to see Jake standing in front of me with a gun pointed at my head.

"If I can't have you, no one can!" He instantly aims the gun at Brennan, and a loud bang rings through my ears.

"No!" My eyes shoot open, and I see Brennan hovering over me with concern in his eyes.

"Ellie." He tucks my damp hair away from my face and kisses my forehead. "It's okay. I'm here."

"It's happening again," I whisper through a cracked voice, trying to steady my breathing. "These dreams."

"They're just that. Dreams." He nods and gazes into my eyes. "He can't hurt you anymore, baby. I know I promised that before but this time it's true. He's gone, and I will always make sure you are safe."

I nod in response and bury my face into Brennan's bare chest. He smells so good, and it instantly soothes my shaking body. How did I go so long without his embrace? He wraps his arms around me and lays back down beside me.

"I'm sorry," I say after a few minutes of silence.

"You have no reason to be sorry." He strokes my back as he speaks.

"I'm so broken."

Brennan immediately sits us both up and faces me, taking my face in his hands.

"You are not broken, Ellie." His eyes show a look I've never seen before.

It's distraught and pained, and yet there's a fire to them that makes my entire body shiver with endearment. This beautiful man cares about me so much. For whatever reason, with all my baggage, he chooses to be with me and do whatever it takes to keep me happy and safe.

"You are the most beautiful person to enter my life since my children were born, and I couldn't ask for anyone better to be by my side." He runs his thumb along my cheek, taking in my entire face as he talks to me. "You have been through so much over the years, but you were so strong through all of it and pushed through it until the end. That doesn't make you broken, Ellie. That makes you tough, tenacious, and strong, and those are some of the things I love about you."

I nod at his words and glance down at the quilt covering our legs. He's right. I've been through so much and look where I am now. I didn't think I deserved this kind of happiness after everything and yet here I am, sleeping beside a man whom I've come to love and care about immensely.

"Ellie," Brennan whispers, causing me to look back at him. "Please don't ever apologize for your past. You are who you are now because of it. It has shaped the woman you've become, and to me, that woman is perfect. Scars and all."

His words are my undoing, and I pull his face to mine as a tear escapes my eyes. His lips crash onto mine in a passionate kiss that sends butterflies throughout my body. His hands tangle into my hair, and we slowly lay back down, not breaking the kiss.

Brennan shifts himself, so he's on top of me without putting too much force on his shoulder. His hand runs down my body and finds its way up my shirt, stopping just below my breasts. I let out a small moan, and I feel Brennan smile on my lips.

"I want you, Elle." He whispers, closing his eyes and keeping his face just inches away from mine.

I don't think he realizes what he's done, and for just a split second the name throws me off, but that feeling vanishes immediately. Brennan would never hurt me, and I know that with every fiber of my being. He can call me that for the rest of my life and I wouldn't mind one bit.

"I'm all yours," I whisper, running my hand through his dark hair.

He doesn't hesitate one second, and his lips are immediately back on mine, kissing me with a hunger that drives me crazy. As we kiss, we slowly remove each other clothes until there is nothing between our bodies to hold us back.

He gazes at me from head to toe before moving any further, and once his eyes meet mine again, he smiles.

"You are so beautiful," He tenderly sighs as he runs his hand up my side. "I love you."

"I love you too."

Brennan kisses me once more, and we throw ourselves into a movement of passion, pleasure, and satisfaction. Our bodies move in sync with one another and the only sound that fills the night is our breathing and soft moans. My body responds to his so perfectly like he is a part of me and our souls connect as one. I'm not sure how long it lasts, but it is completely incredible, and I am left wanting more.

We lay together, naked and gazing into each other's eyes. This moment couldn't be any more perfect. Brennan has this way of comforting me in every situation without making me feel vulnerable. My eyes begin to close, and I'm about to fall asleep again when he whispers in my ear.

"Ellen?"

"Hmm?" My eyes remain closed as I listen for Brennan's voice again.

"Marry me."

My eyes immediately open and I lift my head slightly to get a better look at Brennan, who is watching me with anticipation.

"What?"

"Be my wife." He smiles as he rubs my arm gently. "I know I said I wanted to date and make this work, but I know for a fact that I don't want to spend another day of my life without you. I want you by my side always, and I want us to grow old together. So, please do me the honor of marrying me."

At first, I can't find the words but soon enough a smile breaks out on my lips, and I rest my hand on his face, rubbing his cheek with my thumb.

"Okay."

Brennan's smile grows wider, and he leans up to kiss me. He then leans over me and pulls out the drawer on the end table, removing a small box. He hovers over me and opens it to reveal a gorgeous white gold solitaire ring. I throw my hand over my mouth in awe.

"You've been planning this?" I ask in astonishment.

With everything going on, how did he have time to plan this? Let alone buy the ring.

"Well, someone once told me that there are these rare occurrences where two people couldn't be more perfect for each other, and I'm not one to ignore those signs. I bought it the day we returned from the Poconos." Brennan removes the ring from the box as he speaks. "I was going to ask you after your sister's wedding, but then everything turned into such a mess."

"I can't believe this."

I can't help but smile as he slides the ring onto my finger and plants a kiss on my forehead. I'm unable to fathom the idea that he was ready for this after the vacation a few months ago. I really haven't been alone in my affections.

"I love you so much, Brennan, and I can't wait to start our life together."

"Me neither." He plants kisses all over my face and then beams at me with pride. "I love you."

"Hmm, Ellen Grant." I lay back down with a smile. "Has a nice ring to it."

"Indeed, it does." Brennan links his fingers with mine and lays back down beside me. "It doesn't have to be right away. We can wait however long you want, but I just want to commit myself to you."

I stare at Brennan and think about how different this feeling is. I know that he said we could wait because of what happened with Jake, but this is not the same situation.

"Brennan, I could marry you tomorrow and spend the rest of my life knowing that wasn't a mistake. I appreciate you thinking of me, though, and I would like to wait. But I want you to know that I don't compare this to anything I've ever done. We may be moving fast, but this is true. I've never had true before, and I can say without a doubt that you're the man I want by my side for the rest of my life."

"Good, because I couldn't live without you." Brennan kisses my nose and smiles. "And I actually have another offer to make you."

"And, what would that be?" I ask with a huge grin.

I'm already emotionally overwhelmed with tonight, and I'm interested to hear what else he has to say.

"It's a lot to ask, so don't feel like you have to say yes." He says, stalling.

"What is it?" I ask seriously this time.

He seems really nervous and I'm not sure where this is going.

"Once we're married, I thought it might be nice if you, um," Brennan pauses for a second, gathering the courage to ask me what's on his mind. "I thought maybe you'd want to adopt the kids. You know, legally become their mother."

"You want me to –"

I can't finish my sentence. My mind is racing as I process what Brennan has just said.

"I remember what you said about Eamon when we were in the Poconos, and I thought about how nice that would be for Sophia and the boys. For them to have a mother to care for them the way they need. Not to replace their real mom, but to continue on in her place." Brennan explains himself and I just watch him with a smile.

I sit up again and look around the room in silence for a moment, allowing my thoughts to wander. This is such a big deal, and I almost can't believe Brennan is offering it to me. I never thought I'd be a mother. After my hysterectomy, I had accepted the fact that I would never hear the word "mommy" or have children to raise. But, Brennan wants to give me that opportunity, and I couldn't be more grateful.

Brennan sits up with me and I smile at him as a tear escapes my eye. He wipes it with his thumb and watches me curiously.

"Are you okay?" He asks, searching my eyes for a response.

"It's just," I swallow through the lump in my throat, trying not to sob like a big baby. "I never thought this could happen to me. I've just accepted that I wasn't meant to be a mom, but now I can be."

"I've told you before, you'd make an amazing mother." Brennan smiles. "And I want nothing more than for you to be one to my kids."

"I'd like that," I smile and kiss him on the lips once more.

"Does that mean you'll do it?" He asks hopefully.

He's adorable when he's excited about something.

"Absolutely." I nod excitedly, and Brennan beams with pride.

"You have no idea how happy that makes me." He kisses my cheek, and then rests his forehead against mine. "We're going to make a great family. I know life has been a bumpy, broken road for both of us, but we've got this chance to change all of that."

"I look forward to it." I kiss Brennan again before we both lay back down and watch each other.

We silently stare into each other's eyes, enjoying this special moment. It's amazing how things can change in just a few, short minutes. This is the man I'm going to marry, and I'm going to be a mother to some amazing children.

"Get some sleep, beautiful." Brennan whispers. "I love you."

"I love you, too. Goodnight Brennan." I watch as he closes his eyes and slowly dozes off. He looks so peaceful, and I can't help but wonder how I got so lucky.

He's right when he says that life has been a broken road for us. We've both been through some hard times, but we really do have a chance to turn that all around. Life is about to be completely different for all of us, but it's going to be incredible.

I still can't believe how much my life has changed over the past few years, and I look forward to beginning this new journey, leaving everything behind us.

Although we can't escape from our pasts, we embrace them, and learn from them. Our pasts make us who we are, and lead us to where we are going. I'll always have some respect for the broken road that led me right here, to this moment, where I belong.

275